REACHING

A Novel by
Julie McDonald

Sutherland Publishing
Sutherland Printing Company, Inc.
Montezuma, IA 50171

All rights reserved
including the right of reproduction
in whole or in part in any form
copyright © 1988 by
Julie McDonald

1st Printing 1988

ISBN 0-930942-12-4
Library of Congress Catalog Card Number 88-61287
Manufactured in the United States of America
by Sutherland Publishing, Ft. Myers, FL 33908
a Division of Sutherland Printing Company, Inc.
Montezuma, IA 50171

A boat is reaching when she sails more or less across the wind...Sailing craft usually attain their highest speeds when reaching.

- Collier's Encyclopedia

"For Erika, Jill, Emily and Betsy, whose reaching is ahead of them."

reaching

A Novel

This was my summer of fleeing my body to live in the future, then rushing back to clutch at the present and secure the past—of puzzling over how to introduce myself in places where I had no assurance of welcome. "Margaret Langelund? Who's she?"

All through the hot months I typed briefs and letters at Gregory Sommer's law office, and it certainly was hot in those windowless upstairs rooms on the east side of the Square. A rotating fan blew onionskin copies every which way unless I remembered to weight them with a chunk of petrified wood Mr. Sommer had collected on a long-ago vacation. The dead, electrically-driven breeze carried the scent of old leather book bindings and the clean, male smell of Sommer himself that was so different from any olfactory signatures I knew.

Those came to me powerfully at home during the evening sewing sessions when Mom, Grandma and Aunt Kamille gathered in our dining room to prepare my college wardrobe. Mom was Lady Esther face powder, Aunt Kam was Djer Kiss talcum, and Grandma was a potato scrubbed for baking.

Despite our lowering the windowshades in the heat of the day and cooking on a small kerosene stove instead of the kitchen range, the dining room was hot and sticky. The glass chandelier that looked like melted pink and green lollipops must have achieved that form on nights such as these, I thought.

The three women argued about darts and seams, using Danish terms when English didn't seem to communicate, and the only thing they said to me was, "Turn!"

I turned, always too much or not enough, and was corrected bodily by the hem measurer who had issued the terse order through lips clamped tight on straight pins.

Seized by vertigo, I touched the table for support and winced when the pins grazed my skin as the garment was pulled over my head. Then I slumped in my rayon slip with the shiny stripes (from the Montgomery-Ward catalog) until my body was required again. I did not feel undressed in this company and had no need of modesty.

Neither did Aunt Kam. She picked up her skirt—a cotton print of small blue roses—and fanned her thighs. Grandma, however, wore long sleeves winter and summer. Her skirts were long too, but she never seemed to feel the heat—not like Mom, whose upper lip was beaded with sweat.

I was supposed to be printing my name on cloth tapes to be sewn into my clothes, but I was tired of writing "Margaret Langelund" over and over and worsening the dark stain of permanent ink on the writing bump of my middle finger.

The garment in production was a bright melon sheer wool two-piece dress with a peplum to disguise my hips. Aunt Kam called them "voluptuous hips," but I thought they were shaped like a guitar and hated them. They certainly didn't go with my slender top half.

"Why am I built like this?" I said, "None of the rest of you are."

"I don't know," Mom said. "I never saw your father's mother and sisters, but I suppose that's where you got it."

So! It was the fault of a bunch of strange women in Denmark. I pushed aside the Danish white cookies on one of the plates the Farleys left behind to look at the figure painted on it—an exotic woman reclining on a couch beside a stream. Why couldn't I look like that? A single, smooth rise from the dip of the waist instead of the double hump of a Bactrian camel?

Since the operation in Rochester, I'd had to get used to a completely new body—more of it. Pretending to be Hedy Lamarr was much harder, if not impossible. Now they had to let out my cousin Marianne's hand-me-downs for me instead of taking them in, and when they were finished with the one new garment I would take with me to Iowa City (except for the ill-chosen purple crepe I'd bought to celebrate winning the scholarship), I'd have to try on that whole armload of stuff draped over the back of a chair.

"How about some lemonade?" Grandma asked, removing her thimble and sticking her needle into the spool of melon thread.

Mom nodded gratefully, biting off a thread with her teeth.

"Use the scissors," Grandma said, as she always did.

Aunt Kam continued to work the foot treadle of the sewing machine, and it still said, "Bismarck! Bismarck! Bismarck!" the way it always had as long as I could remember.

I could see into the kitchen from where I stood. Grandma took the bright lemons from the Norge that had replaced the old ice box and cut them with one decisive slash of her favorite knife, the one with the age-blackened blade. Her hand, pressing and turning on the juicer, hid the yellow completely but released a tangy, citrus smell as the juice ran into a pitcher of tawny, mottled pottery that I considered to be ugly. Aunt Kam said it was valuable every time she saw it used, and I wished that Grandma would give it to her and get it out of my sight.

The lemonade was served in the thin, golden glasses with raised leafy swirls that went with my parents' best dishes. Now that most of them had been broken, we used the survivors for everyday. Grandma brought me the limp cap of a squeezed lemon half to bleach the ink stain on my finger, just as I knew she would.

Everything in this house was so predictable, I thought impatiently. I was more than ready for something new.

Yet, as we sat at the table, pushing the fabric, thread and scraps toward the center to make room for our glasses and as the tartness of the lemon clutched at two spots under my jaw, the moment seemed precious and worthy of preservation.

Especially after what Aunt Kam said next. As the four of us sat sipping and staring into space, we were both together and apart. Then Aunt Kam cleared her throat the way she did when she had something important to say, and we all cast blue, green and hazel glances in her direction.

"Karl is selling the hardware store."

"Why?" Mom asked. "Now that the war is over, he'll be able to get something to sell."

Aunt Kam shrugged. "I guess he's just tired of working so hard—of being totally responsible."

"What will he do?" Grandma asked.

"Sell cars for Reimer Andersen."

Hot as the night was, I felt the chill of change. Of course I wouldn't be here to see it. Maybe that was the problem. I could go away confidently only if all that I was leaving behind could be frozen as it was, waiting until I came back. That was what I wanted, I thought, and yet I hated "Little Boy Blue," the poem about the toys waiting hopelessly and endlessly for the dead kid who "kissed them and placed them there."

I said, "But Reimer Andersen sells Plymouths."

Aunt Kam nodded, plucking a bit of lemon seed from her lips. "So?"

"How can Uncle Karl sell Plymouths when he thinks the Chevy is the greatest car in the world?"

"He has that all worked out. He says he thought that because he knew more about Chevys, but now that he has read up on Plymouths, he thinks they're even better. That's why it's so important to inform oneself."

Grandma poured more lemonade all around, asking if Karl had a buyer. Aunt Kam said he did. I couldn't imagine walking past the hardware store and seeing somebody else's name above the door.

"May I put some clothes on?" I asked.

"No," Mom said, "we're not through with you. Let's try on that navy blue dress of Marianne's next."

It was tight in the hips, which was no surprise, and I had to take it off to let Grandma release a seam with a razor blade. Then I put it on inside-out and let them pin away while I took my mind elsewhere.

I had been accepted by the State University of Iowa in Iowa City, and it seemed as far away as New York City to someone who never had been farther east than Des Moines. The brochure showed Old Capitol, an impressive golden dome; august-looking buildings with pillars where classes were held; smiling girls with arms piled high with books talking to good-looking males without pimples. I would be even more special—one of the Girls of the Century who entered SUI in its centennial year.

Out of sheer habit, I placed my idol, Hedy Lamarr, in the university scene, and somehow I had trouble making her fit. *Too bad, Hedy*, I thought, abandoning her to her glamorous fate outside the halls of ivy.

At length we had worked through the pile of clothes on the chair, but I had not progressed as fast in my daydreaming. I didn't have enough facts to go on, I decided, and like Uncle Karl reading about Plymouths, I needed more information.

However, my friend Lotus Hess had been taken to visit Simpson, the college she would attend, and she wasn't too excited about getting there.

"What's it like?" I had asked her.

"Methodist."

"That's no answer."

"The heck it's not! If you don't like it, ask somebody else."

It was impossible to fight with Lotus or push her around, and I hoped I would find another friend as good as she at the university.

Among Marianne's discards was an all-wool bathing suit in bright, Halloween orange, and I asked Mom if I could wear it to the pool that Sunday.

"If it gets into the mid-90s, I'll think about it," she said, worried (as always) that I'd catch cold at the heavily-chlorinated municipal pool.

The mercury did me a favor. After church, dinner and a full hour for digestion, I was permitted to collect my swimming gear and leave with Lotus. We struggled into our suits in the odiferous locker room, getting the bottom parts in place before removing our slips. I felt fat, especially in such a shrieking color, but Lotus was fatter. I couldn't swim, but neither could she. We waded in to get wet, and I was grateful for the wool that didn't turn clammy. Lotus' suit was heavy cotton, and it felt like wet laundry, she said.

Lying in the sun on the rough concrete deck and seeing a spectacular light show on the screen of my closed eyelids, I alternated between thinking ahead to the fall and simply surrendering to a pulsing awareness of my body. Boys who knew me didn't give me a second glance, but several strangers who were diving off the high board and horsing around looked at me in a way I understood immediately. How could I, when I'd never attracted such a look before? I decided it was something that all women just knew. And, that much decided, I exempted the Jorgen women. They were uncommon, pure, elevated, and I wasn't sure whether I wanted to throw in my lot with them (as I had so far), or join the rest of womankind.

My old yellow bathing suit had looked better on me than this one, I thought, but it was too small. Also, it reminded me of Albert Rettig—Albert the Pious—who was responsible for my first visit to a real lake and ruined it for me by mooning around after me the whole time. Albert was married now, but I couldn't imagine him doing the unimaginable. At this point, I believed that sex was only for the beautiful and the damned.

Someone was nudging my thigh. Lotus, I thought, but when I opened my eyes to look at her, she was motionless and asleep in the sun. The nudge came from a set of toes, large and male.

"Did you want something?" I asked coolly, noticing that the owner of the toes was not attractive enough to invite notice.

"Just passin' by, Blondie."

Blondie? He had to be from out of town. Nobody in Harlan found blondes at all rare. I turned my head from him, then turned over on my stomach, feeling the orange wool catch on the concrete and the pounding of my own blood somewhere deep in my body.

Lotus spoke lazily, "You sure do have a strong sex drive."

Startled, I said, "Why do you say that?"

"Guys don't come around anyone who doesn't."

"But how can they know—especially when they don't know the first thing about you?"

"Energy. You have to have a lot of energy for that. You've got all kinds of it, and it shows."

"Lotus, you're nuts, do you know that?"

"Am not," she said flatly and promptly fell asleep again.

I drowsed too, then woke and dipped myself into the rank, disinfected water to cool off. The locusts were humming their monotonous song, and even the screaming little kids had settled down under their towels to suck their raisin-textured fingers for awhile.

As I came up the ladder from the pool, I happened to glance toward a shaded bench to the south and thought I recognized Mom. Just when I decided it couldn't be, I knew that it was. Her presence embarrassed me—more this way than if we had come to the pool together and parted at the nastily antiseptic foot bath outside the women's dressing room. It seemed like spying. I refused to look at her, and yet I couldn't resist a quick second glance.

During the few moments that my eyes were elsewhere, a man had approached and was standing there talking to her. She was looking up at him and smiling in a way that was unfamiliar to me where she was concerned—the way a woman smiles at a man. I'd learned about that from movies.

The catch in my chest was gone almost before I was aware of it— the tight, sharp fear of change. I looked away, concentrating on the too-blue floor of the pool and telling myself that I'd soon be so far away that she wouldn't be able to follow me and watch me—or disapprove of the wonderful unfolding of my future.

And what would happen here when I was gone? Grandma would see to it that everything stayed the same. The next time I looked, Mom was gone. So was the man.

When I came home sunburned and filled with the lassitude caused by hours in the open air, Mom was sitting on the porch swing reading *The Upper Room*, a devotional booklet from the church. Grandma was rocking in the wicker chair, using a cardboard fan from Schack's funeral home to move the dead air of late afternoon.

"Did you have fun?" Mom asked.

"Did you?" I countered.

Her eyes left my face and focused on the leafy vines that screened the porch. I saw the tiny, secret smile that a casual observer would have missed.

"Who was that man?" I demanded.

"Magnus Nygaard. I was just telling Mama about running into him. He and his wife went to the Wisconsin Ridge church when we did."

Relieved, I nodded and went in the front door, through the house and out the back door to hang my suit and towel on the clothesline near the grape arbor. I could hear Mom and Grandma talking, Mom saying she should be sewing name tags into my clothes, and Grandma saying she'd have to take every stitch up with her nose in heaven if she did it on Sunday. Some things would always stay the same.

After the last wash before my departure came out of the old Maytag, I had to keep everything clean to pack. Finding something to wear wasn't easy, but I was getting by in a faded cotton skirt and Mom's blouses. Then the invitation arrived.

The note was on pink paper with an embossed seashell, and it was signed "Florine Hammond." Balaam couldn't have been more surprised by his uttering ass than I was to be asked to tea by Judge Harvey Hammond's wife.

The Hammonds lived in a big, beautiful house on Baldwin Street with fairytale turrets and mullioned windows. I never had crossed its threshold, but I had imagined lifting the heavy, brass doorknocker and snuggling into my furs to wait for admission—Hedy Lamarr, the eagerly-awaited guest.

"What kind of a party is it?" Mom asked.

"I think it's just me. She says we have something to 'chat about.' "

"Well, I guess you'll have to wear the new dress. Try not to spill on it."

"I won't spill!" I said indignantly, yearning for the independence that was just a few days beyond my grasp.

The appointed day was too hot for sheer wool, but that couldn't be helped. After Labor Day, one was supposed to wear fall clothes. I walked north to Baldwin Street as slowly as I could to keep from sweating, going a block out of my way to find the shadiest route.

Tea? We drank elderberry tea when we were sick but never consumed the stuff for pleasure. Coffee was the beverage to enjoy, freshly-ground at the A & P and jewel-clear from the raw egg broken into the rich, brown grains.

I knew very little about Florine Hammond because she was younger than the mothers of my friends (younger than her husband, too), didn't go to our church (she was Episcopalian), and didn't shop at the A & P. She and the Judge had no children, but they attended high school class plays and sports events, and she was on the library board. She also played golf at the Field Club, and I remembered seeing her come in off the course while our Girl Scout troop was encamped in the ballroom of the Club, army cots in long ranks along the dance floor. Her thick golden hair was braided with a scarf of royal blue chiffon and coiled high on her head like a crown.

"Who is that?" I whispered to Monica. Monica knew all the people on what Mom called "Silk Stocking Street" because her dad was a doctor.

"Mrs. Hammond. She can't get a caddy anymore because she cusses so bad."

"I don't believe it! She's too gorgeous to cuss."

Monica shrugged, "So don't believe it! That's why they don't ask her to join P.E.O., too."

"What's P.E.O.?"

"I don't know. They've got a bunch of secrets, and they don't let Catholics in because they're afraid they'd tell when they go to confession."

"You don't tell stuff like that at confession, do you?"

Monica shrugged again. "*I* wouldn't, but you never can tell about someone who doesn't have any halfway decent sins to offer."

At any rate, I had admired Florine Hammond from afar. She drove a cream-colored convertible, the only open car in town; her clothes were at least as expensive as my cousin Marianne's but in straightforward colors—none of the celery, nougat and shrimp bisque shades that Marianne favored and passed down for me to explain. Mrs. Hammond had a bright, challenging gaze that measured whatever it met and seemed to find it wanting. This, I decided, was divine discontent.

Gregory Sommer, my boss, called her "Carol," and when I looked puzzled, he told me to read *Main Street* by Sinclair Lewis. Like many of his suggestions for my edification, this one was filed for "future disposition," one of his own favorite designations. If ever I'd dreamed of this summons from Florine Hammond, it wouldn't have been.

As I turned up the Hammonds' front walk, I smoothed my peplum, licked my Persian Melon lips and checked out the tight roll of my pageboy hair. I wished I had carried a purse, which would give me something to do with my hands, but I really didn't need one. I never carried or used a house key, I didn't smoke, and I didn't have a cold that would require a supply of handkerchiefs.

When I raised the heavy bronze knocker, it whined in its hinges, and bringing it down on the metal plate produced such an insignificant rap that I had small hope of being heard. Through the screened windows on the porch came the low hum of a fan, but I heard no footsteps, and the pleated chiffon covering the glass oval in the door yielded nothing but my own reflection. I tried the knocker again and waited, beginning to feel as I had during the agony of selling Girl Scout cookies.

Just when I was ready to turn and go, believing that Mrs. Hammond had forgotten, the door opened. She gestured to me to come in while she retrieved the phone receiver stretched to the limit of its long cord and laying on the polished tile floor. The rest of the apparatus was in an adjoining room. Our phone hung on the wall, and you couldn't move two feet away from it.

I stood in the entry hall, hands behind my back squashing my peplum, while she listened and rolled her eyes. She was wearing a "transitional" dark cotton that made my sheer wool seem all wrong, but I realized that I owned nothing that would be any better.

"Someone's here, Annabelle, you can tell me the rest later. All right, good-bye." She disappeared into the next room to hang up the phone and returned with a rueful smile.

"Philistines!"

The Philistines were all over the Bible, but I hadn't expected to encounter them in this house. I smiled back and waited for my next cue.

"Come into the parlor," she said, "it's cooler there."

It was. Many shades of blue and white, the room was furnished with antiques. Aunt Kam had asked me to take a good look at the "Hammond family things" and describe them to her. She had taken a sudden interest in "fine, old pieces." I tried to look and remember without being obvious, and even *I* could tell that Florine Hammond had altered the usual feeling of "fine, old pieces." The deep, wing chairs were upholstered in geometric prints, and the oval picture frames held paintings that were nothing but brush strokes of color. Aunt Kam would be astonished at the sight.

Mrs. Hammond watched me take it all in and waited. I couldn't call it "nice," or "pretty," and I didn't know *what* to say, so I simply waited too.

"Do sit down," she finally said, "take the Chippendale. It's more comfortable."

Which one was that? I had spent my life with no-name furniture.

"Oh, I'm comfortable anywhere," I said, backing up until my calves hit something and lowering my peplumed posterior with great care.

Florine, as I called her mentally, collapsed gracefully into one of the big chairs, looking like a book illustration. Her small feet, delicate even in red espadrilles (I knew what they were called from riffling through old fashion magazines at the dentist's office), scarcely touched the floor.

"So," she said, "you're the winner of the Garner scholarship."

"Yes. If I hadn't been, I wouldn't be going to college at all."

"Why not? No aspirations?"

"No money."

She nodded almost brusquely and said she'd get the tea. I'd heard that the Hammonds had a hired girl who got dressed up like maids in the movies, and I was disappointed to miss this phenomonen. Maybe it was her day off.

At least this gave me a chance to *really* look around in Aunt Kam's behalf. Mom and Grandma wouldn't be interested in such things, but Aunt Kam made much of being a "lady" and would have given anything for the credentials to join the D.A.R. or that other bunch from which Florine was excluded, according to Monica. For all I knew, they were excited about antiques too. I had a feeling that *none* of them would admire Florine's handling of the Hammond heirlooms. I didn't think they looked too good either, but I rather enjoyed the unexpectedness of them. For instance, that tiny, fancy table of dark wood with a mirror cut to fit the top and reflect the pantaloons of a porcelain figurine that resembled Vivien Leigh. "Vivien's" fragile hand was positioned on the fat belly of a brass idol.

Just as I was craning my neck to read the spines of a stack of books on another table, noting that there was no "Public Library" stamp on the page bottoms, Florine returned with the tea tray. I'd been hoping for iced, but it was hot.

She poured from a soft blue-gray pot into cups with no handles, saying, "There's nothing like hot tea to cool one off—or to warm one up, for that matter."

Her hands, hardened by golfing, no doubt, were equal to grasping the cup without pain, but I had to stifle a gasp when I took mine. The tray held nothing edible, which was a disappointment. When she invited someone for tea, she really meant it, whereas a Danish invitation to coffee promised (and delivered) much more. What did this woman want of me?

Florine sipped, eyeing me broodingly above the rim of her cup. Then she said, "I knew Bill Garner very well. His death was a great loss."

"That's what everyone says. I didn't know him."

"Nobody here did. First he went to prep school in the east and then to Harvard. If he *had* come back, they wouldn't have understood him."

And if he hadn't died, I wouldn't have had a scholarship, I thought, realizing that this observation was unspeakable. What did she want?

She seemed lost in thought or memory, staring at the fringed and tasseled draperies as if I weren't there, but then she snapped back suddenly and said, "I suppose you know that Mary Lois Engle isn't going to school this fall?"

"No!" I said, genuinely shocked that the valedictorian of our class would back out with all arrangements made so far in advance. Mary Lois had been the one to make me feel miserable with all her talk of campus life when I thought it was not for me.

Florine smiled thinly. "In that case, you won't know why, either, and you'll never believe it!"

"Why?"

"Because she's in line to be Worthy Advisor in Rainbow, and she wants to go through the chairs before she begins her education. If you ask me, she'll *never* begin if she doesn't do it now."

I was speechless. Mary Lois and I never had been friends, but circumstances had thrown us together enough for me to be aware of her and interested in her. She had been the perfect girl all through school, from the Shirley Temple look-alike of kindergarten to the top student and piano virtuoso of our senior year. I was a Rainbow Girl too, but I'd never give up my future for it.

"I suppose you're wondering what my interest is in all this and why I asked you to come and see me?"

I nodded, trying to think what I could say if she asked me to change Mary Lois's mind. Almost anyone else would have been a better choice, considering the way we felt about each other.

"Margaret, have you thought about pledging a sorority?"

"No."

"Well, think about it. They always count on me to send someone good their way—someone to raise the grade average in the house—

and since Mary Lois has chosen to fail me, I'd like you to consider it. Greg Sommer says you're really very bright."

"Oh, I couldn't!" I said quickly, remembering the information about Rush Week that had arrived in the mail. When I got it, I decided that I didn't have enough clothes to appear at that many events and be weighed in the balance. Besides, I wouldn't have the money for the dues or whatever.

"Margaret," she said patiently, "don't say no so quickly. I'm sure that you'll see the advantages of the Greek way of life when you've investigated it more fully."

"No, really, Mrs. Hammond—I can't afford it."

"I could help."

"My mother would never allow that."

"She wouldn't have to know."

I laughed, knowing how rotten I was at keeping things from her. "What if your sorority didn't want me?"

"There would be no problem about that," Florine said, adding darkly, "there are ways."

"You're very kind, but I can't."

"Oh shit!" she said. "There's nobody else!"

Stunned by the word I'd never heard from a woman's lips, I thanked her and left in a hurry.

When Mom and Grandma wanted to know what it was all about, I told them, and they were surprised to hear about Mary Lois. I protected Florine by burying the word I was sure she didn't mean to say aloud. As I started to take off my dress before I ruined it completely, it occurred to me that she hadn't admired it. I didn't like it as much as I had before and wouldn't blame Mrs. Hammond for being glad I wasn't pounding on the door of her sorority house, mad to get in.

Aunt Kam asked Grandma if she'd like to come along and "help take Margaret to college," but Grandma shook her head and said, *"Nej, nej!"* That meant that the serious good-byes would begin sooner than I had anticipated. Somehow, I had expected that everybody would come along, postponing the inevitable.

The other thing I felt was a tiny bubble of relief which I wouldn't have admitted to anyone. That bubble, like the last one to rise in a glass of stale gingerale, held the image of a small woman from the Old Country wearing oval glasses framed in thin gold and dressed in a high-necked "waist," a long skirt and heavy lisle stockings walking into the slick-brochure perfection of the SUI campus. She wouldn't fit in.

Aunt Kam and Uncle Karl would be OK. Marianne had given Aunt Kam a subscription to Vogue, and Uncle Karl had bought a new suit when he was elected president of Kiwanis. I wasn't too sure about Mom, though. She made do with stuff she'd had for years, insisting that telephone operators should be more concerned about sounding pleasant than looking "spiffy."

I knew what I would wear on the day of sailing out, as Grandma called it. My last check from Gregory Sommer had bought a lavendar pullover and a deep green pleated skirt of heavy wool at Mardee's Frockery, and I had a new pair of saddle shoes.

Everything was ready for loading when Uncle Karl pulled up in his pale green Plymouth. A battered foot locker that had belonged to Uncle Stig held almost everything, and the rest went into a pouchy suitcase like the ones old-fashioned doctors carried. Alas, no one had given me a baby-blue Samsonite for graduation.

I hated the suitcase, originally black but now worn to tan, raw leather in spots. It had been in the store room of every house we'd lived in, and I'd never known whose it was in the beginning.

Grandma ran her fingers over the scars on the thing and said, "It was brand new when Peter took it to Chicago in '93, but Stig gave it some hard use when he ran away to join the carnival. I should have given it a swipe with some black shoe polish."

"No! Then it would smell."

She shrugged with a dry smile. "It's up to you whether you baby your nose or your eyes—but I'll just give it a swipe."

Mom said, "It's getting pretty hot. Don't you want to wear a blouse in the car and put the sweater on later?"

"I'm OK," I lied. The lavendar wool was altogether too heavy for the warm, hazy September day, but, as Grandma so often said, "Beauty must suffer."

"You women about ready?" Uncle Karl called. He whipped out his handkerchief and rubbed the fingerprints off the finish of the car trunk. We could see why Aunt Kam called the Plymouth his "new sweetheart."

"All except for the lunch," Mom said, hurrying into the house for the basket packed with sandwiches, apples, cookies and two tea towel-wrapped Mason jars filled with lemonade. Thermos jugs cost money and were used too infrequently to justify the investment.

I had hoped that just this once we could stop at a restaurant along the way, but Mom wouldn't hear of such an extravagance. Besides, she said, the food in those places was nasty.

I had hugged Grandma, who responded with a brusque pat on the back, and was climbing into the back seat to sit with Mom when somebody yelled my name.

"Margaret, wait!"

"Gee whillikers, now what?" Uncle Karl groused.

It was Merrilee Adams, my friend from the commercial course taken by those who were not college bound. Until I won the Garner scholarship, I had been one of them.

I heard Aunt Kam's sniff and resented it. So what if Merrilee had gotten pregnant when she shouldn't? That was one mistake she'd never make again.

I hadn't seen Merrilee all summer—not since graduation, when she said, "Well, it's all over for me, but not for you, I guess." I heard that she got a job at the REA, and once I even called the number to hear her say, "Rural Electrification Association, may I help you?" She sounded so unfamiliar that I hung up in confusion.

Now she was running awkwardly in high heels, panting with the effort. I went to meet her, taking whatever we would say to each other out of Aunt Kam's hearing.

"God, I almost missed you!" She thrust a small package into my hands.

"Thanks, Merrilee, you didn't have to—"

"Just wanted to—for old times, you know?"

I knew. The long conversations on the high school steps, sitting on stacked mattresses in the corner that was her bedroom, helping her capture and scrub her younger brothers and sisters, admiring her prom formal—and all the time begging her to tell me the Mystery of Life. She had to know after having a baby, but she wasn't telling.

"I'll write you a letter," I promised, thinking that I might have a few mysteries of my own to offer soon.

"Aren't you going to open it?"

I pulled at the yellow ribbon, trying to ignore the clarion call of the Plymouth's horn. Uncle Karl was getting fed up with waiting. When the white tissue paper parted, I saw the heart-stopping cobalt blue of an Evening in Paris bottle.

Merrilee couldn't know of my younger yearning for such a magic blue bottle—or of my disappointment in the fragrance it held once I smelled it. My eyes smarted with tears as I gave her a quick hug.

"Thanks!"

"That's OK. You look great—like a real college girl. Hurry up, now. Your uncle's about to throw a fit."

I climbed into the car, careful to smooth my dark green pleats, and took a deep breath of the new car smell that everyone seemed to appreciate so much. I hoped it wouldn't make me carsick.

Uncle Karl turned down 9th Street to take Highway 44 out of town, tooting his horn at pedestrians he recognized. Of course there wouldn't be any he didn't recognize. The pale green Plymouth was a head-turner, as there hadn't been all that many new cars in town since the war ended.

Acutely aware of the combined prickle of the plush seat and my wool pleats, I tried to ease the window open just a crack. Uncle Karl was lighting a Lucky Strike, and I wanted to snatch a quick breath before his first exhalation.

"I feel a draft!" Mom said, folding the lapels of her blouse over her throat.

Turning sideways to hide the operation with my body, I cranked the window up, grateful for the well-oiled silence of the handle.

"That's better," Mom said.

We passed several of the spots where I had done much of my dreaming—the creek where crawdads bubbled to signal their presence, the tree I had climbed to watch sunsets on the way to and from getting the milk, and the swimming pool park where I had played summer concerts and once in a great while wallowed in heavy chlorine.

I had wished myself away from all these places, but now that I was really leaving, they were invested with a special glow that made me want to jump out of the car and repossess them.

We headed east, and when the Plymouth had purred its way up the first hill, I turned to look at Harlan one last time. The daytime view wasn't as spectacular as the nighttime look of a tiara resting on dark velvet. Now the town looked like a bracelet in need of polishing set with a soap-dulled gem that was the water tower.

Aunt Kam turned in the front passenger seat and reached for the tissue-wrapped package in my lap. "Let's see your present."

As I handed it to her, she saw what it was and released her grip, letting the bottle fall back into my pleated lap.

"The poor girl probably thinks that's quality," she said.

Uncle Karl turned on the radio to get the news, which saved me from having to devise an inoffensive response or turning loose the offensive one that would come to me without effort.

Evening in Paris was a dream, and I thought it was wonderful that Merrilee still was capable of dreaming after all she'd been through. Some of Aunt Kam's standards were ridiculous—like her notion that "only trashy people have peaks in their tablecloths." What were you supposed to do with a tablecloth, hang it on the wall between meals? Whip out the flatiron every time you set the table? Of course none of us ever let our resentment of Aunt Kam show, knowing it would bring on one of her choking fits if we did.

We rounded the breathtaking curve at Jacksonville, and I took one last look at the porch of the general store where there had been a shootout before I was born. And in the cemetery next to the Lutheran church was the grave of a girl who had taken poison when she found out she was in Merrilee's situation. People would gossip about her forever, but she wouldn't be around to hear it. Mom said Merrilee could live it down. "Live" was the word that mattered.

Mom and Aunt Kam were having their usual argument about who married whom and lived on which farm, and that went on between Kimballton and Hamlin.

The highway crossed the railroad tracks in the middle of this flat, sparse town where no Pied Piper ever could have lived, and soon we were in the beautiful hills skimmed by the Ridge Road.

Guthrie Center, Panora, Dallas Center, Grimes, and then Uncle Karl turned south to pick up Highway 6 and drive through Des Moines on Euclid Avenue. We stopped at the Koffee Kup, and while Mom and Uncle Karl argued about the check, I headed for the restroom.

I had been trained to put toilet paper on the seat to avoid "nasty diseases," but it kept falling in or onto the floor, so I took the giant risk and sat unshielded. The small enclosure smelled so strongly of disinfectant that I was sure no germ could survive. While I sat there breathing shallowly, I added a few words from the lipstick scribblings on the wall to my look-up list.

As we left Des Moines, my excitement mounted. Going east always had meant adventure, just as traveling west had meant going home, and now we were in new territory, going farther east than I had ever been.

Colfax, Newton, Grinnell and Brooklyn. None of these towns looked as strange as I thought they would. When we reached Ladora, Uncle Karl said he was hungry. He looked for a park but at the urging of the women, settled for a cemetery.

Mom spread the scratchy Army blanket on a hillside and we settled ourselves among obelisks so old that their porous stone looked like partially-consumed popsicles—that stage when you've sucked out the liquid and most of the color.

We were used to socializing in cemeteries, and we knew the etiquette. You never used the top of a flat tombstone for a table unless it belonged to a relative, you were sensitive to the boundaries of each grave and never stepped on one, you pulled a weed if you were sure it was one, and you never left trash behind.

The sandwiches were *rullepølse,* a Danish spiced meat roll so tedious to make that it was reserved for high occasions. Grandma had done it as a surprise, Mom told me, rolling and sewing the beef flank, pork slices, onion and spices to soak in cold brine for ten days, and then cooking it for two hours in the heat of dog days. How could it be that I hadn't noticed?

"I'll bet you won't taste this again for a long time, Margaret," Aunt Kam said, lifting the top slice of homemade white bread to admire the paper-thin meat dotted with coarse pepper.

I agreed absently, having discovered that the occupant of the nearest grave had been just my age when she died. Her name was Lovilia, and she was somebody's "beloved wife" as well as the mother of the infant whose grave was marked by a stone lamb that had lost its definition to a century of weather.

I risked imagining myself cut off from life just now—just when I was at the brink of all discovery. The thought was unbearable, and I turned from it to a pitying curiosity about the manner of Lovilia's death. Better her than me.

We pressed on through Marengo, South Amana, Homestead and Tiffin, where I was enthralled by a sign marking "The Lark Supper Club." The building was fairly ordinary, but what did that matter? The name was the thing, evoking Hedy Lamarr swinging her hair in a dark cloud as she turned to greet someone on the way to her table for two.

The day had grown hotter, and I was suffering in my wool, but when we reached Iowa City, I saw that others were doing the same. That made it all right.

The thing that was all wrong was the length of my new green

skirt—just below the knee. Everyone else's hemline plunged past mid-calf.

"I think they call that the New Look," Aunt Kam said. "I read about it in *Vogue* and would have suggested it for your sheer wool, but I didn't think it would catch on out here."

Mom sighed deeply, and I might have succumbed to despair if I hadn't looked up just then and recognized the gold dome of Old Capitol. It was even better than the brochure, much more beautiful in its slender simplicity than the one in Des Moines that reminded me of a fat woman wearing too much costume jewelry.

That dome offered the promise of what I'd come to Iowa City to find and made hemlines seem relatively unimportant.

Uncle Karl had studied the directions for finding Currier Cottage 15 while we were eating lunch, and he brought the Plymouth to a smooth stop beside a low building of corrugated metal that looked like a hog house.

"This must be it," he said doubtfully.

"It *does* say fifteen," Aunt Kam said.

I just stared. Cottages were cute, little houses in fairytales or the retreat of "Sleepytime Gal" and her true love. This couldn't be one.

"Go up and check, Margaret," Mom said.

I got out of the car, shutting the door gently. Nothing made Uncle Karl madder than having his car doors slammed. I had to stand aside and wait while another girl and her father staggered up the steps from the sidewalk with luggage and garment bags. Her New Look skirt swirled around her lower shins like a trumpet flower.

A tiny brunette with a clipboard appeared in the doorway saying, "Welcome to Cottage 15! Which one are you?"

"Sue Benton," said the beautiful, fashionable girl.

I returned to the car to help with the unloading. Uncle Karl insisted on managing the footlocker by himself, though Mom and Aunt Kam thought he shouldn't. Their attempts to help were a hindrance, and their muttering in Danish embarrassed me.

I got to the door first, carrying the leprous-looking satchel, and identified myself to the girl with the clipboard.

She checked off my name and told me she was Boots Ryan, the proctor.

Mom came inside, swept the salmon-walled interior with a glance, and plunked a cardboard box of my belongings on a lower bunk. "Better take this one. You might fall out of the upper."

"I would not!" I said in a furious but low tone, hoping that the dazzling Sue Benton hadn't heard. It seemed that she hadn't. She was busy cramming wonderful-looking clothes into the cardboard wardrobe she'd picked out down at the other end of the cottage near the study desks.

Two more girls arrived, one with her parents and the other with parents plus the hometown boyfriend. Boots made the introductions, yelling out names and pointing with her clipboard. When it was over, I couldn't remember which was which.

Aunt Kam started to unpack the footlocker, but I told her I'd do that later. I wanted them out of there before anyone else came.

Mom seemed to understand that, but still she was reluctant to leave. She looked at Boots Ryan doubtfully, as if Boots were a babysitter of dubious qualifications, and moved sideways to the door. I was afraid she might decide not to leave me there.

Uncle Karl hurried out, eager to light a cigarette. "Looks like you're all set," he said, "guess we'd better pull out. You ready, Kam?"

My aunt seemed caught in the doorway, looking back into the cottage. She joined us with a series of quick, little steps.

"It's such fun to see all these lovely, young things," she said. "Oh, to be young!"

I nodded, as wistful as if I were her contemporary, not theirs.

Mom grasped my upper arm loosely, staring into the distance with a heavy, hazel gaze. "Well—"

We were blocking the sidewalk, and two couples holding hands walked wide around us. I saw us through their eyes and didn't like the picture. Then, hating my disloyalty, I hugged my mother and wept, gulping in the scent of her Lady Esther face powder as I sobbed.

"Write. And send your laundry," she said, gently but firmly removing my grappling arms.

Uncle Karl was waiting behind the wheel, but Aunt Kam was still there on the sidewalk. She pinched my chin with hard fingers and said, "Jorgen women do not make public scenes!"

The reminder of the standards of the maternal line did the trick. I froze mid-sob and forced a smile. We exchanged brief hugs, they got into the car, and I waved. Then I turned away to avoid watching them out of sight, which would invite bad luck.

I returned to the cottage and climbed into my lower bunk, looking out through the bars of the headboard like a caged animal—an animal bereaved by removal from its native place.

The downward bulge in the upper bunk mattress was registered by my homesick eyes but not identified. It shifted, and an upside-down face spoke to me.

"Hi! I'm Venus Craton from Davenport."

Fascinated by a mouth moving where eyebrows ought to be, I told the mouth who I was and where I came from.

"Where's that? Never heard of it."

"Out west," I said, hoping to make it sound at least as far as Denver.

Venus jumped down and sat on the lower bunk across from mine. No one had claimed that one yet, and I asked her why she hadn't taken it.

"I feel safer up high."

She wasn't exactly plump, just rounded everywhere like a loaf of rising dough. Her hair was dark brown and crinkled, her nose was sharp, and when she spoke, she cocked her head to one side like a brightly curious bird.

"No food in the dorm tonight," she said. "Want to go out and find something?"

"Sure, if you know where."

She nodded with city-girl assurance, and when we had collected cottage keys from Boots, we walked toward the Pentacrest. Venus told me they called it that. She seemed to know everything. Pointing, she said, "That's Commerce, that's Physics, that's Old Dental, that's MacBride and that's Shaeffer."

Old Capitol caught the last gleam of sunset as the surrounding buildings settled the dark importance of their bulk into the twilight. I wanted to rush right into one of them and learn something but didn't dare to say so.

When we came into the glaring light of Hamburg Inn, I observed that Venus was decently dressed but no more fashionable than I was. Apparently, it would be us against the world.

We ordered hamburgers and Cokes and exchanged information about our families. She had a brother, a sister, an invalid mother and a father. She was the first member of her family to go to college, encouraged by a high school counselor who helped her put together some scholarships.

We had no counselors in Harlan. If you got into trouble, a teacher or the principal whaled you, and if you couldn't figure out what to do with your life, that was your tough luck.

"What's your major going to be?" she asked.

The answer surprised even me. "Journalism. What about yours?"

"Don't know for sure. Miss Suderman thought I was artistic."

"Are you?"

She blushed, and I decided that Western Iowa directness might not be the thing around here.

I picked up my check with an odd sensation. Never had I bought a necessary meal. At home, restaurants were primarily for strangers in town. The locals used them only for incidental and recreational eating. I knew that I would be paying for my meals in the dorm, but that was different. I wouldn't be handing over money three times a day.

It was dark when we came out into the street. Venus sniffed at her blouse sleeve and wrinkled her nose.

"The only trouble with that place is that you smell like it for days after."

We walked along in companionable silence until the darkness

encouraged her to ask something personal, "Do you have a boyfriend?"

"No, do you?"

Her face was a pale, moving blur as she shook her head. "That's why some girls come here, but not me!"

Back at the cottage, everyone had moved in. Nine girls and a proctor would share four sinks, two toilets and two showers. Venus and I came in through the door from the alley, and whoever was speaking didn't see us.

"Would you look at that? Evening in Paris! My God, does anybody actually *use* the stuff?"

Hot humiliation rose from my cheeks to the top of my skull and then plummeted through my body like a falling elevator.

"And that clock!" There was a pause in which the speaker evidently picked up the offending object. "Big Ben! This thing ticks louder than the real thing in London!"

Venus had checked out my possessions well enough to know that the property under discussion was mine. She flashed me a quick look of sympathy and cleared her throat loudly.

"Somebody there?" asked the voice.

Venus grabbed my unwilling arm and marched me down to our bunk area, where she announced both of our names to the back of a shapely body bent to set down my Big Ben. The legs probably were just as good, but how could you tell in the New Look?

The figure in gray flannel and white angora whirled, and I'm sure my jaw dropped a mile. The black hair, green eyes and bright, full lips came as close to the Hedy Lamarr ideal as seemed humanly possible.

"Hi," said the most beautiful girl I'd ever seen, "I'm Reva Rosendorf from Sioux City."

Then the person she'd been talking to emerged from the shadows of a lower bunk. She said she was Sheila Swift from Cape Girardeau, Missouri.

A musky, heavy scent that seemed more than a little wicked seemed to be emanating from Reva. I told her that a friend had given me the Evening in Paris just as I was leaving home, making it clear that I had not chosen it.

"What kind are *you* wearing?" I asked her.

"Faberge."

I sniffed, envisioning ripe melons and turbaned slaves waving huge peacock fans over a recumbent Reva lazily eating grapes. I couldn't bring myself to say, "Nice!" and end this stupid conversation, so I just nodded.

Reva ended it, edging past me in the narrow space between the bunks. When she was in the clear, she twirled on the ball of one foot, setting the flared hemline of her long skirt in motion. It was beautiful. She peeled off the white angora swearter, let the gray skirt drop in a pool at her feet and eased into a satin robe the color of the darkest peonies in Aunt Kam's backyard. Everything she owned was opulent, I thought, feeling more despair than envy. What would Reva think when I got into the flowered cotton pajamas Mom had made for me?

Sheila lay back on her bunk, arms folded behind her head, and regarded Venus and me with a vague smile. She was a transfer from a junior college, she told us, and she supposed they wouldn't keep her in a cottage full of freshmen for very long. If they did, she'd appeal to her oldest sister's husband. He was in the Iowa State Legislature.

I hadn't finished unpacking, and I was hanging up clothes in the heavy cardboard wardrobe beside my desk when three more girls came in. I happened to have the purple dress with the silver sequin butterflies in my hand, and I thrust it between two other garments like a guilty secret.

The newcomers were Dot Greer from Spencer, Nita Lund from Waterloo and Kay Albers from Anamosa. They had been swimming at Lake MacBride all day, they said, taking advantage of Kay's brother's car which would have to be returned the next weekend.

Dot was short and muscular, almost mannish-looking with her cropped hair and severely-tailored clothes. She came from a family of doctors and planned to enter medical school herself.

Nita was even blonder than the Danes I'd grown up with. Her hair was straight and long, and she tilted her head downward to peer from beneath long, straight bangs with blue eyes that were pale to the point of eeriness. She laughed a lot, sounding slightly frantic when she did so.

Kay Albers was tall, rangy and sleepy-eyed. She looked like a girls' basketball player and seemed like a person who could be imposed upon readily.

"Hey," Nita said, "what do they call you?"

"Margaret."

"The whole thing?"

I nodded, and she shrugged. Then she said, "Hey, Margaret, do you know how to tell whether you had a good time on a date?"

Her eyes glittered, and I answered warily that I supposed I did. Dot rolled her eyes, and Kay added a grin to her sleepy-eyed expression.

"You just *think* you know," said Nita. "Here's how you really find out. When you come in, throw your pants against the wall. If they stick, you had a good time."

Dot exploded with laughter and Kay joined in. I wasn't sure whether they were laughing at what Nita said or at how I reacted to it. I knew that my face had reddened for the second time that day and that I had no ready response.

"Ever hear that one before?" Nita pressed.

"Nope," I said, "that's a new one on me."

The entrance of Rosemary Horstmann got me off the hook. She was from Monona and engaged to a fellow from home who had just one more year at the university. Rosemary wore a plain white blouse like the ones that go with gym shorts. She didn't have to worry about the way she looked because she had Charlie, who had just smeared her lipstick with a lingering good-night kiss outside the cottage's alley door.

Venus came to her desk, which was beside mine. She fussed with a cup filled with pens and pencils and straightened the edges of some magazines. I introduced her to the others, getting everything straight but Nita's last name. I figured she was lucky I remembered *any* of her name, considering the way she'd startled me. I'd see to it that she never caught me off guard again.

"Well," said Nita, "keep your legs crossed!" She and the other three headed for the bunk area, leaving me alone with Venus.

"Just one more to go," I said.

Venus was tight-lipped, almost white around the mouth. "I suppose we'll have to listen to that stuff all year."

"You mean Nita?"

"I can't stand sex talk!" Venus said with quiet intensity.

"I've never heard much of it."

"My mother told me how men rip and tear you. They do it first, and then the babies finish the job!"

"I'm sure it's not always that bad—"

"My mother has slept sitting up in a chair for years. She has asthma."

"But you don't get that from—"

"Oh *don't* you? I have a sister—Betty Lou. Mother told her the same thing she told me, but would she listen? Oh no, Betty Lou had to get married. She didn't even graduate high school, and I was so ashamed! Nobody's ever going to touch me that way!"

"Is Betty Lou happy now?" I asked, thinking of Merrilee and her refusal of a husband she couldn't love.

"How *could* she be?" Venus cried.

"Well," I said, "I'll bet you'll meet someone who'll change your mind about all that."

Venus dumped the pens and pencils from the cup and fenced a rectangular enclosure with them, "If I ever do meet anybody I can stand—if I ever marry, we'll work out an agreement. Maybe I could put up with it once a year—do it on New Year's Eve to get it out of the way."

How could Venus's mother name her after the goddess of love and then fill her with such dread? I hadn't been told much about love, but at least I hadn't been made to believe that it was awful and to be avoided at all costs. Very little of it went on among the Jorgen women because the men of the family died young. Venus's father was still alive, and I wondered about him. For the first time in a long while, I wondered how my life would have been different had my own father lived.

I thought about taking a shower, but Reva had disappeared into one of the stalls half an hour before, and Rosemary had plunged into the billowing steam to claim the other one shortly thereafter. Boots Ryan was yelling at them to hurry it up.

Nobody had studying to do yet, so Sheila, Dot, Nita and Kay had a bridge game going, and I saw that they had dragged my old foot locker between two lower bunks to use as a table. Dot and Nita were, in fact, sitting on my bed.

Venus yawned and said she was going to call it a day. "If those two hog the showers all night, I'll take mine in the morning."

I sat at my desk staring at the peach walls until she came out of the bathroom in a long nightgown, toothbrush in hand, and said, "It looks like Dante's 'Inferno' in there. Goodnight."

It seemed that I could put off changing into my homemade pajamas no longer. Unfortunately, they were in the foot locker being used as a bridge table. I decided to wait.

My head was filled with so many new impressions that it felt like one of those small books of drawings that become "movies" when you flip the pages as fast as you can.

I thought of home. Grandma would be unbraiding her hair, brushing it and re-braiding a single plait. Mom would be smearing Ponds cold cream on her face and reading a bit from her Bible while it sank in. I should be there too, brushing my teeth twice because I had yearned for one of Grandma's filled cookies after the first brushing. Tears almost came to my eyes at the thought, but I forced myself to consider the matter coldly. Would I give up this for that? Absolutely not.

Someone was knocking at the door, and Boots Ryan jumped up, grabbing her clipboard. "This had better be Elena," she said, "I've got a heavy date as soon as I get all of you checked in."

It was. Elena Pavkovic from Joliet, Illinois, was delivered by her mother, two sisters and a speech therapist. The sisters were beautiful (one married and one single), but Elena was the loveliest with the whitest skin I'd ever seen, eyes the color of purple-blue irises, and long, dark hair. The mother was a wearier, sadder version of the daughters, and the speech therapist gave a sandy-colored impression. Her voice had the same inflections I'd noticed in Reva's.

The therapist, whose name was Vida Golden, was telling Boots about "Elena's handicap. She's totally deaf—it happened when she got the mumps at the age of sixteen."

Boots looked worried. "How do I—I mean, can—can she—"

Vida Golden waved an impatient hand. "No problem. She lip-reads beautifully."

"Sorry to be so late," Mrs. Pavkovic apologized, "but we stopped to visit friends in Rock Island, and time just slipped away from us."

"Oh well," Boots said, "she should have one last fling before she has to keep hours. This is Margaret Langelund."

Elena kept her eyes on Boots's lips as long as they moved, then followed the proctor's gesture to me.

"Hello, Margaret." Her voice was low and a bit foreign-sounding.

I told her I was glad to meet her, feeling that I was making exaggerated motions with my mouth to help her understand.

She laughed. "Don't do that! It's easier for me if you talk to me just the way you do to anyone else."

After her family and Miss Golden left, I helped Elena unpack. It was late and I was tired, but I couldn't get into the trunk that held my pajamas anyhow.

The bridge players had turned on the radio, and I almost said something about how loud it was before I remembered that Elena couldn't hear it at all.

Now *I* was the one with a hearing problem. Elena's low voice was buried in the music from the Aragon Ballroom and in the Friendly Grainbelt beer commercial.

I did manage to learn that her family was Serbian, and that she had learned lip-reading at a small college. She didn't intend to tell every Tom, Dick and Harry that she was deaf, either.

"You don't need to think that it's all bad—not being able to hear," she said. "If you ever want to eavesdrop on somebody across the room, just let me know. Anything I can see, you can hear!"

"What will your major be?" I asked.

"Journalism."

"Really? Mine too, I think."

Finally I applied to the bridge players for permission to tilt their table, snatched my pajamas and retreated to the bathroom.

Boots had been picked up by Steve, considering her duties to be finished with bed check, and the radio was turned up high. Vaughan Monroe was singing "Racing With the Moon."

I hadn't grabbed my slippers from the trunk while I had it open, and the concrete floor was no comfort to the feet. Reva was at the long mirror, towelling the steam off with one hand and patting a mud-like substance on her face with the other. Her pajamas were white silk piped in the peony-red of her robe, and she looked at mine in disbelief.

I didn't know what to say to her, but she seemed kindly-disposed toward me and made small talk. "I don't know why we have to come down this early. We have to go right home again for the High Holy Days."

"High Holy Days?"

"Yeah, Rosh Hashanah and Yom Kippur."

I remembered baby-sitting with Rivka and Esther Edelstein—talking about the New Year that came in the fall and the Day of Atonement. It simply hadn't occurred to me that Reva was Jewish.

The Edelsteins were not beautiful, but Reva was—even with a mudpack on her face. Her eyes were living green lights and her full mouth, scrubbed clean in the long, long shower, was rosier than some were with lipstick.

She had been looking at my reflection in the mirror, and now she turned to look at me directly, "What's the matter, didn't you ever see one before?"

"One what?"

"A Jewess."

"Of course I have! A number of them." (The number was three, but she didn't have to know that.)

"Yeah? Well, the way you were staring made me wonder."

"That's because you remind me of Hedy Lamarr. I used to collect pictures of her when I was a kid."

"Oh yeah?" Reva smiled, cracking the drying mask, and I said goodnight, hoping to quit while I was ahead.

Nita and Dot were sitting on my bed, still playing cards, but they allowed me to climb in and be short-sheeted by their firmly-planted posteriors.

"Bid!" Nita yelled at Kay, who was her partner.

"I'm thinking," Kay said mildly.

Dot put her arm around Nita's waist and buried her face in the long, silky hair.

"Quit trying to look at my cards!"

"I'll do anything to get what I want," Dot said.

The atmosphere was charged, but I was too tired to figure out why. I was glad when they got up and let me push my feet to the bottom of the bunk.

The radio blared on. "Ahhhh!" said a male voice that made me want to scream, "Friendly Grainbelt beer!"

I was too exhausted to sleep, especially with all that noise. As I watched the shifting lump that was Venus in the upper bunk, I knew that she was awake too. Elena was the lucky one. She couldn't hear a thing.

Just before I drifted into sleep, a startling thought came to me. Could Hedy Lamarr be Jewish?

Swayed by the prevailing opinion in the cottage, I almost skipped the freshman tea in the Union. We'd already been to a tea at the impressive home of the president of the university on Church Street, and while I had done nothing there to disgrace myself, I had felt neither happy nor comfortable. Furthermore, I was running out of things to wear to such functions.

Venus was going with Elena, and she urged me to join them. She generously offered to let me borrow a dress of Elena's.

"It won't fit."

"Yes, it will. You're smaller around the waist, but you can belt it."

"Maybe Elena doesn't want me to wear it."

Elena, who was good at keeping up with the ping pong match of a conversation without looking like Barney Google, spoke in her curiously flat inflection.

"It will look good on you, Margaret."

The dress was iris-blue wool, and it *did* look good on me. Despite the color of my eyes, I never wore blue. Marianne, whose hand-me-downs were the mainstay of my wardrobe, never bought it. The greatest asset of the dress, however, was its New Look length. I loved the feel of the hem low on my legs.

Shaky on our high heels, we cautiously made our way down the steep hill to the Iowa Memorial Union and melted into the crowd at the canopied entrance. The only canopy of that sort I had seen was the one at Schack's Funeral Home.

At the beginning of the receiving line inside the ballroom, I gave my name to a woman with a strong jawline, and she passed me along to a fat, friendly-looking dean of something or other. It was hard to hear, and for a moment, I was envious of Elena's lip-reading ability. Then the system broke down altogether, and I was caught in the penetrating gaze of a dark-haired man who claimed the hand I didn't offer.

"I'm Ansel Judd," he said, "dean of the law school."

I told him my name and added, "I used to work for a lawyer."

"Oh? Who?"

"Gregory Sommer—in Harlan."

"I remember Greg well. Brilliant! Say, you do look like a nice Swedish girl!"

I opened my mouth to correct him with "Danish," but closed it because he was still speaking.

"My wife is Swedish, so I admire that nationality."

I tried to smile encouragingly, though I was remembering the prejudice against the Swedes that seemed to run deep among the Danes. Somebody in Grandma's family had married a Swede, and all flaws in the fruit of that union had been attributed to Swedish genes and influence. Should I tell him that he'd given me the wrong label?

"Say, young lady, would you like a job?"

"Why—yes!"

"Excellent! I'm writing a textbook, and I need someone to type the manuscript. As soon as you're registered, let me know your schedule, and we'll work something out."

I thanked him and moved along quickly, embarrassed at causing a bottleneck in the line. I decided I could clear up the matter of my non-Swedishness some other time.

I told Venus and Elena about the job offer as we were eating tiny sandwiches that seemed to be filled with grass. They said it was great but wondered if I would have time to work. When would I study?

Already mentally composing a letter about the good news to Gregory Sommer, I wasn't worried. He was the one who had asked, "Do you want to go to college so much that you'd sleep in a culvert and raid garbage cans if you had to?" I had said I did, and he told me I'd have no trouble finding a part-time job. I'd tell Mom first, though. She had said I could go to Iowa City, but she didn't know how long I could afford to stay—not even with the money I'd saved, the Garner scholarship, and a tuition scholarship for the children of World War I veterans that Mr. Sommer had dug up.

Venus looked at me with undisguised envy. "You have a job already, and you didn't even have to ask!"

"I think it was Elena's blue dress."

Now that I had stopped distorting my mouth with exaggerated motion for her sake, Elena could read my lips perfectly. She smiled.

"Do you feel like someone else in it?" Venus asked.

I shook my head, wondering if the grassy sandwich filling had given me green teeth. Grandma would get a kick out of those sandwiches. Her favorite biblical character was Nebuchadnezzar, the Old

Testament king who ate grass with the oxen for seven years—until he learned to acknowledge the power of the Almighty.

"That's why I never borrow clothes," Venus said.

I shrugged. I was used to being me in Marianne's clothes—all but the slinky black dress that I threw down the abandoned cistern. Venus asked the oddest questions.

On the way home, we overshot the cottage to pass a few sorority houses. We had learned to tell people we preferred to be Independents, but we were also curious about how the other half lived.

I hadn't learned to read Greek letters yet, but Venus could. We passed the brick house with a striped awning where actives wearing dark, round-necked sweaters with pearls were singing to a group of rushees on the lawn, and she intoned, "Gamma Phi Beta."

Farther up the street was a colonial house with a rounded balcony supported by Gone-With-The-Wind pillars. It was gabled in the shape of the three triangles which Venus read as "Delta Delta Delta. You call them the Tri Delts."

Florine Hammond never had said which sorority was hers, and now I wondered. The Tri Delts weren't doing anything visible, and I said, "Let's go home. My feet hurt."

Venus stared at me. "Do you know what you just said?"

I repeated it, and she shook her head in wonder. "How can you possibly feel at home? You've only been here a couple of days."

I had no answer for her, but somehow I felt that my inchoate yearnings would be satisfied in this place, and I would not long to be elsewhere.

Venus emerged from registration white-lipped, I was fairly shaken, and Elena was fine. Elena had to focus her concentration to know what people were saying, and that shut out the peripheral confusion that drove the rest of us wild.

The Field House contained acres of tables with course signs, and the trick was to find the ones you needed before enrollments were closed. A few would-be students had fled, we were told, deciding that the college experience was not worth such trauma.

Since I had decided to study journalism, I was amazed and chagrined that I couldn't get down to it immediately. I needed a sound, liberal arts background first, they told me. Core courses, a language.

I emerged from that madhouse with a block schedule listing English and American Authors, Western Civilization, Man and Society, Spanish conversation, gym and concert band with 7:30 a.m. classes daily and afternoons free. Those I had managed to save for Ansel Judd.

The whole cottage descended on Iowa Book and Supply to buy textbooks, and then we went our separate ways—Nita, Dot, Sheila and Kay to the Airliner to drink beer; Rosemary to meet Charlie; Sue and Reva to shop for clothes; Venus and Elena back to the cottage to look the books over; and I to the Law School to present my schedule to the dean.

I entered the building, climbed some stairs and wandered about until I found the right door. Even though I had been bidden, I felt diffident, and the feeling increased when I put my books down on the high counter in the outer office and cleared my throat in the hope of being noticed.

I'd never seen a Sherman tank, but descriptions I'd heard matched the woman seated at a typewriter near an outside window. She was solidly built and gleamed with hard efficiency. At length, she raised her eyes.

"Yes?" The voice was surprisingly languid.

"I'm Margaret Langelund. Mr. Judd asked me to see him about a job."

"Did he indeed!" She looked at me for a long moment, then got up like the Queen Mary leaving a harbor berth and went to an inner office.

The dean came out immediately with the Sherman tank at his heels. "Well, now, Margaret! You did remember! Come on in." He pushed the swinging gate open for me and held it. "Did you meet Regina Schultz, our most excellent office manager?"

"How do you do?" I said, wondering if she were Miss or Mrs. She didn't seem the type who would tolerate a wrong guess.

The dean extended an arm like a stage courtier, inviting me inside. I showed him my schedule, which pleased him, and he told me what my salary would be, which pleased me.

"When would you like to begin?" he asked.

"Right now?"

"Splendid! We'll have Regina find you a place to work and get right down to it."

I followed him again and heard him tell Regina, "She's to type the manuscript of the Evidence text, but I'll let you use her on the side."

Regina's response to that was a sharp look. She took me to a typewriter behind the big safe and withdrew, letting the dean explain the form he wanted typed from a sheaf of hand-written pages plus casebooks containing passages indicated in the draft.

"Do you think you can read my writing?"

"I hope so. May I ask you if I can't?"

"By all means! Well, I guess I'll leave you to it."

The silence after his departure lasted for quite awhile, and I was able to concentrate on the material. Then Regina spoke.

"How did *you* get to him? Was it horses, or what?"

"Horses?" I dented the page I was reading with my fingernail to keep my place. Regina obviously was the kind of woman who expected full attention when she spoke.

"He has a mania for the beasts, and he assumes that anyone who feels the same is possessed of every good quality. He's been talking about finding a typist for his book for ages, but he never got around to it, so something must have pushed him over the edge."

"It was my Swedish face," I said, wanting to bite my tongue for compounding the mistake.

"Well, let's hope your Swedish fingers can hit those keys! The dean proposes, but *I* dispose!"

It was then that I noticed two other women in the office. A look of complicity is almost as palpable as a tap on the shoulder, and I felt it from both of them. Regina introduced them as wives of law students working to support their husbands.

Hilda Crawford was small and mousy. She worked with a burrowing earnestness and seemed afraid to speak. Gwen Burt was a bounteous blonde who spurned the New Look to show her excellent legs. She caught my glances at them and said, "They're not bad for an old lady of twenty-six!"

After I had worked for more than an hour, I asked Gwen where the women's restroom was, and she said she'd show me. Her passage through the halls caused law students to bump into each other and never notice the collision.

"We share with the female law students," she explained, pushing inside.

"How many are there?"

"Five."

A skinny one was wiping her hands at the sink, and Gwen introduced me to Honor Brubeck. Then in her smooth, little-girl voice, Gwen asked Honor, "Gettin' any lately?"

Honor snorted mirthlessly. "I refuse to answer that on the grounds that it may incriminate me. *You* don't look deprived!"

"Well, I guess not! It's just as important as eating."

Honor backed to the door and made a basket with her wadded paper towel.

"Then damned if I'm not starving to death!"

Gwen laughed, dropping to the leather couch to elevate one elegant leg and admire it. "So long, Honor Bright!"

I entered one of the two stalls and attended to my business, congratulating myself for even recognizing the subject of that interchange. Where I came from, sex was not discussed as casually as the weather. With any luck, I'd learn something about it at last.

I kept my Big Ben alarm clock under my bunk close to the wall so no one would take it and hide it, or I never would have made it to those 7:30s all week. The nights were loud with radios and bridge until well after midnight, and if I hadn't been excited about learning things, even the loudest alarm couldn't have pried me from my bunk to dress sleepily and dash half a block to the Currier Hall dining room for breakfast before class.

"Why don't you skip breakfast and sleep longer?" Kay Albers asked.

"Because my brain won't turn on until I eat." I didn't bother to elaborate on the habit formed by years of force-fed oatmeal and toast.

That earliest class was Man and Society, a course that seemed like a roundup of self-evident information. At least it provided a gradual awakening that readied me for the genuine excitement of George Mosse's lectures in Western Civilization, always referred to as Western Civ.

We were told constantly that most institutions of higher learning would not waste a scholar of Mosse's stature on lowly undergraduates, so we'd better appreciate our good fortune.

Mosse was short, dark and Levantine with a heavy accent called Prussian by some. Knowing no accents but Danish, I only knew it wasn't that. The voice rolled richly into MacBride auditorium, reaching the highest rows in perfect audibility. The message was one of infinite riches, hitherto undiscovered by me. Scattered bits of information began to fit together. The previously mysterious became reasonable, if not inevitable. At the same time, matters I had believed to be quite simple became more complex.

This huge lecture course was filled with former soldiers, and you could almost see them putting the lectures into the context of the European war theatre they remembered. I had been nowhere and remembered nothing germane, so I was content to thrill to Mosse's rolling pronunciation—like the way he said "Savonarola," a magic, deep-toned name that I divorced from its owner to savor simply for its sound.

As if that weren't marvelous enough, I was madly in love with my English and American authors teacher. I, a non-swimmer, would dive deep into Chaucerian waters for his sake or consider "Richard IV" endlessly if it pleased him. The question was, why did he please me? He was of a medium height, black-haired and blue-eyed, and thin with a caved-in chest.

Nita said she was sure he was a faggot, and when I responded to the term with puzzlement, she explained with half a dozen alternate definitions and added, "My God, Margaret, where have you been all your life? All screwed up in a fruit jar? Get it?" Though I was bothered by Grandma's admonition, "Don't let the sun set on your wrath," I didn't speak to her for days.

My Spanish conversation class was about as intimate as they get—two war veterans and me. One of the men opted for the lisping Castilian, which left the tough ex-sergeant to engage me in conversations about drinking beer. I became fluent in asking directions to the bathroom.

All those former soldiers were serious about school and working hard, and since most classes were graded on a curve, the rest of us "kids" had to fight hard for our grades.

Many of the veterans lived in quonset villages called Finkbine Park, Riverdale, Riverside, and Hawkeye in "cottages" just like ours. I would walk past, eyeing the laundry on the clotheslines; the kids in sand boxes in the bleak, little yards; the pregnant women farther from the New Look than I was. What I saw made me glad that I was still free.

Gwen said it wasn't such a bad life. They had parties—even dress-up affairs—and got together for cards and potlucks. Once in awhile they even went to movies, but most of the men who had soldiered in Italy weren't crazy about going to see "The Well Digger's Daughter." That picture seemed to play endlessly at one of the downtown theaters.

Although I'd managed to be excused from gym most of my school life because of my assorted operations, the university wouldn't let me off the hook. The fierce phys ed department head with elephant legs and hawk features gave me a stern lecture.

"You must condition your body if you ever expect to bear children!"

"I'm not ruling that out altogether," I said, "but generations of women in my family have had children without taking gym."

In the end, I opted for archery, golf, and some indoor exercising. With the kind of days I put in, I was so exhausted that I'd lie down on the exercise mat "just for a minute" and wake when one of those elephant feet nudged me to get up.

One night soon after the Friendly Grainbelt sign-off, somebody crawled under my bunk and took my Big Ben. When I awoke, it seemed unusually light, and it was. A horrified glance a Sheila's clock told me that I'd missed my first class entirely, and Mosse's Western Civ lecture would be over in five minutes.

"Who took it?" I roared.

Nita raised her pale head and squinted at me. "We did. Makes too damned much noise."

My face started to twist and tickle with unshed tears, and Nita said, "For God's sake, if it means that much to you, it's outside next to the steps—alley side."

"It's not the clock," I said, sniffing.

"Then what the hell is it? You've got a nerve waking me up at this obscene hour! I don't have a class until afternoon!"

Why try to explain to Nita? Venus might have understood, but Nita never would grasp what it was about those unforgetable lectures of Mosse's. He made us feel we had participated in the whole span of Western history.

Too bad it wasn't the day for the discussion leader, Ralph Harrison. I wouldn't have minded missing his session in a quonset near the Pentacrest.

After my last class there, I felt him behind me and knew he was going to speak to me. Without turning, I saw the tweed jacket; trousers charred spottily by burning clots from his tilted pipe bowl. Sighing, I turned to face the sour expression of a low man on the academic totem pole.

"You have a good mind," he said.

Surprised by his praise, I thanked him.

"Too bad you're female."

"A mind is a mind," I said in a tight voice.

"Yeah, but all the promising girls go the same route. You're trapped by your bodies. All the juice goes to the womb."

Figuring my womb was none of his business, I defended my privacy by attempting to invade his. "Are you married?"

He nodded morosely. "Yeah, I wrecked one brilliant gal. Patty had some fine insights into American history, and now her greatest challenge is figuring out whether the baby is wet or hungry."

"That's a shame. Maybe she'll get back to it when the baby is older."

"Yeah," he said, sounding a bit worried that his brilliant gal might do that. "See you Thursday."

I crossed Clinton Street to the main campus, pausing to let the pedestrian traffic of changing classes swirl around me while I marveled at being part of it. The gold dome of Old Capitol glowed benignly at Shaeffer Hall, MacBride, the Physics building, and University Hall as if they were high-achieving children. Even Old Dental building, which marred the pale stone Pentacrest with its red brick antiquity, seemed bursting with post-war energy.

Even more wonderful was the long, low art building across the river with its arched colonnade and the carved legend, *Ars Longa, Vita Brevis Est*. I'd had just enough Latin to know what it meant. The building seemed like a temple to me, and I wouldn't have been surprised to find it inhabited by Maxfield and Parrish, the white-gowned beings in the picture that once hung above my parents' bed.

The only art I'd ever had in school was short periods of drawing and coloring with my regular teacher, but the art students here had learned what they knew from specialists—real artists. I would walk through the building just to smell the oil paint that seemed to promise so much, wishing that I could blend into the scene but knowing that I didn't. My nails were too clean, and I felt that everyone knew I'd never seen original art before—just encyclopedia pictures of famous stuff like the Mona Lisa and the print that a lot of Iowa farmers hung above their cream separators—a lonely wolf on a snowy, moonlit hill looking down at a house with smoke rising from its chimney.

Venus talked me into going to the Mabie Theater for the first time. "It doesn't cost anything," she said, "you just show your ID."

We saw "The Glass Menagerie" by Tennessee Williams, and I, who had never seen anything more ambitious than a high school class play, was struck dumb by my total immersion in the world of the Wingfields.

After Tom's curtain speech, "Blow out your candles, Laura—and so goodbye...," I was too affected to applaud with the rest of the audience. "Blue roses, blue roses, blue roses."

Venus said something to me, but I seemed to see her through the wall of a glass bubble, hearing nothing. She said it again.

"He went to school here, you know."

"Who?"

"Tennessee Williams."

"Oh. Yeah, I saw that in the program." I wanted her to be quiet so I could think about the sad gallantry of the Wingfields' lives. However, it was important to know that the man who had written this play had gone to classes right here—where I was. Once he had been just another student—like me.

I'd also have to reconsider the scornful dismissal of drama students by most of my cottage mates. At the sight of a girl in barefoot sandals and a tunic like that of a heraldic page outside Whetstones, Nita, Dot or Kay would snort and mutter, "Oh, *she's* a DA!" I had recognized Amanda Wingfield as one of the Currier Hall waitresses, and from now on, I would be intensely interested in her every move.

The revelation of new wonders in visual art and theater had to be balanced by a loss of some kind, I supposed. Grandma always was reminding me, "The Lord giveth and the Lord taketh away," so I wasn't surprised when I discovered that my level of musicianship wasn't as high as I had believed it to be.

Somehow, when you join the high school band at the age of nine, grab the first chair in your section the minute its owner graduates and keep it until you get your own diploma, you come to believe that you are pretty hot stuff. You even cherish hopes of Juilliard.

First chair in the University Concert Band's clarinet section clearly was not to be mine, and when I showed up for my first private lesson with a graduate student in the music department, I was told that I had a lot of wrong techniques to unlearn. Pity the big frog taken from a small puddle and suddenly dumped into a lake.

The compensation for my demotion was the chance to sit slightly nearer the trombone section and have an unobstructed view of Arthur Blair, a tall, pale former soldier who wanted to be a high school band director. I became aware of Arthur at the Baptist student house, a Sunday night hangout for those of us looking for a cheap meal when the dormitories weren't serving food.

Arthur was not aware of me. He played with the Bo Williams dance band—trumpet, trombone, keyboard and drums. They called him "Art," which seemed wrong to me—a name for someone who worked in a lumberyard. Arthur was soulful in the extreme, suffering the after-effects of some unspecified war wound, and when he played "Danny Boy" on his trombone, he could make the stone angels in the cemetery cry. Even the one in the Iowa City cemetery used for the virgin test, I supposed.

Nita thought I was such a hick that I'd believe that tale, and her pale eyes glittered as she told it to me.

"You have to go there just at midnight and touch the statue in the magic spot."

I said, "I'm not going to ask where *that* is!"

Venus, looking tight-lipped, deliberately dropped a coffee can filled with hair curlers to drown Nita's voice, but it came through.

"On the clit, that's where. It's hard to find it under that marble robe, but men can't do it when there's *nothing* between!"

Nita was sitting on Sheila's bunk, and Dot moved in from behind, curling her body around Nita's hips as if she were a hound dog.

"Knock it off, Greer! I'm educating Margaret."

"You and everyone else," I said. "I'm going to the library. By the way, Nita, have you ever pushed the magic spot on that angel?"

"Sure, lots of times."

"How long does the angel stay black?"

She shrugged. "Who knows? Once my date gets a load of those black wings, we're off. Who wants to screw in a cemetery?"

On the way to the library in the strong-smelling chemistry building, I thought over Nita's last remark. Our family considered cemeteries quite suitable for all sorts of social occasions. When we were near our own dead, we talked about them affectionately, and that was the next best thing to having them with us. Daddy seemed almost alive at those times, and I even felt that I knew the ones who had died before my birth—like Grandpa Peter.

Nita probably was right. The act that she called "screwing" wasn't something you'd do in front of your relatives, living or dead.

I imagined myself standing before the stone angel with Arthur—then with Dexter Burton, my English and American Authors instructor—but I couldn't imagine myself pressing the magic spot. Those guys would just have to guess about my virginity!

Venus, who had not been "popular" in high school, was determined to savor all the experiences the university had to offer, and I was her chosen companion because I was available and not much of a threat. Sue, Reva and Sheila had a Greek social life, Dot and Kay hung around with Nita when she wasn't flunking the angel test, Rosemary was involved with her fiance, and Elena spent most of her time at the speech clinic.

"There's a tea dance at the Union tomorrow afternoon," Venus said. "Let's go."

We arrived in the small fountain room overlooking the Iowa River "a fashionable 15 minutes late," according to Venus, and I immediately remarked, "There's no tea."

Venus laughed and said, "They call it that because of the hour."

We found two chairs along the window wall and sat down, I in a black dress that had belonged to my cousin Marianne and Venus in a white Gibson Girl blouse and black skirt. Venus tossed her head and paired an animated expression with the most mundane remarks about sending her laundry home and buying a new bottle of Yardley's lavendar hand lotion.

I tried to look as if I were listening to her in utter fascination, but I was really looking past her at the piano player, Leo Cortemiglia. I'd never had a chance to study Italianate good looks anywhere but the movie theater, and looking at Leo was a treat. He was—suave. That was the word. His hands moved in a caressing glide on the keyboard as he played "Someone to Watch Over Me," and he smiled faintly at everyone and no one.

When the dancers blocked my view of Leo, I told Venus, "I think I'll stand up. My skirt is too short to sit."

She shot me the quick look I had learned to interpret—the one that said, "You're letting me down, but that's what I expected."—and nodded with a bird-like bob of her head.

Leo had started to sing. I edged closer, so caught up in his "—turns out to be—someone who'll watch—" that I didn't notice the man who was trying to speak to me. He touched my elbow with the unheard question still in his eyes.

"Dance?" he said.

I hadn't since my cousin Davy, masquerading as an out-of-town stranger, had taken me to the senior prom. That hadn't been so bad, but I'd gone all stiff and shaky when I danced in the Hess' dining room with the Merchant Marine I had a crush on during the war. Other girls melted into their partners and allowed themselves to be led, but I'd been taught to dance by a girl and was so tall that I was always the "male" partner among the wallflowers. I decided to risk the humiliation. I didn't know this guy, and if he walked out of my life, so what? He'd never been in it.

He was tall enough that I needn't slump. I warily placed one hand on the black shoulder of his suit jacket and let him take the other in his cool, dry grasp. His thumb rested on my rings, then shifted to reveal them. They were sky-blue turquoise set in gold. One had belonged to Mom and the other to Aunt Kam. The rings were mute chaperones, reminding me that I was one of the Jorgen women.

"My name is Lew Browne," he said.

I bumped into his foot, apologized and told him who I was. His pale hair was a strike against him, I thought, stealing another look at the piano player. As far as I was concerned, blond men were a bore.

However, Lew's thin face and haunted expression counteracted his coloring. Like Desdemona, I was ready to love someone for the dangers they had passed.

"Were you in the war?"

"Yes."

"Army?"

"Navy."

"So you're here on the G.I. Bill?"

"No, I teach here."

"Oh? What?"

"Greek and the Bible."

"Then you must know Dexter Burton," I said, enjoying saying the name of my English and American Authors teacher.

"Sure, I know Dex."

"Does *he* ever come to these things?"

Lew shrugged.

"If I were in your class, would you ask me to dance?"

"Probably not."

I sighed and listened to the music again. Leo had segued into "All the Things You Are," which made me think of the jukebox at Cronk's in Denison and a farm kid named Speed. Lew was pulling me closer for the slow tune, and he had a metallic smell about him. If I leaned on him too hard, I was sure I would overbalance us, despite the feeling of strength in the wiry arm around my back. It seemed to me that we were pulling and hauling like a badly-matched team of mules.

Venus was still sitting where I left her, smiling into the middle distance, and I told Lew, "I do want you to meet my friend, Venus Cather. We both live in Currier Cottage 15."

"I don't care where *she* lives. How about dinner?"

"Well, I—Venus and I usually go to Roger Williams House on Sunday nights."

"She can find the way, can't she?"

"I—I suppose so. But I'll have to tell her. Will you come with me? And would you dance with her just once before we go?"

He nodded, dancing with me toward her. After the introductions, they moved back on the polished floor. As I was observing that Venus bounced when she danced, the music changed to a tango, and they gave it up.

We said our good-byes, and Lew and I started for the Jefferson Hotel. I wondered what Venus would have done if she were the one invited to dinner?

"I used to know a sailor," I said, "so I can imagine how you looked in the uniform."

"I was a lieutenant commander."

"Oh. Then I guess I *can't* imagine it. He was just a plain sailor."

"You know what attracted me to you?"

I laughed shortly. "My legs? They were practically the only pair in the whole place that showed."

"No, good as they are, that wasn't it. Your black dress is what did it."

Marianne must have been right about the allure of the "little black dress," I thought. Personally, I hated it, but Venus said the draped purple was too much for a tea dance.

"At least we match," I said lightly.

We passed the women's gym, the geology building and the law school. I wished that Gwen could see Lew Browne and render an opinion on him. She seemed to know everything in the world about men. We crossed the street near MacBride and angled across the campus to Clinton Street. I saw a few people I recognized and greeted them, but Lew spoke to no one.

After rounding Whetstone's corner, I glanced at Lew in the harsh streetlight and thought he looked like a mortician in his black suit. The light was red at the next corner, and I turned to look at the windows of Dombey's Boot Shop while we waited. I wasn't even aware of the sudden buzz in the control box for the signals, but Lew heard it, grabbed my arm and pulled me down. I landed on my knees and ruined my stockings, no small mishap, considering my financial condition. I decided God was punishing me for choosing dinner with this strange man over an evening at the Baptist student house.

"My God, I'm sorry!" He helped me up, pulled out a handkerchief to dab at my bloody knees and then swatted at the knees on his trousers.

"Why did you—?"

"Too much sea duty, I guess. My nerves are shot, and I hit the deck at the slightest sound."

We found a booth at the Jefferson, and Lew ordered for me without consultation—as if he were my father. I rather enjoyed that, having been without a male parent since I was four.

I had considered taking Greek and the Bible rather than English and American Authors, and I questioned him about the course to find out whether I'd made a mistake. It seemed that he had a different view of the Bible than I did, and his long pronouncement about Greek comedy and tragedy wasn't nearly as interesting as what I knew about the Greek myths. Lumping all of that together as literature seemed odd to me, and I said so.

He laughed. "It's perfect for me. I can have my hell hot or cold, depending on my mood."

I knew something about the frigid hell of the Greeks, and I said, "Yes, but the hot one is real and the cold one is just made up."

"What if they're *both* just made up?"

The challenge was almost too much for Margaret the Missionary, but I managed to do no more than smile pityingly and address myself to the Dover sole the poor, benighted soul had ordered for me.

Lew delivered me at the alley door of the cottage with no attempt at a good-night kiss, but he asked if he could see me Wednesday night. I agreed uneasily.

The next morning Boots brought in a brown paper bag with my name on it. It was a pair of stockings tied in a loose slip-knot like a noose.

Tuesday the paper bag contained a book of poems by A. E. Houseman, and Wednesday there was a withered rose. The whole cottage was intrigued by these tokens.

Venus had asked about my scraped knees, but I didn't want to explain, so I just said I stumbled and fell.

"Did you like him?" she asked me.

"He's all right, I guess."

"I thought he was kind of strange."

Ha! I thought, *and you saw him when he was acting normal!*

When Lew called for me that night, he pressed a small gold star into my hand. "From my uniform."

I thanked him and pinned the star on my lapel.

"Thanks for the stockings—and the poems and the rose. It must have been colder last night than I thought. The rose was a little withered."

"It was supposed to be."

I couldn't imagine why, so I simply asked, "Where are we going?"

"Let's just walk along the river for awhile first."

He offered his arm for the steep descent of the hill to the riverbank and then guided me north, where the lovers were not so numerous. It was quiet until the dark shape of a canoe slid past and a girl's soft laughter floated across the water.

"It's so peaceful here," he said, "almost as peaceful as the grave. When I saw you in that black dress, I knew—"

I moved away from him slightly, as carefully as one backs away from a dangerous dog. "You knew what?"

"Do you like Wagner?" he asked.

The question seemed irrelevant. Brandon Bardell, my once-respected high school band director, had told me that Wagner's music was schmaltz, and it certainly had been unpopular during the war. I was unfamiliar with it, and I admitted this to Lew.

"Then you must hear the 'Liebestod'! It will make you understand the richness, the beauty, the passion of the only kind of love that makes sense in this crazy world! Come listen to it with me!"

"I can't. You were late picking me up, and I have hours."

"You'll never have to worry about hours again, Margaret," he said almost hypnotically. "You're perfect! I knew it the moment I saw you—all that bursting life in black! Every hair on your head lives exuberantly—you bring so much to the culmination!"

I didn't really understand what he was saying. I was afraid to understand. I broke and ran, sliding on the damp grass as I scrambled up the incline from the water. South. I had to go south.

"Margaret!" Lew shouted.

He sounded like Heathcliff played by Orson Welles. Afraid that I couldn't out-run him, I threw myself down beside two dark shapes and begged, "Please, let me hide!"

"What the hell!" the man growled, but the girl said, "She's in trouble, Don," and flipped the edge of their blanket over me.

Pressed against the cool, damp sod, I could feel the vibration of Lew's running feet. It seemed like forever until the girl said, "Hey, all clear! Want us to walk you home?"

"For God's sake, Barb!"

"I'll be all right, thanks."

I ran back to the cottage and threw myself face-down on my bunk. I wasn't crying, but Boots came and sat beside me.

"Are you OK?"

"I guess so. Boots, did you ever know anybody who was in love with dying?"

"No, but sooner or later I probably will. All kinds of nuts are running around this place, and most of them blame it on the war."

"And I thought he wasn't wounded."

"Those are the worst kind, they say."

I carefully unpinned Lew's star from my lapel and put it away. It seemed that his mind and his body wanted two different things, and Lew struggled between the survival instinct of hitting the sidewalk at the innocent buzz of a traffic light box and trying to arrange a suicide pact.

In the morning, I found a note from Lew shoved under the cottage door. "If you're not willing, it's no good. I'm disappointed in you, Margaret. *Vale!* Lew."

Reading over my shoulder, Nita said, "What's the matter, wouldn't you screw?"

"Nothing that simple, Nita."

Apparently Lew had other such disappointments, as he went on teaching his classes in a perfectly normal way, I was told.

My encounter with Lew Browne gave me an even stronger determination to live—to experience all the things I'd only read about and more. His cool touch had not chilled me in the least. And that was the second black dress of Marianne's I got rid of in my lifetime. The first one went down the cistern at home, and this one was given to the maid who cleaned the cottage too seldom.

After my experience with Lew, I wasn't eager to go to another tea dance, but Venus was certain that the next one would make all the difference for her and begged me to go with her. I argued that since the "little black dress" was in the closet of the cleaning woman, I had nothing to wear.

"Why don't we take the silver butterflies off the purple?" she suggested. "It wouldn't look too bad plain."

We snipped and pressed, and the dress looked like one of those connect-the-dots drawings in *Child Life*, but Venus said the lights would be so low that no one would notice. I tried it on with my saddle shoes.

Sue Benton regarded me with amusement and said, "Sexyyy! Want to borrow my black suede pumps?"

They fit me, more or less, but the heels were so excruciatingly high that I felt like a Chinese woman with bound feet. While I was tottering around the cement floor of the cottage in them, Nita rushed in, blowing her blonde bangs out of her eyes and fairly quivering with malicious excitement.

"Guess what I've got in here!" she said, holding out a small brown paper bag. She shook it, producing a soft thump that gave us no clue.

When the thing rolled across Dot Greer's desk, Kay Albers yelped, "God! What is it?"

An eye, that's what it was; a big eye that stared at us balefully after coming to rest against Dot's pencil cup.

"I swiped it from the biology lab," Nita said, "and I'm going to put it in Boots's bedroom slipper."

"It'll give her a heart attack!" Kay said.

Nita laughed, picked up the eye and yelled, "Catch, Margaret!"

I wasn't good at catching anything, but the eye hit my purple-clad stomach, and I instinctively pressed it to the crepe to keep it from falling. It felt cool and viscous, and I looked down quickly to see if it had stained the fabric. It hadn't, but as it regarded me from my palm, it seemed to know something.

"God, Margaret," Kay said, "how can you stand to touch it?"

"It's just a cow's eye. No worse than picking up a steak."

I fired it at Nita in an awkward, overhand throw. She dodged, shrieked and finally retrieved it with a "potholder" of toilet paper.

Boots was tiny, and the toe of her scuff slipper was just big enough to accommodate the eye. The band of woolly stuff over the instep looked like a fat, pink eyebrow.

"How juvenile!" Venus said. "Let's get dressed and get out of here before we get mixed up in this."

Somehow I got down the hill in Sue's pumps and tottered into the River Room, where I gratefully found a chair on the sidelines. A small combo was playing this time, and when the dancers shifted to give me a glimpse of the musicians, I caught my breath with a mixture of dread and delight. It was Bo Williams at the piano, a drummer and my darling Arthur Blair on trombone.

Arthur would hate being called "my darling" by me, even mentally, I supposed. If I scared him in a skirt, sweater and saddle shoes—and it seemed that I did—the draped purple crepe and four-inch heels would fill him with absolute terror.

"Let's move over there," I said to Venus, pointing at some chairs hidden from the bandstand by the fountain figure.

"What's the matter with here?"

I pretended not to hear her and moved, leaving her to follow if she wished. She came after me, giving me quizzical glances as I stole peeks at Arthur through the bent arm of the statue.

Suddenly my view was blocked completely by a tall, swarthy man who seemed to be asking me to dance. I considered refusing, not wanting Arthur to see me, but Venus was nudging me from behind. It was simpler to stand up and move into his arms.

"I am Abdul Adid."

I told him my name and said, "Where are you from?"

"Egypt."

"But I thought—" I broke off, fearing that I was on the threshold of an insult to his nation.

"You thought Egyptians were little people, is that not so?"

I nodded with an embarrassed laugh.

"Any person who is photographed with the Great Pyramids will give such an impression."

His smile was broad, white and gat-toothed. Dexter Burton had lectured so exhaustively on the gat-toothed condition of the Wife of Bath that I had grown wary of anyone whose front teeth were widely spaced, and as Abdul's arm tightened around me, I stiffened. He seemed to enjoy that.

"What are you studying?" I asked.

"The hydraulics. We have many dams in Egypt."

He was an excellent dancer, overcoming my tendency to lead with sheer muscle, and he was big enough to hide me from Arthur Blair as long as we were dancing in the right direction. Arthur was soloing on "Canadian Sunset," which caused me to melt in Abdul's arms until I realized what I was doing and straightened up.

I remembered the stacks of National Geographics the Farleys had left in the house on Willow Street—the acrid, inviting scent of the thick, shiny pages. The ones I liked best featured the Sphinx, the pyramids, the palms and yes, the small, dark people seemingly clothed in white sheets or portions thereof. I was sorry that I hadn't waited to finish my letter to Mom so I could tell her I'd met a real Egyptian.

"May I take you to dinner?"

"Well, I—"

"You have other plans?"

I remembered my agreement with Venus. If either of us got an interesting offer, no notification was necessary. We just wouldn't be at the canopied Union entrance where we'd arranged to meet at 5:30 and walk home together. I really had hoped Venus would be the missing person, because she needed to find someone. She hadn't had a date since she arrived on campus, even in the post-war flood of available men.

"Thank you," I said, "I'd like to go to dinner."

I excused myself to comb my hair and scrub my Revlon lips to make way for a new layer of crimson. Under the harsh lights, I looked pale and world-weary. It occurred to me that purple might not be my color and blood-red lips not quite the thing for the purple. The distant sound of Authur's trombone made me wistful.

Abdul was not alone when I joined him. His friend, whom he introduced simply as Ali, was about half his size. Ali stared at me unblinkingly.

"We will go to the Mad Hatter," Abdul said with a quick glance that Ali interpreted as an order to open the door.

Ali positioned himself on the other side of Abdul for the walk up the hill. I got the feeling that he didn't want to be any closer to me.

"Are you from Egypt too?" I asked, bending forward to catch his reply.

"Yes."

"From Cairo," Abdul added, "and I come from Alexandria. Ali's English is not—not much practiced."

"Well, yours is certainly good."

I'd never been to the Mad Hatter—just passed the door wishing someone would take me there. It was up some stairs, and while I'd been taught that gentlemen ascended first, Abdul and Ali stood back and waited for me. I felt self-conscious about the exaggerated sway of a purple rear that my borrowed footwear was causing. To make it worse, they talked to each other in Egyptian, probably commenting on that very thing.

The restaurant was full, and while we stood in line waiting for a table, I inspected the "Alice in Wonderland" decor and the waiters in the same cheap approximation of formal attire that small high school bands use—no coat. I saw no one I'd ever seen before, but we were attracting a few stares.

Seated at last, we studied the large menus decorated with Alice, the White Rabbit and the Hatter himself. I was appalled at the prices. If Abdul wanted to leave without ordering, I was ready to go quietly. He didn't look at all disturbed, however, and I couldn't tell about Ali. He was too small to be seen above the menu.

The background music was "Deep Purple" with a vocal. When Abdul recognized it, he flashed his gat-toothed smile and said, "You were sitting there all purple-sailed like Cleopatra on the Nile."

I smiled uncertainly at being compared to a boat but decided he meant well. Then the waiter appeared, standing there with the nerved-up impatience of the overworked. I hastened to choose the cheapest thing, chopped steak, offering the order to my escort in the approved manner. Abdul ignored me, and the waiter wrote it down.

"And you, sir?"

"Coffee."

The pencil formed a fast "C" and remained poised, but Abdul looked away, sending an almost inaudible whistle through the gap in his teeth. The waiter turned to Ali.

"Also same."

"Just coffee?"

Ali nodded emphatically.

"In that case," I said, "please change my order and make it three." I glanced at the wall clock and saw with chagrin that it was too late to pick up a 35-cent supper at the Baptist student house.

"No," said Abdul, "you must have dinner."

"But if you aren't—"

"Please, I love to watch a woman eat."

The waiter was all but yelling the White Rabbit's line about being late, so I gave in.

"If it's a religious thing, I—"

Abdul shook his head. "We are a long time from Ramadan."

"Don't you enjoy eating?"

"Enormously. Sometimes at home in Alexandria I will spend three hours at my lunch. Perhaps someday I will invite you there, and we shall eat fillets sliced from the side of a living fish—and pomegranates."

I grieved for the poor fish, but the word "pomegranates" was so wonderful that it transformed Abdul into someone who might walk along the bank of the Nile with Hedy Lamarr. It was at this moment that I considered him worthy raw material for my "perfect man" factory.

cellophane packets of crackers. I offered them to Abdul and Ali, and they refused. The chopped steak with broccoli and baked potato tasted good, but I could scarcely heap praise upon food consumed under the gaze of the two coffee drinkers. I tried to offer them the roll basket, but they waved it away.

Eyeing the lengthening line of people waiting for tables, I ate as quickly as I could without swallowing the bites whole. Mom, who before my birth had encountered some advocate of chewing each mouthful two hundred times, would be horrified if she could see me. And I wasn't feeling too terrific, either. My dinner felt like irregular concrete chunks stacked between throat and stomach.

The ever-watchful waiter dropped the check the minute I put down my fork. Abdul glanced at it casually and produced a twenty-dollar bill from his breast pocket, removing my dread of a long dishwashing stint in Sue's excruciating pumps.

We walked back to Cottage 15 in silence. In the bright light above the alley door, I offered my hand to Abdul and thanked him for dinner. He kept the hand, spoke to Ali in Egyptian, and pulled me down the steps and into the shadows. Ali had disappeared, and I was in the tight embrace of a stranger who looked like (but obviously wasn't) a eunuch in a Cecil B. DeMille movie. His tongue was probing so deep that I expected the worst. I struggled, and just as I was at the brink of suffocation, he turned me loose.

"You do not like me?"

"I like you, but we hardly know each other! You wouldn't even tell me why you didn't eat!"

"Ah," he said reflectively, "I will telephone to you."

"Good-night!" I scrambled back up the steps, putting myself together as well as I could. The lower part of my face was one big smear of Revlon, I was sure. Fortunately, I made it to the bathroom to scrub before anyone realized I'd come in.

Venus heard the water running and came in, wanting to hear all about it.

"I thought human beings were alike all over the world," I said, "but now I'm not so sure."

"You know something? It seems that you think that when you're a kid, and then you go through the finding-out stage that gets you all mixed up, and then when you've had a lot of experience, you're back to what you thought when you were a kid."

"How do you figure that?"

"My high school counselor told me. She's been everywhere."

"I never even *had* a counselor—had to figure everything out for myself."

"Well," she said, "so far, so good."

Boots came in for bed check at 10:30 and went out with Steve again. Those of us who wanted to sleep couldn't because Nita was hooting and laughing with Dot and Kay about what would happen when Boots got ready for bed and slid her foot into the scuff—or tried to.

Even the wild bunch had dropped to sleep when Boots finally did come home and let out a shriek that woke the whole cottage.

We all sprang from our bunks and turned on lights, and there was Boots—mouth swollen from kissing, bra around her neck like a Hawaiian lei, pink-browed calf's eye in her hand. She was screaming her head off.

"Who the hell did this?"

No one spoke.

"For you, Langelund," Nita said, holding the phone out languidly, "some guy with a foreign accent."

"He has almost no accent!" I snapped as I grabbed the receiver. "Hello, Abdul."

"This is Margaret? From the west of Iowa?"

"Yes." He *did* seem to have more of an accent today. For once in my life I'd done Nita an injustice.

"You would like to go in a canoe on the river?"

"I thought they'd put the boats away for the winter."

"Ah, those boats, yes, but we have one at the hydraulics lab. Will you go tomorrow night?"

"If you're a good swimmer. I'm not."

"Ah yes, I spend my boyhood in the Mediterranean."

We arranged a time that would put us on the river at sunset, and this also meant I would miss dinner in the dorm. Even if he offered it, I simply was not going to eat another meal while Abdul drank coffee, so I smuggled enough rolls and fruit out of the Currier dining room at lunch to stave off starvation. Venus helped, and we laughed at the unsightly lumps in our sweaters that jiggled as we ran the half-block back to the cottage.

What to wear was the next problem. My wardrobe consisted of clothes for class, church and scrubbing floors but nothing for the so-called leisure hours. I had no leisure. Elena offered her dark green wool slacks, and the always-obliging Sue made her plaid jacket available. When your top and bottom halves are different sizes, your borrowing opportunities are enhanced by living in a nine-bunk cottage.

I was getting pretty excited about it all by the time I reported for work at the law school.

"Got a heavy date?" Gwen asked.

"Really heavy! He has to be at least 6-foot-2, and he's built like a Mack truck. He's an Egyptian."

"You gotta' watch out for them."

"You know any?"

"Nope, but I do know they're a passionate type."

"If the canoe tips over, I'm dead! I'm just learning to swim in gym class, and I know I'll never be able to do it well enough to graduate."

"Are you kidding? You mean you can't get your diploma if you can't swim?"

"That's right. So many lengths, tread water for fifteen minutes and I don't know what all."

"Well, I'll be!"

That was as close to an oath as Gwen ever got. She was sexy but wholesome.

"Where's the stuff I'm supposed to type for the Dean?"

"He told me to do it. Too dirty for you today."

"Heck!" I said, because I was wholesome too.

At the appointed hour, a firm knock sounded on the door, and Nita and Kay both raced to answer it. They fell back at the sight of Abdul in a heavy turtleneck sweater and tight pants that displayed his potential.

Hoping to escape while Nita was still speechless, I grabbed Sue's jacket and hurried toward Abdul, but she recovered in time to advise me, "Keep your legs crossed!"

I slammed the door in a hurry, hoping he hadn't heard. We set off toward the river, looking at each other approvingly. We did make a handsome couple, and I no longer had the sense of creating a ridiculous picture that I had felt entering the restaurant in my purple dress accessorized by Ali.

Abdul was carrying a portable radio, and he handed it to me so he could pull the canoe close to shore. It had drifted to the end of the rope that tied it to a slender tree. Getting in seemed like a precarious undertaking, and I was all for pulling it down to the dock on its leash, but he brought it alongside and bodily deposited me in it before I could worry further.

"I will paddle," he said, springing into his place with almost no rocking and tilting. "You have not the experience."

"Right. I'll handle the radio dials."

We moved out into the current, and he paddled against it without strain. The sunset to our left was bars of orange, pink and what I supposed to be pomegranate red. Surely the Nile could provide no better display.

Abdul said, "The Koran speaks of 'bright and large-eyed maids like hidden pearls' who reward the 'foremost of the foremost.'"

I enjoyed the sound of the words but ignored their meaning. Eyes closed almost to slits, I was imagining us in Egypt. Our camels would be waiting, tethered to palm trees near the Sigma Chi house, and as soon as we came in off the river, we would proceed to a banquet of many courses in a desert tent about as far away as University Hospitals, where we would be entertained by belly dancers. The radio was playing the "Sword Dance" that Venus hated because it once was her background music for being violently sick.

I didn't see Abdul slide to his knees, didn't know he was close to me until I felt his breath on my cheek. Then his mouth suffocated me once more, and his hands moved under my jacket.

I turned my head sharply to get the words out, "Please stop!" I couldn't defend my upper torso because I was clinging to the seat for dear life. The radio played on; "Deep Purple," of all things.

Abdul had gone deaf, it seemed, and his hands were pressing lower. I twisted and dodged, and he pulled back enough to give me a glazed look and a warning.

"Those who do not swim must sit very still."

The explosion of outrage I felt had to do with a sense of invasion. Abdul didn't know me, didn't *want* to know me as anything other than a body to be appropriated. He acted so *entitled* to pursuing his intentions that it made me furious.

"Why do you think that what *you* want is all that matters?"

The hands pressed and kneaded my thighs, moving upward and inward. "The Koran also says that 'men stand superior to women.'" His mouth covered mine again.

I lurched from his grasp, shouting "No!" and tipped the canoe. The shock of the cold water and the strains of "Deep Purple" gurgling into silence told me that the unthinkable had happened, and Abdul would be too angry to save me.

I came up sputtering, turned over in a float and geared up my elementary backstroke. Expecting Abdul to overtake me and hold my head under, I couldn't afford to glide after each stroke. The extra action warmed me a little, but when I clambered out on the muddy riverbank, the air struck my sodden wool clothing like a blast from Greek hell.

One fearful backward glance told me that Abdul had made a successful dive for the radio and now was trying to right the canoe. Then I ran, part of the Iowa River squishing in my shoes.

Reva, who spent most of her time at the SDT house, was the only one home when I reached the cottage. Everyone else was at dinner. When she answered my frantic pounding on the door, she was touching her pulses with Faberge.

"What—??"

"Lost my key in the river."

She stood aside to let me in and closed the door after me.

"I got tipped by an Egyptian," I told her through chattering teeth, staring at the widening puddle at my feet in dismay. I also had that crawly feeling in the solar plexus I got when I told a lie. I was the one who had done the tipping, but that seemed too complicated to explain.

"Get that stuff off!" she ordered. "I'll turn on the shower. You ought to have something hot to drink, too."

I was amazed by Reva's wholehearted solicitude. Her date knocked, and she told him to wait outside while she towel-dried my hair and wrapped me in her own peony-red robe.

"This is really nice of you," I told her.

She shrugged with that magnificent smile of hers and said, "So who'd make a better Jewish Mother?"

"He said something that made me so mad—I—I don't really know how it happened, but all of the sudden, I was in the water—" I giggled suddenly, "and so was he, and the radio was playing a slow foxtrot for the fishes."

"What did he say?"

"Men stand superior to women. He said it was in the Koran."

"Ha!" said Reva, "They don't, but it doesn't hurt to let them think it. But what were you doing out with an Egyptian? *We've* known they were bad news since before Moses!"

"I guess I've read too many national geographics. I'm sick about what I did to Sue's jacket and Elena's slacks."

"Don't worry, the cleaner can fix them up. And if I were you, I'd make him pick up the tab."

"I don't ever want to see him again," I said, worrying about whether I had enough money to pay the cleaner. "Hadn't you better go? Your date is probably having a fit out there."

She waved an elegant, red-nailed hand airily. "Sherwin will live. Sure you're OK?"

The shower was pouring steam into the main part of the cottage by now. "Yeah. After I soak in some heat, I'll be good as new."

She threw her fur jacket over her shoulders and waved. Before the door shut, I could hear Sherwin's querulous voice and her reply. "It was an emergency, Sherwin!"

I caught a severe cold, the borrowed clothes were restored to an approximation of their original condition, and I decided not to write home about the incident. Mom and Grandma both were worriers inclined to fret over what *might* have happened but didn't.

Thinking it over, I decided that an assault on my virture by the right person might be acceptable—Arthur Blair, perhaps, or Dexter Burton. It would have to be someone who also cared about what went on in my head. My only regret about Abdul was unsatisfied curiosity. Now I'd never know why he and Ali just sat there and watched me eat. When you'd never known people who were different, you thought everyone was just like you, and I was learning that this wasn't so.

Though I was still curious about myriad differences, I was glad to return to the safety of Roger Williams Fellowship. Here, I could admire Arthur Blair to my heart's content, and common Christian courtesy would require him to be civil to me. Not that he came to the house that often. Bookings with the Bo Williams combo kept him pretty busy.

But Harley Schippers was always there, and I fell into the habit of dating him when I had nothing better to do. Harley had the broad, mashed face of a bulldog. His height caused me to put the high-heeled shoes away, and he had a deep voice that was impressive until something amused him. Then he went into wheezy paroxysms that sounded like a seizure.

Harley was a talented photographer, and he posed me on the Union bridge across the Iowa River, leaning on the lampposts along the shaded path to the Quadrangle, on the steps of Old Capitol, trailing a finger along the keyboard of the grand piano at Roger Williams House, waving an Iowa pennant in the stadium, and all dressed up for a formal dance with a gardenia in my hair. In short, he provided me with evidence that I was a coed, giving me pictures to document my letters home.

A chaste kiss at the cottage door was Harley's reward for all his attentions, and I found it as exciting as kissing the back of my own hand.

Venus observed all of this and finally asked with that bright, birdlike expression of hers, "Don't you think you're getting his hopes up for nothing?"

"What hopes?"

"He's obviously crazy about you."

"You're imagining things."

So I thought until the night Harley took me to hear the music in the basement of Hotel Jefferson. Bobby Cotter was singing there with Larry Barrett's orchestra, and I was so caught up in her sad, smoky version of "I Cover The Waterfront" that Harley had to repeat himself to get my attention.

"Margaret—I really *am* serious about this."

"About what, Harley?"

"I'm going to need someone to help me entertain my business clients, and I—I thought it might as well be somebody that I—"

Bobby Cotter sang with a catch in her voice, "...for the one I love to come back—to me."

Why couldn't it be Harley? He yearned for me the way I yearned for Arthur Blair, and Arthur probably yearned for a woman who yearned for someone else. It was as if we all were running in an endless circle, never catching the one we were pursuing. If just one person in that circle would turn and run to the arms of the pursuer, *somebody* could be happy. But I simply couldn't be the one to turn. He was waiting—and with such pathetic hope. Belatedly, I realized that he had been outlining his excellent future prospects while I was covering the waterfront with Bobby Cotter. He didn't see how I could refuse.

"Harley, I'm just a freshman. I'm not ready to think about anything like that."

He snapped his fingers. "*Knew* I was bringing it up too soon, but I wanted to get my bid in."

I bent my Coke straw into one-inch segments, folding it into a packet that sprang into an angled corral when I let go. "Don't Fence Me In!"

"Well," he said, smiling with less certainty, "you can think about it."

I looked at my watch. "I think I'd better get back, Harley. I have a test tomorrow."

"Tomorrow's Sunday!"

I blushed, grateful for the dark room. "I—I meant Monday, but even so—"

As we left, Bobby Cotter was beginning "Can't Help Lovin' Dat Man O' Mine." I wondered if I'd *ever* find one to love 'til I died.

Harley walked me to the darker door between the cottages, and as he reached for me to administer the usual good-night kiss, I said, "Harley, I don't think we should see each other anymore."

"Don't tell me that. I didn't mean to scare you, Margaret, and I won't push."

"It's not that, Harley. You shouldn't waste your time on me. You should be looking for someone who *will* do your business entertaining or whatever. I can't."

"Forget the business part, then."

"No, Harley, we'd better forget it all. I just don't feel—I mean, I—"

"You don't love me," he said in a flat voice.

"That's it—and I'm really sorry!"

He turned away, and then he began to sob. I could see tears glinting in the streetlight that pierced the tree branches.

"Oh Harley, please, don't!" Our family being short of men, I'd never seen one cry, and I was appalled.

"This just can't be the end," he said in a thick voice.

"We'll see each other—at Roger Williams and all kinds of places." I wiped the tears from one cheek with the flat of my hand, which he caught and kissed.

"But you've *got* to go out with me!" Fresh tears gushed.

"All right, Harley, just stop crying!"

He pulled himself together with remarkable speed, stepping behind the tree to blow his nose and returning to claim the good-night kiss that I had hoped would be the last.

I went inside thoroughly disgusted with myself for being such a coward—for being the type who pulled off adhesive tape bit by bit, thus prolonging the misery. One of my secret ambitions was to become a tape ripper.

Venus listened, then said, "Too bad you couldn't get the job done. 'When half-gods go, the gods arrive.'"

"What does that mean?"

"Just what it says."

"Who said it?"

"Ralph Waldo Emerson. Another of us Unitarians. That line is from 'Give All to Love.'"

"Wish I could find a love that *wanted* it all!. Why can't I find someone who wants the whole package?"

"I can't even find takers for the parts!" she said.

The prospect of going home for Christmas filled me with a mixture of yearning eagerness and anxiety. Being totally responsible for myself for almost four months had been exhausting, and I looked forward to yielding (temporarily) that new independence to the all-powerful women who had sent me out to find it. On the other hand, I would be offering my new self like papers brought home from school; only this time, Mom and Grandma would do the grading.

I could have pressured Roger Andersen into giving me a ride home. His mother had taken an interest in me during high school, and a short note to her hinting of my need would have done the trick. Not that Roger was a mama's boy, but he knew better than to cross Athalia Andersen. However, Roger's hard-drinking, woman-chasing, fraternity-man facade gave me a pain. When I heard girls speak of him with admiring awe, I was tempted to tell them he had wet his pants as late as the sixth grade. I didn't, of course, because I knew how I'd feel if he told anyone what I used to be—the wallflower of the western world! Coming to the university had been a liberation for us both.

Mom sent me Greyhound bus fare, fortunately, because I had used all but a dollar or so of my small check from the law school for basic existence and a few Christmas presents.

No matter what I chose for Grandma, I knew she would say, "I'll never live to use it." Her dresser drawers held a twenty-year accumulation of things she'd never live to use, a twist on the bridal hope chest. I bought tortoise shell combs to secure the wispy strands of hair that escaped from the knot twisted high on her head. I admired the combs set with rhinestones but passed them by, knowing she would scorn the glitter.

I wanted something beautiful for Mom, but I almost felt her beside me when I paused to look at the costume jewelry. She was shaking her head, and I continued my search until the sensation subsided at the hosiery counter. I could hear her say, "You can always use stockings." Even now that we could buy as many pairs as we pleased, the wartime sense of their preciousness lingered, appeasing my desire to offer her a treasure.

I was still wistful about the jewelry, but Mom never wore it—not even her wedding ring. The delicate cameo on a gold chain my father had given her was mine now, and so were the robin's egg-blue turquoise rings she and Aunt Kam had bought for themselves when they were young. I wore them together like a wedding set, a reminder of the women who stood behind me no matter what.

Everyone in the cottage had left before I started to pack. I planned it that way, not wanting them to notice my embarrassing luggage. Among the baby-blue Samsonites, the suitcase my grandfather had taken to the Chicago World's Fair in 1893 looked like a fugitive from a museum. Unfortunately, it had been made to last. The catches worked perfectly, and though the lining resembled the whorled endpapers of antique books and smelled old, it showed little wear.

I wouldn't need many clothes at home, unlike Nita and Sue, who would be going to formal dances. Slacks, sweaters, a skirt or two, a dress and two pairs of shoes should do it.

I'd need to study, so I packed all my books, putting some of them with the dirty clothes I meant to carry in their cloth and cardboard mailer to save postage. At least I would be well-balanced for the long walk to the bus station in the snow.

Venus had asked, "Why don't you call a cab?", and I had just stared at her as if she had made an obscene suggestion. Where I came from, there were no cabs, and years of carrying heavy sacks of groceries home from the A&P had convinced me there was no other way.

I stopped only a few times to switch hands on the laundry and suitcase and brush snow from my hair and lashes. Mittens cushioned the handles, sparing my palms. Passing Whetstone's drugstore, I longed to stop for hot chocolate, and there was time, but I couldn't afford it.

Not one person I knew was on the streets that night. In fact, very few people were out at all, and the carols over the loudspeaker at the bank seemed forlorn without an audience. "O Little Town of Bethlehem," which I considered to be the saddest of them all, was playing, and I brooded over its minor melody and the portentous phrase, "the hopes and fears of all the years." The words flung themselves at the golden dome of Old Capitol and sank into its core.

I didn't want to leave this town of infinite possibility, fearing that something indescribably wonderful would happen in my absence. On the other hand, I knew that I needed to go home and sort out the bombardment of new experience in this place.

With the students gone or going, the campus was like a church on Monday morning or a movie theater at 10 a.m.—suspended and waiting. Before I rounded the corner that would put the Pentacrest buildings out of sight, I turned and promised them, "I'll be back. Wait for me!" I knew that this was the behavior of a young child or a primitive, but that didn't bother me.

I hurried on, recalling Thoreau's advice, "walk like a camel, the only beast which ruminates while walking." I intended to spend a lot of time with Thoreau over the holiday (Dexter Burton had intimated he would loom large in the final exam), and I was actually looking forward to it.

As soon as Mom sent the money, I had bought my bus ticket, and I could almost feel it pulsing in my billfold inside the shoulder bag that left both hands free. I set the bags down, straddling them as a safety measure while I found the ticket and clamped it between my teeth.

The bus was half-hidden by clouds from its exhaust, and the driver emerged from the eerie steam to stow my bags. I could take my choice of seats and chose one next to the window, placing my Western Civilization textbook on the aisle seat to discourage occupancy. I didn't feel like talking. As my eyes grew accustomed to the dark interior, I saw a man farther up the aisle looking back—looking at me. I turned to the window and studied my reflection. Mom always said, "Never look a stranger in the eye. It's asking for trouble."

"Why?"

"When you look at someone, it's like unlocking the door and saying, 'Come in!' The eyes are the windows of the soul, they say."

Doors and windows. I sighed, thinking that I could spend the rest of my life identifying all the "theys" who said things that interested me. I had discovered that it was possible to look most of them up—except the ones that ended in the stone wall of "Anonymous."

The man was hanging half out of his seat now, trying to window-peek. A flash of headlights through the side window revealed that he was wearing an old Army coat, and that did it. I'd had all the war veterans I could take in Iowa City. Many were driven, drunken, desperate men trying to make up for lost years. They worked hard enough in their classes to create a fierce grading curve, and they were so used to being the occupying forces in foreign countries that they thought they could still get whatever they wanted for a candy bar or a cigarette.

I put my head back against the seat and pretended to be falling asleep, but my eyes were slitted enough to watch the passing landscape through Tiffin, Homestead, South Amana and Marengo. The dark shapes that were cattle against the snow, the farmhouse lights and the continuing tracery of telephone wires lulled me until I no longer pretended.

The stop in Des Moines woke me, and I went inside the bus station to await my turn in the restroom. Everyone in the waiting room looked exhausted and worried, or maybe it was only the bleaching fluorescent lights that created that illusion. The black woman ahead of me was carrying five or six satchels looped together with a piece of rope, and she had to move sideways to get through the narrow door marked "Women." Someone put money in the jukebox. I listened to "Sentimental Journey" all the way through and then tried to understand a garbled announcement on the loudspeaker. What if I missed my bus? Mom would be frantic. Just as I was turning to go back to the bus, the black woman come out. I reclaimed my place in line just in time.

This was the first bus station toilet I'd encountered, and it epitomized "sin and degradation" with its nasty odors, crumpled paper towels all over the floor and graffiti inside the stalls. Having been warned about germs too vile to identify in public toilets, I covered the seat with paper which slid into the bowl and to the floor. I worked at it until I got it to stay put and sat down to contemplate the "cave drawings" around me. I didn't even understand all of the inscriptions, but I picked up the tone the way one tunes into cursing in a foreign language. I wouldn't write my name on that olive drab metal. It would be like leaving a part of oneself in a smelly prison. Besides, as Grandma always said, "Fools' names and fools' faces are always seen in public places."

When I emerged to wash my hands, I saw that the gooey bar of soap was gray with other people's dirt, so I held it under the faucet before I took off my turquoise rings to use it. The rings tended to collect soap in the hollows of their mountings.

The closed door seemed to clarify the loudspeaker, muffling the crackling. I heard my bus called and rushed out, regaining my seat in plenty of time for departure. I pulled my knees up, wound the strap of my purse tightly around my arm for safety's sake and went to sleep again.

I didn't realize my loss until the bus had stopped at the Saylor Hotel. With a glad leap of the heart, I realized that I was home. By sleeping, I had missed my favorite view of Harlan, the necklace of lights seen from the hills east of town, but here I was on the Square. Colored lights made a giant Maypole of the courthouse, and the streetlights cast that golden light that tinged all my memories. But everything looked so much smaller. I stood in the aisle, buttoned my coat and started to draw one mitten on when I realized that my ring finger was bare.

A vision of the blue stones in their mellow gold on the gray whorls of dried soap flashed into my mind, and I let out a cry that made me glad I was the last person left on the bus. Numbly I climbed down and claimed my bags to trudge home. When the lights of the square dimmed, giving me a cloak of darkness, I began to cry.

With each step I took, the rings became more beautiful and more precious—harder to lose. My carelessness was a betrayal, making me unworthy of family trust. By the time I reached the jockey hitching post at the O'Neills', I was sobbing in earnest.

Mom rushed the length of the porch to meet me, still knotting the tasseled tie around the flannel cotton robe they always borrowed for one of the Wise Men in the Sunday School program.

"Margaret! What happened?" She snatched my suitcase and the laundry bag, tossing them to one side and feeling me all over as if she were looking for broken bones.

"The rings! I lost the rings!"

"What rings?"

"Yours and Aunt Kam's—the turquoises. Oh Mom, I could die!"

She exhaled noisily and pulled me inside. "Don't wake Mama—if we haven't already."

I had, of course, and she came into the kitchen in her long flannel gown with the Chinaman's pigtail hanging down her back, sliding the thin, gold earpieces of her glasses into place. *"Nuh, suh!"* she said.

"It's all right, Mama. She just lost the rings Kam and I gave her. I thought she'd been attacked."

Grandma went to the refrigerator and got out the milk, then went to the pantry for a pan of fresh cinnamon rolls—the kind I liked best. Roll-ups with raisins and lots of brown sugar.

I was still standing there in my coat, scarf and mittens. She divested me of my wraps as if I were a kindergartener, saying, "Things do not matter very much, Margarethe. Eat, now."

I sat down to chew and swallow sorrowfully. The loss of the rings as things didn't bother me as much as what that loss seemed to symbolize. They wedded me to my family, and now there was a breach caused by my carelessness.

Looking around me, I saw shabbiness I hadn't noticed in September: the couch covered with an army blanket and piled high with second-hand newspapers from Aunt Kam; the rack of plates, a hairline crack crossing the pudgy form of Moses in the Bulrushes; the scars in the sky-blue paint of the big trunk my father had brought from Denmark. I loved every flaw, but I was glad Nita couldn't see them.

Mom wrapped a flatiron in a dish towel to warm my feet in the cold bedroom. After living in the over-heated cottage, I wasn't sure I'd make it through the night. I stubbed my toe on the heavy iron, which started me crying all over again, but I finally stopped shuddering and went to sleep. My dreams were fragmented and distressing. Lew Browne coming at me like Dracula and suddenly becoming someone I trusted—or wanted to trust—Arthur Blair. Gregory Sommer, the lawyer I worked for when I was in high school, speaking to me in a hollow voice from a great distance, "Wait until all the facts are in—facts, facts, facts!" Standing outside myself to watch me struggle in the cold water of the Iowa River.

My cousin Marianne came home for Christmas, and I admired her Rosalind Russell career woman style. She asked me how I liked college but didn't really want an answer, so I just said, "Fine."

Aunt Kam really did want details, and I edited my experience before providing her with them. After all, I wasn't going to offend her with Nita's classic vulgarisms or describe the hot love life of my graduate student cottage proctor.

When I went uptown in the daylight, it seemed that the buildings on the Square had shrunk. The bank that had seemed so grand with its Greek columns looked loveable but slightly foolish now—like a little girl playing dress-up. I went in because my friend Wyonne was working there. She was allowed a break, and we went to Levendahl's drugstore for a Coke.

Close as we had been in high school, we seemed to have little to say to each other. Venus, Boots and Nita meant nothing to her, and I wasn't interested in her purchase of a set of Wearever aluminum cookware on the installment plan. When I told her about Lew Browne and the "Liebestod" and Abdul and the canoe, she thought I was making it up.

"How's your love life?" she asked, "I mean *really*."

"Still looking. What about you?"

She sighed. "I suppose I might as well marry Harold Volmer and get it over with! I'm sick of going to showers for other people!"

"Do you love him?"

She shrugged, "Not much to pick from around here."

"Then go somewhere else."

"Too much trouble."

"Remember when we used to go out with those sailors, Gene and Duane?"

"Yeah," she said with wistful smile, "those were the days!"

"Do you know that you sound about forty?" I turned away from the hurt in her eyes and quickly asked, "How's your brother Max?"

"He's a surgeon now."

I nodded, remembering how he used to dismember bugs "to see how much they could get along without."

Wyonne had to get back to the bank, and I stayed in the booth, comparing the molasses pace of Levendahl's with the electric bustle of Whetstone's in Iowa City.

"Why, Margaret Langelund!"

I recognized Mary Lois Engleman's voice with a start—my accompanist, my antagonist, my classmate.

"You don't look any different," she said, sliding into the booth.

"Did you expect me to turn black and old gold?"

"Well, your tongue's as sharp as ever."

I shifted my eyes to an old farmer who was opening a snap purse with stiff, chapped fingers to pay for a prescription. What could I possibly have to say to a valedictorian who had postponed college because she couldn't bear to miss being Worthy Advisor of the Rainbow Girls after working her way up through the chairs?

"We're initiating Wednesday night, and I've got a new formal," Mary Lois said. "Don't you wish you hadn't dropped out at Faith?"

I shook my head, remembering the monotonous, white-clad marching around the Masonic Hall above Norgaard's drugstore to the music of "I Wish You Were Jealous of Me." The promised mysteries seemed much more promising before they were revealed.

"I just don't understand you!" Mary Lois said.

"You're not alone. I seem to do better in Iowa City."

"Well, why don't you just go on back there?" she got up and flounced off, leaving me to stare into my empty Coke glass.

Then, feeling a hovering presence, I looked up into the face of Albert Rettig, the pious swain of my high school days. He was a younger version of the old man with the snap purse.

"Hello, Margaret, how are you?" He shuffled his heavy boots and thrust his hands deep into his pockets. A fine layer of sawdust on his glasses obscured his eyes, but I remembered that they were pale blue.

"I'm fine—I guess. How about you?"

"Can't complain. Well, I'd better get along. Leah needs some medicine for the baby, and Dad wants some two-by-fours from the lumberyard. Glad I saw you."

He left me readily, willingly, as I once had prayed he would do. Now, even though I didn't want him to stay, I felt a letdown. I paid for my Coke and walked toward home, stopping to see if Lotus Hess had time to visit.

Lotus was home from Simpson, and she at least had some inkling of what college life was all about, but it scarcely seemed marvelous to her.

"Dorm food stinks, doesn't it?" she said in a voice voluptuously muffled by a mouthful of her mother's famous burnt sugar cake.

Restless and unable to get through to anybody, I went home, picked up *Walden*, and opened the oven door on the cook stove to toast my feet while I read. But even Thoreau, the famous loner, began to pall.

Florine Hammond might be the answer. When I had gone to see her at her command in the late summer, I had sided with the community in perceiving her oddity. Now it was possible that I had jumped the fence.

I put on my coat once more, noticing the look Mom and Grandma exchanged when I told them I'd be back soon. Snow threatened, making the afternoon dark, and the walk to the big house on Baldwin Street was a cold one.

Roger Andersen's car, a red Chevy with an SUI window sticker, was parked in front of the Blairs' a block from Florine's, and I wondered why he'd be visiting that elderly couple. As far as I knew, he wasn't related to them.

I was relieved to see soft lamplight glowing from the depths of Florine's house and the roof of her Chrysler visible through the glass top of the garage door. Then it occurred to me that she might not be glad to see me, considering the way I had spurned her sorority.

Even so, I rang the bell, listening for footsteps on the terrazo floor of the hall. There was no response. I rang again, shivering in the foggy cloud of my own breath and marching in place to ward off the penetrating cold.

Then I saw movement on the stairs—slender, tanned legs breaking a navy blue robe as Florine took two steps at a time. I heard her throw back the door bolt.

"Mrs. Hammond, I thought I'd—I mean, I'm sorry if I woke you."

"No, you didn't wake me. I was just reading and recuperating from the hordes of Attila. The Hammonds breed like rabbits, and they were all here for Christmas. What can I do for you?"

I turned up my palms helplessly. "I—I don't know. It's just that coming home feels so strange, and I thought maybe you'd understand."

She stood in the open door, pondering, and then threw it wider and said, "Come in for a quick cup of coffee."

I took off my wraps, following her to the kitchen. She operated like a pharmacist in that big, bright marvel of efficiency. When the coffee was brewed, we moved to a small den filled with modernized Hammond antiques where a fire was burning in the grate.

"So tell me about it," she said, cradling her cup in both hands. Her eyes glittered, and her hair was falling from its usual careful arrangement, but she made no attempt to fix it.

Before I was well into my recital, I heard a thump upstairs and raised my eyes to the ceiling.

"The judge is home with a cold," she said, and I wondered if she could be getting one too. She looked flushed and only half-listened to what I was saying.

Just as I launched into an account of my experience with Lew, the back door slammed and she stiffened.

"My God!" she said, "What time is it?"

Before I could answer, the judge looked in on us, healthy and smiling as he beat the snow from his hat.

"It's really coming down!" he said. "You two look mighty cozy in here."

Florine became very still, as if she were holding her breath. The back door slammed again.

"Guess I forgot to latch it," the judge said, turning.

"I'll get it!" Florine moved so quickly that the dark robe swirled.

"I guess I'd better be getting home," I said, and the judge told me not to hurry off on his account.

"Florine enjoys young people," he said.

She reappeared and urged me to stay, but I said, "I really can't. We eat early. I'll just go out the back and cut through."

"We'll have lunch and really talk," she said quickly, nervously.

The back steps had been swept hastily with a broom, but a chain of footsteps circled the house and led to the dark rectangle where Roger Andersen's car had stood. He could be her son! All right, so I had sighed over Balzac's contention that the last love of a woman and the first love of a man was an unbeatable combination, but when you knew the woman and the man, it was revolting.

I plodded homeward in the blackest disillusionment and refused to answer when Mom asked me what was wrong. She was too innocent to hear such a thing, "Florine enjoys young people!"

Then expecting to be appreciated for the glad news of ecumenism I was bringing to my church from Iowa City, I was startled to be accused of worldliness and liberal heresy. I came home to rant and rave about narrow-mindedness, and Mom said the church people couldn't be blamed because that was all they knew.

"And that's all they *want* to know," I said bitterly.

What little of the holiday remained I spent with my feet in the cookstove oven and *Walden* on my lap. Thoreau's pure, unmessy

Nature was the only antidote for my unhappiness. Consequently, I got a wonderful grade on my English and American Authors final.

While most of my cottage mates were whiling away afternoons at the Fieldhouse, playing bridge in the seats they had staked out for the basketball game those nights, I was typing the dean's Evidence textbook. Venus, Elena and I would gulp down our dinners and hurry over there to relieve the others while they grabbed hamburgers. It worked out well, because we three didn't play bridge and couldn't afford hamburgers.

The favorites of Cottage 15 were Murray Wier, a firecracker of a forward; Roger Finley, a slow, towering center; and Charlie Mason, a fast, tireless guard. Their style on the court had something to do with their popularity, but even more important, their names could be spelled backwards and emerge pronounceable by the elect: Yarrum Reiw, Regor Yelnif and Eilrahc Nosam. They had more trouble with Jack Spencer, the team captain who was known as "Thin Man," not that they appreciated his athletic ability less.

I never used the "backward" names for the players nor joined Nita and Kay in speculating about the sexual prowess of the men in the gold satin trunks, but I shared the general excitement of a winning season. The over-heated Fieldhouse grew steamy as a crowd garbed in damp wool wedged itself into the bleachers. The odor of pool chlorine and cigarette smoke mingled with that of wet wool and sweat to create a smell that would have been disgusting at any time but game time.

Lettermen in their old gold sweaters with big block I's did whatever ushering was needed. Venus and I didn't know many of them on sight, and we played the game of guessing their sport. The football players were easy, huge despite their unpadded condition, but track, swimming and baseball athletes were harder to sort out.

I had focused on a slender blond who looked like a high school kid. He was coming our way. "Swimmer?"

Venus shook her head. "Not enough shoulder."

The man in front of me shifted, bumping into the knees I was working hard to keep out of his back. Smoke from his cigarette streamed into my eyes and made them water.

"Sir," said the letterman we had been observing, "you'll have to put that cigarette out."

"Go to hell!"

The letterman retreated, shoulders narrow beneath the old gold sweater, but he soon returned with a massive football player. He pointed out the smoker, and the problem was solved without words. A large, old gold arm raised like a piston rod and a broad thumb and middle finger flipped the cigarette from mouth to polished floor. The slender usher ground it out with his heel while the big athlete pointed to the No Smoking sign, and then both of them were gone.

Venus laughed uneasily. "It's all in who you know."

"Whom," I said, wishing I had asked the smaller guy what his sport was.

"Here they come!" Nita screamed, nearly breaking my eardrums, "Yarrum! Yay, Yarrum! Regor! Regor!"

The one game I missed was our loss to Minnesota, and that was because I was detained at the law school. I hadn't worked for the dean long enough to be really confident about the routine, and it had occurred to me that Regina liked to keep all of us slightly off-balance and dependent upon her. The technique didn't work with Gwen, but the quiet, mousy Hilda Crawford could be intimidated easily. I was wary but infinitely curious about the fascinating collection of eccentrics that made up the law school faculty. Observing them, I could see why Regina always said, "The mind of a lawyer is a strange and fearful thing."

Steve Carr was the prime attention-getter with his untrimmed hair of straw yellow and an English accent. I was amazed to hear that he came from Wisconsin and had picked up his speech patterns during a brief time at Oxford. Carr held up his trousers with a length of rope and wore a Tyrolean hat pierced by bright fishing lures. He lived with his wife and a large brood of children in a trailer.

Ernest Dunker, a former Office of Price Administration official, was slow of speech but deadly with the delayed-reaction insult. The students called him "the O.P.A. S.O.B." and mimicked his slightly cross-eyed gaze. According to Regina, Dunker's children threw the table silver at dinner guests.

The rotund Edward Cepik adorned the hill of his vest with a Phi Beta Kappa key on a chain. He visited the dean daily to deliver his latest dirty joke, which we all tried vainly to hear from the outer office. One of Cepik's sons was in a class of mine, and I marveled that a purveyor of such low humor could have begotten that sweetly serious boy.

Paul Thayer was my favorite. He never remembered whether he had eaten breakfast and depended upon the counter girl at Whetstone's to tell him if he had been in earlier that day. Once he drove his car to Cedar Rapids, forgot he had it and took the inter-urban trolley home. He built a room onto his house, neglecting to create a connecting door. But he did remember names and faces. When we met on the campus, he removed his hat (if he hadn't left it at Whetstone's) and said, "How do you do, Miss Langelund?" One of the high points of the law school year was Thayer's annual poetry reading. All his students attended, whether they enjoyed poetry or not, because he would know exactly who was missing. With his dog Assumpsit, a black hunting type, sleeping beside him on the podium, he would read until he was overcome by emotion. Usually it was "John Anderson, My Jo John" that brought tears and forced him to stumble from the room. Then Assumpsit would wake, look around in momentary bewilderment, and follow his master. Assumpsit had learned to look around the hard way. He frequently slept on the wide ledge outside Thayer's office windows a long way from the ground, and one imprudent move was all it took to teach him caution.

At the other end of my rating scale was James Maddox, a sadist who reduced the students to quivering profanity. When Regina sent me to his office on an errand, I expected and got insults with a subtle sting. The first time was the worst because I gave him an opening.

"And who might you be?" he asked.

"Regina's minion."

"Indeed! Get thee to a dictionary!"

I felt heat in my face and throat and lost no time getting back to the big dictionary in the office. Gwen looked up and said, "Oh, oh! Maddox is at it again. What did he call you?"

"Nothing," I said truthfully. I'd done it myself. I found "minion," and when I struck the word "wanton" in its definition, my face burned hotter.

Jim Nathan, the bachelor professor from Massachusetts, came in to ask for a class list, distracting me from my humiliation briefly. He wore cowboy boots and looked at all women in a way that led them to believe they were infinitely desirable. I wondered if he really did, as rumored, dance on table tops after a certain number of drinks?

It was unthinkable to speculate about the foibles of Myron Cantwell, the white-haired former dean. He seemed too Olympian to exist outside the classroom—more a monument than a person, a legend wearing thick glasses. He said he didn't plan to stay long because he'd been invited to teach in "a boneyard for old professors in California."

Carson McGreer, a former Yale Law Review editor, was in his first year of teaching. Younger than many of the war veterans in his classes, he accorded them respect for their experience in return for their recognition of his own superiorities. Sensing that McGreer was too poor to pay the various faculty assessments I was sent to collect, (like contributions to the Red Cross) I by-passed him and invented elaborate excuses to tell Regina.

"They've had some really heavy expenses this month, so he can't afford—"

"Such as?" Regina said stonily.

I stammered, "Well, they—the furnace broke."

Regina gave me a menacing, heavy-lidded look, but nothing more was said.

It was at times like this when I longed to be a Catholic. My friends Wyonne and Monica always could find a way to put a good face on a lie, but I was consumed by conscience no matter how benevolent the reason for lying. Could it be possible that the conscience resided in the shoulder? That was where I felt a physical pain when I drank beer or told lies. Perhaps the conscience rode the shoulder like a falcon, digging in when you tried to shake it.

The least colorful member of the faculty was Jamie Fitzgerald, and that probably was because he lived in the shadow of his exotic wife, Norma. Mrs. Fitzgerald had been a highly-paid advertising director in New York before the marriage that eclipsed her talents. Norma sat in the classroom while her husband lectured, following him back to his office to deliver a nit-picking critique without bothering to close the door.

Once Gwen asked her (with the elaborate innocence only Gwen could manage), "Where did you go to law school, Mrs. Fitzgerald?"

Norma's laugh was brittle. "Nowhere—yet, but I think I'll try to work in Carr and Nathan next semester. I have to do *something* to keep from losing my mind in this backwater."

As the sharp scent of perfume receded with Norma's passing, Gwen murmured, "If she brought a mind with her, she won't have any trouble hanging onto it. They ought to charge her tuition for all the time she spends here already."

The afternoons passed quickly as the Evidence manuscript grew. Struggling against the sleepiness induced by a pasty dormitory lunch, I would plunge into the typing. Before I knew it, Regina would be locking her desk drawers and getting ready to close the office. Her last act was to slam the heavy door of the safe where records and examinations were kept and twirl the combination lock.

The day of the Minnesota game, I felt the tension in the office the minute I walked in, but nothing was said. I typed steadily, forgoing a break I would have appreciated because I had the feeling that Regina was watching me closely.

When Regina had not locked her drawers or closed the safe at the usual quitting time, I was puzzled. I covered my typewriter, thinking I'd have to hurry because of the game. I put on my coat and then wondered why Regina was standing in the door like that.

"Good-night," I said, expecting her to let me pass, but she continued to block the door.

"Hand it over."

"What?"

"Oh, I suppose it's too much to expect that you'd have it on you!" she said sarcastically.

"I'm sorry, but I don't know what you're talking about."

"I think you do," she looked like a female Sidney Greenstreet.

I glanced at my watch, worrying that Venus and Elena would have trouble holding all the seats at the game without my help.

"The Torts exam is missing from the safe. Now don't you think it's a strange coincidence that it was there at 3:30 yesterday, you were alone in the office from 4:30 to 5, and when I opened the safe this morning it was gone?"

"That's circumstantial evidence," I said.

"Don't get legal with me! Carr has to make up a new test whether we get it back or not, but you'd better cough it up!"

"I can't give you what I don't have, and why should *I* want it, anyhow?"

"You've seen the grades. It's worth money to somebody, and you'd know who."

"To whom," I said automatically before protesting, "The others have seen the grades too!" Regina *wanted* it to be me, clearly, and I'd need somebody bigger and stronger and more important to get me out of this—like the big football letterman. When I was growing up, most of my friends ran to their dads for help, but our family of women had to manage the best it could without male assistance.

That's when the dean came to the door. He'd been out somewhere in his hat and coat, and as he asked Regina's pardon and moved sideways to come in, I shot him a look of mute appeal.

"Well?" he spoke to her.

"She won't admit it, naturally."

He took off his hat and nodded to me, gesturing toward his inner office.

"Have a chair, Margaret," he said, hanging up his coat.

I sank into a slippery, golden oak seat and waited. I shifted purse and textbooks to loosen my coat.

"This is serious," he said, whacking his pipe on the metal wastebasket with a resounding clang.

"I know nothing about the test," my voice broke and I fought tears.

"Were you out of the office at any time yesterday afternoon?"

"Yes, around four. I was in the lounge with Gwen."

"Regina was in Mr. Cantwell's office at that time, she says. What about Hilda?"

"She didn't come in while I was here. She had a dental appointment—" as I spoke, I remembered that I *had* seen Hilda in the building just before Gwen and I went to the lounge. She was standing in the recessed doorway of Steve Carr's office across from ours rummaging in what looked like a knitting bag.

"Then it wouldn't have been Hilda," the dean was saying.

"She goes to the clinic at the Dental School. You could call and ask if she was there."

We could see the Dental building through the office window, and the dean kept his eyes on it as he reached for the phone. "That will be all for now, Margaret."

Heart pounding, I went to my desk to wait. I was surprised to see that neither Gwen nor Hilda had left yet. Neither of them spoke.

Then the dean called for Hilda. She was in his office for a long time. When she came out, her face was mottled and her eyes were wet. She stopped at my desk and spoke without looking at me.

"It wouldn't have hurt you as much."

Gwen approached and touched Hilda's thin shoulder while Regina stared, still looking like Sidney Greenstreet. Hilda twisted away from Gwen's hand.

"What could *you* know about the hell I've been through? *Your* husband makes his grades. Larry hates living in that quonset! He always talks about getting out—how much better it will be—but he *can't* get out because he won't—I had to do *something*, didn't I?" She crashed through the swinging gate into the outer office and ran blindly into the hall. Gwen started to go after her, then turned back with a palms-up gesture.

"Clean out her desk," Regina said.

Gwen and I did it, putting Hilda's nail file, a small jar of hand cream and her pens into a manilla envelope with her name on it. She didn't have much that was personal.

By this time, it was too late for dinner at the dorm, and I was too shaken to think of going to the game. Gwen said, "I'll feed you."

Their quonset was bright and more homelike than I thought such a structure could be. Gwen's husband was still at the library, she said, but she introduced us via their wedding picture. I expected her to kick off her high heels and change her clothes before she started to make supper, but she only put on a frilly apron.

"Bob likes me in heels, and there's nobody in the world I'd rather look good for," she said. "Want a beer?"

"No thanks, it gives me a pain in the shoulder."

Her beautiful eyes widened. "No foolin'!"

"Maybe I *should* have taken the blame. I feel terrible about Hilda."

Gwen snorted. "That would be a waste! Larry is a loser, and she'd do well to get rid of him."

"What will happen to her?"

"God knows. Why didn't she think to have a dental student back her story? She's as stupid as Larry!"

I thought of Hilda slipping into the building during a class hour and hiding in the shadows of that recessed doorway, dying a little with every footfall while she waited for her chance. She didn't steal the test to sell; she gambled on the possibility of making her man love her again—if he ever had. I wondered if he had asked her to get the test for him or if the idea were entirely hers? Would I ever love a man enough to do something terribly wrong for him?

Gwen turned on the radio. Iowa was 12 points down. "That's 'cause you're not there, Honey."

I laughed shortly. "Yarrum and Regor don't depend on me much."

"*What?*"

I explained the backward spelling, and she said, "Oh, you kids!"

Bob came home, and because I averted my eyes from their kiss of greeting, it took me awhile to realize that he had an artificial leg. Gwen never had said a word about it, though she wasn't bashful about saying what a wonderful lover he was.

After the excellent meal, I knew I should go home and study, but being in a house was such a good feeling that I hated to leave. When I finally did put on my coat, Gwen stepped outside the door with me and whispered, "In case you're wondering, it was Iwo." I knew that neither of us would ever mention it again.

When did peace truly become peace with no visible reminders of war?

As I walked away from the quonset park, I thought about Gwen and Bob and their marriage. I'd never really seen a marriage up close—except Aunt Kam and Uncle Karl's, and that didn't count because they were so old. Besides, they were relatives and thus immune from sexual consideration. My cousin Geraldine and Vito Scarpelli might have been an exception, but they left Harlan immediately after their wedding and never sent any word beyond a Christmas greeting. One thing I knew for sure. If I ever loved anyone enough to marry him, I wouldn't take the advice of Venus: do it once a year—on New Year's Eve, maybe—and get it over with.

Back at the cottage, I turned on the radio and learned that Iowa had lost to Minnesota, 56-72. Red-hot Yarrum hadn't been hot enough. Then the horrible thought returned to me—I had been suspected of theft. Even though the blame had gone elsewhere, the accusation seemed like a permanent stain.

My second semester schedule allowed me to choose one elective course, and I took Contemporary Protestant Thought. The professor was the least ministerial minister I'd ever encountered, but he seemed to be well-intentioned.

I read Karl Barth and Kierkegaard dutifully and with interest. When I wrote a paper interpreting and commenting on what I had read, Dr. Brattleson asked me to speak to him after class. I hoped it wouldn't take long, because I now had a pupil of my own, a Chinese boy named Wilson Ling whom I had met at the Baptist student house. He asked me to drill him on English conversation, and when I said I had no time, he said he would meet me after each of my classes, and he could practice while walking me to my next class.

Dr. Brattleson was arguing with a tall, stooped fellow who always sat in the back row wearing an Army jacket with the stripes cut off. Bits of thread remained in the holes, tracing the outline of those badges of rank.

"Kierkegaard is showing us that we must move out of the aesthetic, through the ethical and into the religious and Christian way," Brattleson said.

The student scowled. "If he were in this class, he'd get up and walk out. After all, he *did* pray, 'Teach me, O God, not to torture myself, not to make a martyr out of myself through stifling reflection, but rather teach me to breathe deeply in faith.' All you do is make it complicated."

"Kierkegaard *is* complicated, Mr. Keller."

It was raining, and I walked to the window to look out. I had to go up on my toes to see the doorway across the broad stone window ledge. Wilson was standing there, soaked and scraggly as a baby robin. I hoped he could converse while running, because that was what we would have to do to make the next class on time. I had Modern Lit in a quonset three long blocks away. I cleared my throat loudly to remind Brattleson I was waiting. Keller turned to glare at me and left.

"Now, Miss Langelund. What can I do for you?"

"I don't know. You asked to see *me*. You wrote a note on my paper."

He removed his glasses and sucked one stem reflectively. "Hm. Yes. I wanted to ask you if your faith is really as simplistic as that paper indicates?"

"I said what I meant."

"Oh, come now! You're at the age of questioning, doubt and rebellion. Your certainty is too easy—it's unearned."

"I can't help that. It's like the line from *The Messiah*. 'I know that my Redeemer liveth.' And like what Mr. Keller said about breathing deeply in faith."

"Do you have the paper with you?"

I handed it over and watched while he wrote something across one corner. I took the paper back and dashed down the stairs to where Wilson was waiting, shoving it inside a book without reading the message in red ink.

Wilson brushed a wing of wet, black hair from his eyes and smiled brilliantly. "Good day to you."

"No, Wilson, you say, 'Hello' or 'Hi' or 'Hi, Margaret.'"

He pointed at the sky, "High?"

I laughed. "Yes, but this one is spelled differently. It's short for 'hello.'"

He reached for my books, which he always insisted upon carrying, puzzling over "high" and "short."

"We have to run like crazy, Wilson. I'm late because Brattleson wanted to talk to me."

We ran, trying to avoid the puddles but still splashing each other with regularity.

"My friend plays violent in the symphony," he panted, looking at me expectantly.

"Your friend plays *violin*, Wilson. Or maybe it's a viola. No, I guess it must be violin." Somebody who put more accent on the first syllable had confused him.

"*Vi*olin?"

"Vio*lin*."

"Sometime I come to your town? See where you live?" The wing of hair had fallen back into his eyes, but I could see their shy, black gleam as he asked the question.

"Sure, Wilson, why not?"

He looked distressed, which mystified me until I realized he thought I had asked a question of him—one for which he had no answer.

"Wilson, that's just a way of saying yes. You can come to my town. I'll write to my mother and tell her that I'll bring you home with me at Easter, OK?"

"OK," he smiled, bowed, and handed me my books, "see you at 10:50."

Mr. Dagget was dissecting "Hedda Gabler" when I tried to edge into the quonset without being noticed. It seemed strange to me that the term "modern" should apply to a 19th century play, but what did I know? Dagget was a dessicated little man who reminded me of a dried-up insect found on a windowsill when you take off the storms. He was talking about "paper children" and "inspiration as fertilization." The droning of his lecture voice made whatever he said uninteresting, and I busied myself with a tissue, mopping the rain from my notebook and then from my shoes.

The Contemporary Protestant Thought paper fell from my book to the floor, and Brattleson's red words got wet, giving them a bloody look as I read them: "I wish you well in your search. James Brattleson." He wouldn't believe that I wasn't searching and insisted that I be "normal" according to his lights. I was both angry and amused.

I tuned in Dagget just as he was saying we would consider *Crime and Punishment* as soon as we finished the Ibsen play. The rain was coming down harder, threatening to raise the level of the puddle at the quonset's door above the threshold. Dagget said we would dismiss early, and everyone but me was delighted. I had to wait for Wilson Ling.

"Are you coming, Miss Langelund?" Dagget paused at the door with his hand on the light switch.

I shook my head. "I'm meeting someone, but go ahead and turn out the light."

That's how I ran into Dexter Burton again. I hadn't seen him since the English and American Authors final and didn't know that he ever taught in a Temporary. I recognized his silhouette in the gray rectangle of the open door immediately, and my heart actually lurched.

"Hello," I said.

My voice startled him, causing a sudden jerk of his head and shoulders. He hit the light switch.

"Oh, Miss Langelund."

"Thank you for the A you gave me."

"You earned it."

I took a deep breath, unsure of exactly what I would say but certain that it was risky. "Now that I'm not in your class anymore, will you go with me to the Spring Spree?"

"Well, I—uh, when is it?"

"Two weeks from Saturday."

He reached inside his tweed jacket for a small date book and studied its pages.

Please, God, let him say yes! Aloud, I said, "Claude Thornhill is playing."

"Where am I to get the tickets?" he asked.

Hallelujah! Thank You, God! "I'll get them," I said with what I hoped was Hedy Lamarr languor, "it's girl-ask-boy."

He grinned, and the expression was so adorable that I felt an alarming interior melting. "I'm not exactly a boy," he said.

I lowered my lids to half-mast. "If you were, I wouldn't ask you. What time is it?"

"Ten-forty-eight."

I jumped up and hurried to the door, turning for a parting word, "I'll be in touch."

"Right." He touched his temple with two fingers in a kind of salute.

Outside, a dripping Wilson Ling greeted me with, "Short, Margaret."

"No, Wilson. 'Hi, Margaret.' Hi is short for hello."

"Ah!" He practiced it a few times, and I told him he sounded almost American. I was so elated about my date with Dexter Burton that I wanted to make everyone as happy as I was.

Wilson walked me back to the cottage at this hour, and we didn't have to hurry so much—except for the rain. He darted under a sheltering overhang at the chemistry building and motioned for me to follow. He reached inside his jacket and pulled out an object stuffed with excelsior and clumsily wrapped with tissue paper.

"Is for you."

I peeled off the wrappings carefully, revealing a tiny cobalt teapot with flowers painted on its sides, "It's beautiful, Wilson. Thank you."

"Is peach blossom."

"Oh?"

"You peach blossom—in spring."

The teapot sat on my desk while I wrote letters. The first and most important was to Merrilee Adams, my high school friend who'd had a baby before she moved to Harlan and then had become a girl again—for a little while. My thunderbolt of good luck with Dexter Burton brought to mind the talk we had during Christmas vacation when I ran into Merrilee at the library.

I'd been both glad and embarrassed when we met. I liked Merrilee a lot, Mom didn't approve of the friendship, and I was ashamed that I hadn't made an effort to see her.

To make up for that, I lied about nearly using up her gift of Evening in Paris cologne.

"Look," she said in a warm rush of generosity, "if you ever need anything of mine, just ask. You can borrow anything I've got."

Now there *was* something—the seafoam-green formal she'd worn to the senior prom. I remembered it hanging from the ratty light fixture in the Adamses' shabby, little yellow house. I hadn't even wanted to look at it, because I didn't have a prom date, but the dress was the best thing Merrilee ever owned, and she spent a month's salary on it to buy a memory that would last forever. I looked. And I remembered. Merrilee was shorter than I was, but not that much, and the strapless bodice probably would fit me.

I wrote to her and tore up the letter because it sounded demanding. I tried again, explaining that I had had a crush on Dexter Burton from the moment I saw him, and I couldn't believe my luck when he said he'd go to the Spree with me. I wanted to be Spring—

a peach blossom in Spring, as Wilson Ling put it—and that was what made me think of her perfect dress. I promised to pay the postage and be very careful with her treasure.

Then I wrote to Mom and told her that Wilson Ling wanted to visit our town during Easter vacation. I said that I could sleep with her and give him the bedroom with the Farleys' black furniture.

The dress arrived much sooner than I expected it, packed in its original box from the Frockery and swathed in pale blue tissue paper. The outer wrapping was several grocery sacks taped together inside-out and addressed in Merrilee's small, careful hand. Inside the bodice was a note, "I'll be happy thinking of the good time you'll have in this. Love, Merrilee."

Worn with flat silver strip sandals, it was just right, and even the super-stylish Sue Benton admired the way it looked on me.

Then came Mom's letter: "Dear Margaret, About your plan to bring this Chinese boy home with you—I'm not sure it would be wise. This town is small in several ways, and your guest could be made to feel uncomfortable. If you think it over, I'm sure you'll agree with me about this."

I was furious and sat down immediately to write a hot reply. I told her I already had invited Wilson and couldn't take it back, and if anyone dared to be unpleasant to him, they'd have me to deal with. I said I couldn't believe that *she* was prejudiced against anyone who was different or that she feared to disagree with those who were.

Venus asked me if I intended to call for Dexter Burton the night of the Spree, and I said I didn't even know where he lived. The next day I waited for him after Dagget's class to work out the details of our date.

"I couldn't possibly let you do that," he said, "I'll call for you."

I bought him a boutonniere at Eicher's flower shop, he handed me the always thrilling rectangular corsage box, and I wished that I lived in the big dormitory so more people could witness the proud moment of our departure. The flowers were twin gardenias tied with silver—perfect for the sea-foam gown. In a fit of loyalty to Merrilee, I had considered wearing Evening in Paris, but now I was glad I hadn't done it. The scent would fight with the gardenias.

He drove a vintage Chevy with a spic and span front seat and a back seat loaded with books. Nita had cased the car on her way into the cottage and advised me just before he knocked on the door, "He's got a carload of books. Know something, Langelund? You just checked out a faggot."

I scarcely heard her in my eagerness to answer the door. I called him "Mr. Burton" until he asked me to call him "Dex." I couldn't bring myself to do that.

We danced to "Snowfall" rather stiffly, each of us holding back something. We made small talk about the band and the people around us. He told me I looked "very nice," and I thanked him. His eyes were always moving, and I could never tell what they were seeking. He brought me punch, which I drank with slow care to protect Merrilee's gown. It was a long evening, and in the end, I was glad I didn't live in the big dormitory, where saying good night was a mob scene. Just before curfew, kissing couples were plastered against the entire exterior of Currier Hall, and I would have been embarrassed to walk past them with Dexter Burton. As it was, he drove up to the alley door of the cottage, got out to open my door and said good night, making no move to climb the short flight of cement steps with me.

I went inside and numbly removed Merrilee's dress, which I would take back to her when I went home for Easter. Rosemary, Venus and Elena were sleeping; Sheila, Sue and Reva were staying at their sorority houses; Kay had gone home for the weekend; and Nita and Dot were taking a shower together. I sat in my desk chair in strapless bra and gartered hose remembering Grandma's frequent pronouncement, "Expectation is greater than realization." Why had he agreed to go? Because my intensity left no room for refusal, probably, and he didn't want a scene. Would I ever learn not to force things?

Then I noticed the envelope with Mom's handwriting. She must have answered me by return mail, and it was as if I had never written.

She told me that Wilson Ling would not be welcome in our house. That's when I cried—for Wilson, for me, and for Merrilee who thought her dress was magic.

Before I slept, I had to fall back on what Brattleson called my "simplistic faith." I had to believe that God knew what He was doing with my life, even if I didn't.

In the morning when Venus asked about "the big night," I gave her a crooked smile and said, "The half-gods are still around."

Nita gave me the phone message and enjoyed my dumbfounded expression as I read Roger Andersen's name and number.

"He's that big, sexy Sigma Chi, right?"

I nodded absently, wondering what on earth Roger wanted with me? We'd never been friends in the thirteen years we'd been classmates, and after the conclusion I'd drawn about him and Florine Hammond at Christmas, I was sure we never would be. However, I dialed the number and listened to all the commotion at the fraternity house while they tried to find him.

At long last, he said, "Hullo?"

"Roger, this is Margaret Langelund," I said, hoping to get this exchange of question marks off dead center.

"Oh, yeah. I was just wondering if you wanted a ride home for Easter?"

"Sure. That would be great."

"OK, I'll pick you up Thursday noon."

"What about the no-cut rule?"

"Tell 'em you're sick. I do it all the time."

"All right," I said, regretting it instantly, but the bus trip took so long, and even if I bought Roger's gas, I'd save money.

Nita was standing there, waiting for a report, so I explained briefly.

"Wow!" she said, "Clear across the state with that choice piece!"

I gave her the bored, heavy-lidded look that I'd practiced in the mirror and turned my back on her. That was a trick I'd learned from Elena. When she'd had enough of someone, she simply stopped lip-reading, and I had heard her say, "I don't have to argue with you, I'll just turn out the light!"

I wondered if Roger's mother had insisted that he offer me a ride or if he just wanted to pump me about what I knew? Either way, it would be a tense trip.

Easter was late this year, and most of us had done some sunning on the Currier fire escapes. I had the best tan of my entire life and had splurged on a red and white striped seersucker suit and spectator pumps. I would be going home in style.

My cottage mates certainly thought so when Roger gunned his red Chevy into our alley and stopped with a screech of rubber. He honked imperatively, and I snatched up my embarrassing suitcase to run out.

"'Keep your pants on,' Nita said. 'I'll go out and tell him you're coming."

"That won't be necessary," I said, but she beat me out the door and laughingly jumped into the passenger seat before I could get down the steps.

I heard her say, "How'd you like to take *me* home?"

Roger's reply was inaudible, but the cottage door was open, and I could hear Dot Greer snarling. She and Nita hadn't been taking showers together lately, and Dot was smoking twice as much.

I opened the back door of the Chevy and pushed my suitcase and Merrilee's boxed formal along the seat. Nita and Roger were locked into a staring contest, so I climbed in and slammed the door. Calling Dr. Brattleson at home to tell him I was sick had made me feel that way, so I wasn't really lying when I phoned Mr. Dagget with the same message. Nita and Roger had started to Indian wrestle. I closed my eyes until I heard the car door slam.

"Are you coming up here, or am I supposed to be the chauffeur?"

I got out and sat in the seat Nita had vacated. There would be less chance of carsickness up there. Roger didn't speak until we were past Coralville.

"Who the hell was that?"

"I suppose you mean Nita—Nita Lund. She's from Waterloo."

"She comes on pretty strong."

I nodded, and nothing more was said until we came to the Amanas. I was exhausted from months of 7:30 a.m. classes and too much late-night radio, so I slept, waking occasionally to enjoy the white froth of a blossoming fruit tree on a hillside or the young, green crops that looked like embroidery stitches in the brown-black fields. I looked at the cattle grazing peacefully in the pastures and envied their untroubled lives. I even said as much to Roger as we passed the Homestead railroad station.

"Yeah," he said, "but they get slaughtered."

"Maybe so, but they don't have to think about it beforehand. It's a surprise."

"You hungry?"

"Not especially."

"Then we'll wait until we get to Des Moines. Do you know Florine Hammond very well?"

"Not very. I never knew her at all until she asked me to come up and talk about her sorority."

"But you didn't pledge."

"No. Couldn't afford it."

"How did you say no to her?"

"I just did."

He was silent for a long time, and then he said, "You knew I was upstairs that day."

"How could I know that?" I controlled my voice reasonably well, but my heart pounded. What would he do to me if I said I did know?

"Well, *now* you know!" He was furious with himself and with me.

"Have you known her a long time?" I tried to be casual.

"Used to caddy for her."

"Does she really swear as much as they say?"

"More. God, but I hate to go home and face that!"

"Then why *are* you going home? You could have made some excuse."

"You don't do that with Florine."

"Well, you must have loved her if you—"

"No!"

"Then why?"

"At first, it makes you feel like a big shot, and then they start suffocating you—always talking about looking old or having a wrinkle some damned place—asking if you *really* are enjoying yourself. That's when you think, *to hell with it,* but you can't get out. And I don't like doing this to the judge. He's always been nice to me."

"Roger, why are you telling me this?"

"Because you already know. You've probably blabbed it all over town."

"I haven't told anyone—not even my mother."

"Why not? It's damned good gossip, isn't it?"

I shrugged, unable to explain my feeling about the innocence of my family and my reluctance to say anything that would blight it.

"Look, Roger, you've already lied about being sick to cut classes—both of us have. Just go ahead and *be* sick, and you won't have to see Mrs. Hammond."

"Yeah," he said slowly. He cheered up visibly and put a heavier foot on the accelerator, attracting a Highway Patrolman. We got off with a warning.

We stopped at the Koffee Kup on Euclid Avenue in Des Moines for sandwiches and coffee, and Roger poured on the charm for the waitress. Being immune to him myself, I couldn't imagine why she blushed and preened. He was too blond, and his mind took a back seat to his body.

It was nearly dark when we reached Harlan and screeched to a stop under the maple tree at my house. To my surprise, Roger got out and carried my suitcase to the porch.

"See you Sunday at one," he said, "and if anyone should ask you, tell them I looked real sick on the way home." Then he made a burned-rubber getaway to his own house on Baldwin Street.

Mom came to meet me with a hint of hestancy, acting as I supposed she might have done if I had brought Wilson Ling with me. Her refusal to welcome him stood between us.

"How nice that you could get a ride. I suppose that wouldn't have been possible if you hadn't been alone."

"Oh, I don't know. Roger probably would have brought Wilson too. There was plenty of room." But he couldn't have said what he did to me in the presence of a third party.

She took the boxed formal from me, and I picked up my suitcase and followed her inside, smelling the beef and barley soup Grandma was making for supper.

"You're brown as toast!" Grandma said, "Get your clothes changed, and we'll eat."

As I was unpacking my suitcase, I came upon the cobalt teapot wrapped in yards of toilet paper. I unwound it and went looking for Mom. She was cutting bread.

"This is for you," I said, holding the tiny pot in the palm of my hand, "a present from Wilson Ling."

Her color deepened as she took it and said, "How very lovely."

"Why didn't you want him to come? You never *did* come right out and say."

"It's not a thing you *can* come right out and say. If he had been a girl, it would have been different."

I laughed incredulously. "Do you mean to say you think Wilson—Wilson and I? Oh, no!"

Mom waved the big bread knife. "You know how people are, always thinking the worst. We've never had a Chinaman in this town—we don't even have any Negroes—"

"But we did once," Grandma said.

"When?" Mom was incredulous, and so was I.

"There was that little orphan boy whose folks died when they were walking west. The Sechers took him in and named him Ansgar. They even taught him to speak Danish."

"That must have been years ago," Mom said.

"Yes, it was, but he was as Chinese as the day is long!"

"See?" I said, "It wouldn't have been the first time, and what if it were?"

"Oh Margaret, I'm sorry. I should have told you to bring him."

Then I was ashamed of giving her the gift that was meant for me just to shame her, but I wouldn't confess and take it back. Eventually, she would give it to me as she had her cameo and her blue ring. Every beautiful thing she had seemed to come my way. I hugged her until the constraint between us melted, and then we all sat down to the excellent soup.

Harlan was at its best in green and lilac April, and the shrinkage I had noticed at Christmas had corrected itself. The town now seemed to be its remembered size, and the eerie silence of Good Friday afternoon took me back to a childhood state of grace.

Easter Saturday always had frightened me because it was the time when Christ descended into Hell. Even the light looked different— almost like the tail-end of an eclipse. I noticed this as I walked to the Adamses' little yellow house beyond the Square to return Merrilee's formal.

Mrs. Adams invited me in, saying that Merrilee was washing her hair. The small bathroom was so close to the living room that the sharp scent of lemon floated out to do battle with Mrs. Adams's cigarette smoke. Mrs. Adams had a new chenille bathrobe, shrimp-colored with a big, white flower on the bosom, and she was reading *True Story*.

Merrilee's brother Donny waved at me with his good hand, and it seemed to me that his withered arm was shorter than ever. Now that I actually had seen University Hospitals where the long, blue-gray car had taken Donny so many times, I found it harder to believe that they couldn't cure him. The hospital's replica of one of the towers of Oxford crowned the Iowa City skyline, and it carried a charge of omnipotence.

Merrilee presently emerged with her hair in a towel turban and invited me into the corner of the dormitory bedroom that was her "room." She held out her hands for the formal and asked, "Did you have a wonderful time?"

"Yes," I lied, not wanting to disappoint her. How easy it was to be devious when Christ was in Hell. I had picked up an extra dance program someone had dropped in the restroom, a suede-textured booklet of pink and burgundy with a silk cord and tassle, and I gave it to her.

"Oh," she breathed, "it must have been beautiful. Did you have flowers?"

"Gardenias with a silver ribbon."

"I never had a gardenia."

"They turn brown when you touch them, and the way they smell the next day makes you slightly sick. Where are the rest of the kids? Delsey and the boys?"

"You didn't hear about Delsey?"

"No, what?"

"Her appendix burst, and she died. That happened way last fall."

"Oh Merrilee, I'm sorry! Nobody told me!"

"That's OK," Merrilee played with the tail of her shirt tied into a midriff knot. "If I hadn't just washed my hair, we could go out for a Coke."

"Let's just talk. Do you still like your job?"

"It's OK."

"But not like we used to talk about—being in the big city and wearing gorgeous clothes to go dancing after work?"

Merrilee laughed. "Not quite. Once in awhile I take the bus to Omaha to shop and go to a movie and pretend I live there. Lots of times, guys follow me, but I don't want any of that."

"I know what you mean," I said, telling her about Harley, who was impossible to discourage, "maybe both of us will find somebody someday."

"I thought maybe you had when you asked me to send the dress."

"I keep mistaking half-gods for gods, I guess."

Merrilee didn't know what I was talking about, but she responded with that tough, wise nod of hers.

On the way home, I caught a glimpse of Florine Hammond walking past the Golden Rule. To avoid meeting her, I cut back to the north side of the Square and walked several blocks west before I turned south on Ninth Street. Florine had looked quite beautiful, striding along in high heels with a tawny cape billowing out behind her. How could Roger think she was old?

Easter Sunday dawned bright, and I was up early to look at the sun through old film negatives. Grandma insisted that the sun danced for joy on the day of Resurrection. All I could see was spots, but *they* seemed to be dancing, and that was good enough. I wanted the legend to be true as surely as I wanted to believe her tale about the animals using human speech at midnight on Christmas Eve to celebrate the birth of the Savior. Dr. Brattleson would *really* be shocked if he knew about the dancing sun and the talking animals, but I didn't plan to let him in on these family secrets.

We ate hard-boiled eggs, cracking the shells to symbolize the life bursting forth from the tomb, and I obligingly searched for the jelly beans the Easter Bunny had hidden while I slept. Most of them were black, my favorite licorice flavor. I was glad my cottage mates couldn't see my Easter egg hunt. It might have been OK if I had had younger brothers and sisters, but for an only child who was a college student?

Eastern light poured through the stained glass windows of the church, and the lighted picture of the Good Shepherd I had grown up with seemed to welcome me home. Standing and smoothing my seersucker skirt, I sang lustily with the congregation, "Up from the grave He arose!" It was lovely! Why fight it? Why consider it unearned? I hoped that Dr. Brattleson was feeling something similar wherever he was this Easter morning.

And then I walked out with Mom. She introduced me to the new preacher, Reverend Boysen, and he said, "Ah, you're the one who's in Iowa City. Are you keeping yourself unspotted from the world in that sinkhole of iniquity?"

I looked at him sharply, expecting to see a twinkle in his eye or some signal of irony, but there was none. I said, "I do hope so."

"Watch out for the Godless liberals!" he warned, "All this talk of ecumenism sounds beautiful, but the Devil himself was beautiful before he became a serpent."

Mom said, "Move along, Margaret, we're holding up the line. Good morning, Reverend Boysen, that was a stirring sermon."

That's when I realized I hadn't even listened to the sermon. I had been busy reinforcing my childhood faith so I could throw it at Dr. Brattleson the next time he challenged me.

I smiled at the old ladies, nodded at Albert Rettig and his family, and hurried away with Mom. Roger would be picking me up soon.

"Your new preacher thinks he has all the answers, doesn't he?" I said to Mom.

"Well, he's certainly not wishy-washy."

I supposed that I appeared to Dr. Brattleson the way Reverend Boysen appeared to me, and if it were true that "pride goeth before a fall," both of us ought to watch out.

The Daily Iowan headline was big and black, COED FOUND DEAD IN ROOMING HOUSE. Kay Albers read the story aloud to us while we rushed around getting ready for breakfast and class. The girl was Bebe Maxwell from Cottage 14, a neighbor whom none of us knew well, but we saw her daily.

Elena, who could see our faces but not Kay's, asked, "What's wrong?"

Rosemary told her, and she said, "My God!"

Bebe was from Storm Lake, a lushly pretty girl with reddish hair who smiled a lot. An unlikely murder victim.

Kay read on, "'The body, clad in evening dress, was found on a cot in a rented room on Dubuque Street. The remains of a candlelight dinner were on a card table covered with a white cloth and set for two. Police arrested Charles Syrovy, a senior from Cedar Rapids who rented the room in September.' Hey, you guys, anybody know him?"

None of us did, and Dot observed that any male who was a senior had to have something wrong with him. Otherwise he would have been in the service.

"Not necessarily," Sue said, "he could have been a junior when the war started."

I sat through my morning classes abstractedly, thinking of the void created by the death of Bebe Maxwell and trying to imagine how long it would last. For most of us, a world without Bebe would seem normal as soon as the first shock subsided, but her family would go on feeling it indefinitely like the phantom pain in a limb amputated long ago. Gwen had told me about that.

At the law school the talk was about legalities—evidence, whether Syrovy was the only possible suspect, who would take his case.

Even band rehearsal was colored by the death of Bebe Maxwell. We practiced "Finlandia," and Mr. Rutherford let us play it all the way through without stopping to correct dynamics or phrasing. "Considering recent events, a dirge seems to be in order," he said.

After practice, I hurried to catch up with Arthur Blair, falling into step with him outside East Hall. He gave me a tentative smile, and I couldn't believe my good luck.

"How are you, Margaret?"

"Alive."

"Yeah. Some girls aren't."

"Bebe lived in the cottage next to mine. I can't believe it."

"I imagine you've never been exposed to anything like that."

"Oh yes, I have. The woman I worked for in a dress shop at home was shot by her—by her—well, by a man who worked at the bank. Then he shot himself." Somehow I just couldn't describe Chet as Fern's lover, which he was. I could still see the two of them dead—Chet clasping Fern's knees as if he were praying beside the cot and Fern's blood-soaked upper body bent and twisted away from him.

Arthur eluded me so successfully that I seldom got a good look at him, and now I noticed that he had a pasty, unhealthy appearance—probably from something that happened to him in the war. It made me want to take care of him.

"I wouldn't expect you to know about things like that," he said.

I glowed to think that he had any expectations of me whatsoever and asked if he had been playing a lot of dates with Bo Williams.

"Bo has been pretty lucky with the bookings. It's hard to get any studying done. I suppose I could forget school and go on the road with some little band, but the very thought of it makes me tired."

"You *are* going on tour with the University Band, aren't you?"

Arthur sighed. "Guess I'll have to."

We had come to the corner where I had to turn, and I hoped Arthur would walk me home, but he waved and started on toward the bridge.

"Arthur—" I wanted him to turn, but at the same time, I hoped he wouldn't. I wasn't ready to stop inventing his lines.

He turned. "Yeah?"

I wasn't ready for my own reckless words, either. "You don't like me very much, do you?"

"More than I want to."

His answer nearly suffocated me with a mixture of dismay and joy, but I managed to ask, "What do you mean by that?"

"You're the kind who wants to settle down and have a bunch of kids, and after taking Army orders for four years, I'm not about to—"

"No!" I yelled, drawing some stares from passers-by, "That's not what I want at all!"

"OK, OK," he said, embarrassed, "see you."

This time, I turned away first, angry but somehow pleased to have caused him an inner struggle. Pale, stooped Arthur Blair in his faded khaki shirts with the unfaded ghosts of insignia wasn't such a prize. It must have been the sensitive yearning of his musicianship that got me.

At the cottage, Nita was holding forth on something, and Venus whispered, "She's explaining how you play blackout."

"What's that?"

"Just listen."

Nita straddled a desk chair backwards, rocking it for emphasis. She looked like Marlene Dietrich in "The Blue Angel," a film Venus and I had liked better than "The Well Digger's Daughter." She passed her thumb down the side of her throat and said, "There's this place in your neck, see? and if you hit that just right at the same time you rub up some action, you get this light-headed, crazy explosion that takes you right through the roof!"

Sheila asked Nita if she'd ever tried it, and Nita said, "Sure, lots of times. When you're by yourself, you can do it with a noose around your neck—you just have to be careful to stop in time."

I couldn't imagine Venus listening to this without protest, but she was as interested as any of the others. When Nita broke off and went to get dressed for a date, I asked Venus more questions.

"They grilled Syrovy, and that's what he said they were doing—playing blackout. He said it was an accident. He'd done it before, and everything had been OK. This time, she didn't come to."

"At least he went for help."

"Yeah, but then he took off for St. Mary's church. They had to drag him away from the altar."

Most of my life, I had thought one could find sanctuary in the church. There went another illusion.

"And did you hear about the book of poems?" Venus said.

"No, tell me."

"It's called *Desire Me*, and one of the poems is about a dinner by candlelight. Syrovy fixed all the stuff that was in the poem—like lobster and Spanish creme—and they both were dressed up, and then they played blackout and she died."

"And I suppose the 'Liebestod' was playing on the phonograph?"

"The story didn't say."

I wondered if Lew knew about blackout? Love and death. In our family, all the men (except Uncle Karl) were dead, but they were still loved. We went to the cemetery and used their tombstones for picnic tables, telling and listening to stories about them while we ate. A pickle jar might sit on my father's name and the waxed paper that wrapped sandwiches might hide his death date, April 13, 1934, but we felt that he was around.

What I hoped for was love and life—a chance to send the half-gods packing in favor of a man who would look outward with me, fixing on the same focus, and then turn to me in the moment I turned to him, shutting out the rest of the universe. If I could have explained that to Arthur Blair, he would have known better than to think I wanted to "settle down and have a bunch of kids."

Harley Schippers came to take me to a movie, and since he had seen everything else that was on, we went to "Mayerling." Love and death, just what I needed.

We stopped at the Huddle for a malt, and Harley gave a critique of the film, "Not very realistic."

"Harley, it was based on something that really happened."

"Yeah, but it happened to foreigners."

"They're human beings too."

"You sure?"

That irritating, wheezing laughter of his really was getting to me tonight. I sucked up the malt as rapidly as I could, licked the straw clean from top to bottom and played the hands-on-the-bat game of "he loves me, he loves me not" with thumbs and pointers. It came out "he loves me not," a further irritation until I realized that I hadn't designated the "he." It didn't matter.

Harley wanted to hold hands on the way back to the cottage, but I pulled away from him, thinking of the pale fingers of Arthur that curled so lovingly around the bars of the trombone slide.

The kissing couples would be plastered against the outside walls of Currier Hall, and I would forever stand aside, watching but pretending not to see. I walked faster.

Harley caught up with me and grabbed my wrist roughly.

"Let go, Harley!"

"No, by God! I've been patient with you long enough." He tried to kiss me but only succeeded in bumping my nose painfully.

"Ouch!" I struggled in his grip. Hearing footsteps behind us, I was both embarrassed and hopeful that the presence of someone else, anybody at all, would put an end to this ridiculous impasse.

"Maybe you didn't hear the lady?" The voice was male, though not heavy, and sounded Eastern.

"Mind your own business!" Harley said.

The street light shone through a green density of elm leaves, and I could see little more than the outline of the compact figure beside us. Then it moved with amazing speed. Harley uttered a groaning exhalation and went down.

"Allow me," said the voice.

I took the offered arm, and we walked up the hill. When we came into better light, I saw that my rescuer was a head shorter than I was. He wore glasses and had a small, crisp mustache.

"Thank you," I said, turning to peer into the darkness behind us, "I hope he'll be all right."

"I guarantee it. When I choose to get physical, the element of surprise is my only asset. By the way, my name is Hoffman Weir. I'm a geologist."

"Mine's Margaret Langelund, and I'm a—well, I *want* to be a journalist—I think."

"Could I take you somewhere for a drink?"

"No, because I have hours. Besides, I don't really drink. It gives me a pain in the shoulder."

"Extraordinary! What about dinner, then?"

We made a date, and when he left me at the cottage door, he reached for the hand that caused Harley all the trouble and bowed to brush it with his lips.

"Where are you from?" I asked.

"Bar Harbor." It sounded like "Bah Hahbah."

I went inside dazzled, and Venus remarked, "I've never seen you come home from a date with Harley looking like that. What happened?"

I grinned. "Not coming home with Harley makes all the difference. Venus, would you go out with a guy a lot shorter than you are?"

She shrugged. "It depends. If I really liked him, I suppose I would—

and try to do something sitting down. After all, look at Napoleon and Josephine."

Hoffman had a car, and he said we could go out of town for dinner if I wished, but I chose a restaurant at the train depot. I loved trains and all the comings and goings at the station.

His height was unimportant in the car, and I didn't mind the short interval of walking into the restaurant with him. When we were seated, I forgot all about our comparative stature. Hoffman was a brilliant talker. I had a sense of being out with a character in a book and was afraid that I would bore him. When I mentioned that possibility to him timidly, he laughed and said that would be impossible. Even if I never said a word, he would take great pleasure in watching me eat.

"You eat enchantingly."

"Well, I *hope* my manners are all right. My mother really tried."

"Oh, it isn't manners, it's manner. You eat with such pleasure that it's a pleasure to feed you."

"Are you saying that I'm a pig?"

"By no means—more like a Persian cat lapping cream."

Then he talked about geology—the riches of the earth forming for millennia, the romance of surveys in remote countries, the varieties of semi-precious stones in the Lake Baikal region in Siberia. He had been everywhere, it seemed, and that moved me more than Arthur Blair's "Danny Boy" on the trombone.

He kissed me good-night before he got out of the car to walk me to the cottage door. It was a light, affectionate kiss, and the mustache tickled. I thought everything was OK in the short walk to the door until I caught myself hoping Nita wouldn't see us. How could I be so small-minded?

I felt even worse when he said good-night and whispered, "May you wear sea-splashed emeralds around your throat." No one had said anything half so lovely to me in my entire life.

The day we left on band tour I was wearing a corsage from Hoffman. It arrived with a note that said, "Hurry back to me." As I got on the bus, Arthur Blair glanced at the flowers and turned quickly to the window, contemplating his own pale reflection moodily. Arthur was beginning to look a lot like a half-god, but I hadn't fully convinced myself that Hoffman was the vanquishing whole.

We were headed for Illinois, where we would play two concerts before returning to a circuit of Iowa institutions like the prison at Ft. Madison, the mental hospital in Mt. Pleasant and the reform school at Anamosa.

GeeGee Farber, who sat next to me in the clarinet section, invited me to sit with her on the bus.

"How's Princess Reva?" she asked.

"Gorgeous."

"But snotty?"

"Not always."

"Want to play bridge?"

"I don't know how."

"What do you do for fun?"

"Read—or at least I used to. Every time I pick up a book I'm excited about, I feel guilty that I'm not studying."

"Did you read *Desire Me*?"

"Couldn't find a copy. Did you?"

"Yeah, they've got one at the house. It's hot stuff."

"I wonder how the author feels? If somebody used a book of mine as a recipe for murder, I'd never get over it."

"The blackout part wasn't in the book, so it's not his fault. Who sent you the flowers?"

"A guy I'm—dating." I wasn't sure that my meal-a-week arrangement with Hoffman amounted to that, but the explanation would do.

"I was going out with Sherman until he met Princess Reva," GeeGee said.

"Oh? I didn't know that. I'm sorry."

GeeGee shrugged. "So who needs him?"

I looked over at Arthur Blair, who still gazed moodily out the bus window, the passing fields reflected in his glasses like the little books you flip to make a "moving" picture. Could it be that Arthur's resistance to me was his chief charm?

The blossoming orchards we passed were acres of bridal lace, and while I had no wish to marry, I wanted to be in love. That condition forced you to take constant inventory to be sure that you were loveable, and thus created the self-possession I wanted so much. You had to have something before you could give it away, didn't you? As a child, you belonged to your family, and as a wife, you belonged to your husband. In between, you should belong to yourself.

GeeGee crawled over my knees to play bridge in the back of the bus, and I stood up to smooth my band uniform in the overhead rack. I was seized by the impulse to take the empty seat next to Arthur but couldn't figure out how to explain the action. So what? With my heart leaping into the spot behind my goiter operation scar, I ambled down the aisle with elaborate casualness and sat.

Arthur turned to me warily, as if he were afraid I would rape him on the spot.

"You shouldn't be afraid of me, Arthur," I began boldly, "I won't bite."

"But what if I'd like to bite you?" His tone was sardonic.

"Oh, this is ridiculous! We've known each other nearly all school year, and we haven't had a decent conversation yet. What's wrong with you?"

"What's wrong with *me?* The girl comes around in a sweater two sizes too small and asks a question like that?"

My face grew hot, and I took a deep breath before I spoke. "I've never done my own laundry before, and it shrank. I can't afford to buy another one. You act like I did it on purpose!" I started to get up, but he grabbed my arm and pulled me back.

"Hey, I'm sorry! I figured you were just flaunting it."

I crossed my arms over my breasts, crushing Hoffman's flowers in my agitation and uttering a small cry as part of a Japanese iris fell into my lap.

Fortunately, nobody was paying attention to us because the bus was entering the Tri Cities, and they were all looking out the windows.

"Look," Arthur said, pointing at a car in a side street. The young woman behind the wheel of a yellow convertible with the top down wore a broad-brimmed blue hat tied securely under her chin, and the child on the seat beside her had on a miniature version of the hat. Both waved at the bus as we passed.

"Do you know what that says to me?" Arthur asked.

"That she's flaunting it?" I snarled.

His pupils shrank at the hit, but he didn't hit back. He said, "Peacetime. Sometimes in the middle of all the gunfire and the stink, I'd get this picture of a pretty woman heading for the beach in a car like that—big hat and everything—and there she was. Maybe the war really is over."

"Maybe so, Arthur."

We played a late morning concert in some high school in East Moline near a Greek Orthodox church, the likes of which I'd never seen. I took a picture of it. And I'd never been in Illinois before, either. I half-expected to find the ground a different color, like the varying hues of the states on a U.S. map.

As GeeGee and I put our instruments together and waited to tune up, she said, "Don't those high school kids look young?"

I agreed, though I supposed that these city kids were a lot more savvy than I had been a year ago—or was now, for that matter.

We had lunch in the school cafeteria, and Arthur came to sit with me. Amazing.

"Worse than Army chow!" He pushed the pale, watery canned beans to one side and sampled the unidentifiable slab of meat. "Maybe we can go somewhere for a beer and a hamburger later, OK?"

"OK," I said, giving him the Hedy Lamarr look. My loyalty to Hedy had weakened this first year of college, but she was always there when I needed her.

The prospect of going out with Arthur sent me to the top of the

Ferris wheel for a high, magic view of everything around me. My playing was inspired, even in the tough passage with six sharps that always worried me.

GeeGee guessed why I was high. She had looked up from her cards to see me moving in on Arthur on the bus.

"What about the guy who sent the flowers?"

I thought of the note Hoffman had written. It had more urgency than he ever displayed when we were together, but words often gained strength when they were put on paper. One day when I was hurrying across the Pentacrest, I'd met Duane, the sailor responsible for my first shaky, terrified kiss. We recognized each other, but out of uniform, he seemed like a stranger to me. His physical presence didn't affect me. However, I was shaken by the memory of the passionate letters I'd written to a person who no longer made my blood rush. Mentally, I apologized to Hoffman for enjoying Arthur's belated notice, but I really believed that I owed no apology. He couldn't lose something he'd never been given.

We were to stay in the homes of high school band students in Morrison, and when the assignments were called out, I saw Arthur record mine. The kid, a bashful and pimpled youth, had just stepped up to claim me when Arthur intervened.

"If you've got a car, why don't you take her stuff? I'll drop her by in a little while."

"Well, OK, I guess. I'll have to tell my mom, though. She's outside in the car."

"I'll come along and meet her," I offered quickly. Arthur's suggestion seemed a bit rude.

Mrs. Clemmons was a worried-looking woman. Though it was quite warm, she wore a headscarf and a sweater and stood tiptoe in her Red Cross shoes to wave at her son.

"Yoo-hoo, Lamont! Over here!"

Lamont jerked a thumb toward me and said, "This is her."

"This is *she*, Dear, and surely she has a name?"

I introduced myself and stood back to watch Arthur turn on the charm.

"Mrs. Clemmons, I'm Arthur Blair, trombonist?" His voice rose in a question, as if he expected instant recognition—"Oh yes, the *trombonist!*"

Mrs. Clemmons obliged with at least the "Oh yes?", also with a question mark.

"Well, ma'am, Margaret and I are old friends, but we haven't had a chance to talk to each other for ages, and I'd be grateful if you'd let me take her out for a Coke and bring her to your house a bit later? I mean, would it be possible for you to take her things with you now?"

"Oh, certainly, but do you think you can find our house?"

"I've already inquired about that, ma'am."

"Well, I suppose Lamont won't mind. We had expected one of the young men, but—"

Arthur smiled. "Some of us aren't so young, ma'am. I was at Anzio."

"Oh—well—just put her things in the back seat then. Dinner's at six."

"Thank you very much, Mrs. Clemmons," I said, and Arthur snapped a salute as stirring as "Marche Militaire."

Lamont's mouth hung open, and his mother's fingers flew to her lips.

As we walked away, I said, "What about your stuff?"

"I've already stashed my gear. Do you always play 'Mommy' like that?"

"Since when is simple concern playing 'Mommy'? I merely wondered if you would be unencumbered or if I'd have to help you lug something."

We strolled along Lincoln Way, a long and curving street of magnificent houses of the last century. The magnolia trees had dropped their blooms, creating a rotting, brown carpet on the ground, but red and yellow tulips could still be seen on the sloping lawns. I slitted my eyes and imagined the name "Blair" on a brass door plate. Arthur Blair, the distinguished professor of music, would be working with his most promising pupil inside, and Mrs. Blair (me) would be coming home after an exciting day at the newspaper. She (I) would pause on the curving walk and savor the glorious sound pouring from the open windows.

Or it would be fall, and Mrs. Blair wouldn't hear the music until she opened the front door. Then she'd see the fire blazing and the tea for two all set between the wing chairs drawn close to the hearth. The music would stop, the pupil would leave, and after a kiss of greeting, the Blairs would discuss their day.

"We should be hitting a saloon about now," Arthur said.

"I thought you were taking me out for a Coke."

"That's what you tell nice-lady band mothers. Hey, there it is!"

The Tipsy Tap? Not exactly the romantic spot I'd envisioned for my first real tryst with Arthur, but it would have to do. If we had any future and I wanted to reminisce about this, I'd simply omit the name of the place.

The front door was heavy, and Arthur's arm shook almost imperceptibly as he held it open for me. Red neon tubes formed a high molding that was the room's only source of light. The dark forms of the patrons looked like troglodytes around a fire in a cave, and there was enough smoke to support such an illusion. The bitter smell of beer was strong in the air.

I'd never entered a real tavern before, and I turned to Arthur for behavioral clues. He steered me to a booth, its table still wet with rings from bottles and glasses, and instead of sitting opposite me, moved in beside me. My well-padded hip and thigh made a ring box for his bony counterparts, and I shivered deliciously at the contact.

The waitress, peroxided hair pink in the neon, paused with a full tray of empties and said, "What'll it be?"

"Name your poison, Margaret."

I didn't even know the name of a beer. Or did I? The late-night Friendly Grainbelt radio ads came to my aid, and I asked for that.

"We ain't got that."

My eyes moved around the room frantically, reading the signs, but I wasn't sure which were for beer, so I told Arthur I'd have whatever he did.

"Two Buds, then," he said, and that crisis was over.

I hoped the beer wouldn't give me a pain in the shoulder, and that thought led to the consideration of two people who had met in the Baptist student house drinking in a tavern.

As if he'd read my mind, Arthur said, "I'm sure glad you're not going through that 'lips that touch liquor' routine that Baptist maidens seem to favor."

"I really don't drink much. Do you."

"Try playing a gig with Bo Williams without it! But no, I really don't get bombed out of my mind. I can't take much of the hard stuff."

He took my hand and laced our fingers together, making me wish I hadn't lost the sky-blue rings. They'd look wonderful gleaming between his long, beautiful fingers.

"By the way, I'm sorry I made that crack about your sweater. Almost lost you on that one."

"Almost," I agreed, wondering at the timing of his vision of "peace." If that woman had driven her convertible in a different direction, or had the top up, or hadn't worn that gloriously visible hat, we might not be sitting here together now.

The beer came, and the waitress said, "Wanta' start a tab?"

"No," Arthur said, "we haven't got time." He peeled off two bills and told her to keep the change.

"What's a tab?" I asked.

He laughed, startled that I didn't know, and explained, "It's when they keep track and you don't pay every time—just when you leave. At the end of a long evening, you can't even read the figure, let alone figure out whether they've cheated you. I believe in paying as you go."

"Me too." The glass was wet, inside and outside, and I wondered vaguely about germs, but I poured the beer into it anyhow—and got a head that cascaded all over the table.

"Allow me," said Arthur, demonstrating the stream against the side of the glass. Then he poured his own and lifted it. "To you. You're too good to be true!"

I took a swallow, waited for the shoulder pang, and smiled when I felt nothing. The magic difference was Arthur. He turned my face to his and kissed me deeply. The image of red neon bars penetrated my closed eyelids, and I was suffused with joy.

After two beers apiece, Arthur delivered me to the Clemmonses' house. It wasn't dark enough for him to kiss me good-bye, but he did it anyhow. Before he left me, he pressed a tiny, black pellet into my palm.

"Sen-sen, the Baptist's best friend," he said. "See you in the morning."

I was floating, sufficiently unaccustomed to drink to be drastically affected by two beers, but it seemed to me that I was charming. I met Mr. Clemmons, an insurance salesman who looked as worried as his wife; drew Lamont out about his interests (the tuba and stamp collecting) and complimented Mrs. Clemmons on her tuna casserole. Then, pleading exhaustion from our strenuous concert schedule, I said I would appreciate going to bed.

Lamont's bed was what I got. I don't know where he slept, but it couldn't have been much worse than his own lumpy bed. His room smelled sour, too, but I was too wrapped up in Arthur to care. I heard "Danny Boy" in my dreams.

The music stopped the next day. A subdued Arthur sat beside me in the bus briefly—just long enough to say that he was afraid of his feelings for me and didn't dare go on seeing me.

The rest of the tour was a blur. I only remember playing at the reform school in Anamosa and spotting a boy from home shuffling around in the carpet slippers they all seemed to wear.

"Hi, Ronny!" I said, trying unsuccessfully to remember what he had done to be sent to this place.

He looked at me and looked away. Ashamed, I supposed. I felt sorry for him and just as sorry for me. We'd soon be on our way back to Iowa City, and I was wondering how I could bear to be on the same bus with Arthur. After a brush with the gods, it was back to the half-gods.

Hoffman was waiting for me when the bus came in.

The Roger Williams Fellowship planned a picnic at Lake MacBride, and while Venus was eager to go, I wasn't. Harley, Arthur and maybe even Hoffman would be there, and I didn't feel up to all those currents of feeling.

Hoffman's involvement in the group was my fault. I had invited him to several of the Sunday night suppers and had inquired delicately as to the condition of his soul.

"*Somebody* had to create all that geology I'm studying," he said, "and it might as well be *your* God as anybody else."

I sighed in exasperation. "Hoffman, just thinking there might be a God isn't enough. You have to believe that He let His Son be nailed to the cross to save you."

Then Hoffman sighed. "Ah, you Baptist girls!"

I fell silent, brooding over the salvation records of the evangelists of my youth. I didn't have one single soul to my credit. Nobody would listen to me.

Hoffman lifted my chin with one finger and said, "You'll have to work on me like erosion, and that will take a long time, I'm happy to say."

"Oh, why can't you just fall down on the road to Damascus and give me a break?"

"Us hard-core agnostics don't operate that way."

"It's so clear to me! Why can't I make you understand? I can't get through to Venus, either."

"What's her persuasion?"

"She's a Unitarian—believes in a First Cause and Thomas Jefferson—and I don't see how she stands it!"

"Well, maybe you're eroding her unbelief. She keeps coming back here, doesn't she?"

"Just to eat."

"How can you be sure? Maybe even *she* doesn't recognize her attraction to what you have and are."

I gave that some thought and hoped he was right. Daddy B, the

Baptist minister who lived in Roger Williams House with his wife, Momma B, and their four kids, had preached a sermon that was sort of on that subject. He said you didn't have to buttonhole people and ask, "Brother, are you saved?" All you had to do was live as if *you* were. Usually, his text was the Reader's Digest, and he was a smiling, tolerant man who could be civil to a person with a hangover—not at all the stern, "keep yourself unspotted from the world" type. Anyone who was would have gone mad in the "sinkhole of iniquity" that was Iowa City.

Harley had been at Roger Williams House the first night I brought Hoffman, and he glowered, grunting and shifting his eyes when I introduced them. Hoffman behaved much better, giving no sign that he'd ever seen Harley before and extending his hand with a smile.

While I was filling my plate at the buffet table, Harley paused beside me to mutter, "He sounds like he's got a mouthful of hot potatoes."

"Shhh! He'll hear you. That's the way they talk in the East. Everybody can't be from Ottumwa, you know."

Hoffman smoothly closed the gap that had opened between us while he was waiting for them to bring more coffee and said, "You're such a delicious color that I'd like to take a bite of *you!*"

Harley glared and stomped off while I glowed with pleasure. I had acquired the first real tan of my life this spring, lying out on a blanket on the riverbank or studying in a bathing suit on the fire escapes at Currier.

Then there was Arthur, who found me so dangerous. Ridiculous! He showed up every Sunday night for his cheap supper, trying to ignore me, but I always forced him to say "hello" before I ignored him. Not that I didn't notice his increasing pallor and the way his hand shook when he lifted a cup to his lips.

Why couldn't Arthur treat me the way Hoffman did? Why couldn't Harley treat me the way Arthur did? And why couldn't Hoffman be six feet tall? Whenever I was with Hoffman, I found myself hurrying to sit down, and I considered this to be a flaw in my character. If Gwen could be madly in love with a crippled husband five inches shorter than she was, what was the matter with me?

As always, Venus overcame my objections, and we signed up for the picnic at the lake. We had four cars: Daddy B's, Hoffman's and two others, which necessitated wedging eight people into each.

Hoffman gave his car keys to one of the guys, hoping to hold me on his lap. I couldn't bring myself to sit on Hoffman, fearing I would squash him, and I volunteered to hold Lanie Burket, an extremely thin girl from Burlington. Before we'd ridden a mile, I was suffering from the pressure of her unpadded bones.

Fields and trees along the hilly road to Solon were lush, and I thought of Harlan High School seniors capping their fingers with catalpa blossoms and looking forward with a delicious fear to the year I was just completing.

Grandma's garden would be planted, and so would the nasturtiums beside the pump. She and Mom would cook up a mess of dandelion greens now and then to cleanse the blood or whatever the nasty things were supposed to do, and I wasn't sorry to be missing that.

Hoffman turned on the car radio. Faintly, beneath the sound of the wind rushing through the open windows and the laughing and talking of the others, I heard a bit of Brahms—a mellow, clarinet passage. I'd learned one thing for sure this year. I was not the world's greatest clarinetist. My former dreams of Juilliard made me blush. At my first lesson in East Hall, the graduate student instructor told me all the things I was doing wrong, and they were basic. My bad habits were so deeply engrained that I'd never be really good—like Arthur. This revelation set me to wondering about other areas of my life and the heartbreak inherent in being a big frog in a small puddle. I supposed that even if the diminished frog returned to the small puddle, it could never regain its former size. Like Adam and Eve on their way out of Eden, it would carry a fatal knowledge.

Lanie shifted her insignificant weight, pressing my leg against the bag that held my swimsuit and the knitting needles spearing the Pepto-Bismol-pink yarn Wilson Ling had given me. I had started a sweater, but something had gone wrong, and the piece looked like the cover for a miniature dirigible. I thought I might have time to rip some of it up while we were on the beach. I certainly could have used some help from Grandma, who had knitted constantly while tending sheep in Denmark.

Wilson had met me between classes the day before and handed me his customary ivory envelope—payment for his lessons. I would have done it for nothing, but he insisted that honor required him to pay.

"I came no more," he said.

"What?"

"Lessons finish."

"Well, yes, it's almost the end of the semester, so we can stop if you wish."

"Not wish."

"Then why?"

His black eyes seemed to cloud, and he turned from me, biting his lip. The dark wing of hair obscured his eyes as he dipped his head.

"What's wrong, Wilson?"

"No money. My father is in prison."

"What did he do?"

"Learned much. Knows truth."

"That's bad?"

"Communists have other truth."

"Is your mother OK?"

He closed his eyes tightly, and I was sorry I had asked. "My uncle tell me she die."

"Oh Wilson, I'm so sorry! When did you hear?"

"Day before this day. My uncle say she tell me to follow the Tao."

"What is the Tao?"

"Is Truth."

I grabbed his hand, trying to press sympathy into his slender bones. "Wilson, we can go on talking together without money because we're friends—but how will you live?"

"I will sweep dishes at hotel."

"Wash them?" I dropped his hand and made a circular motion on my palm.

"Yesss."

Relieved that he had some means of support, I urged him to continue our conversations, but he refused.

"But you'll have to see the sweater when I finish it. Where can I find you? Do you realize that I don't know where you live—or even where you lived in China?"

"Manchuria," he said, and I had no grasp of the map of China, so it didn't signify. He straightened, took a deep breath and said, "See you around."

"But Wilson, I'm not through with you. You haven't learned enough to—"

He smiled brilliantly and said, "My friend plays *violin* in the symphony. Good?"

"Very good." I clapped, feeling the prickle of tears beneath my eyelids.

I looked out the window at a big herd of Angus grazing peacefully on the clean, green meadows of late spring—"the cattle on a thousand hills" unaware of their ultimate fate—and envied them, not for their whole existence, but for the timeless stretches when they would feel no woes like Wilson's or worries like mine.

What I first took to be the lake was just a small inlet, and the larger body of water was more impressive. The water was dull, gray-green and opaque, not at all like the clean depths of Clear Lake.

Venus was waiting for me at the bath house door. She had been here before and gave me a short commentary on the lake (man-made) and the bath house (built by CCC). We changed into our suits in cubicles open to the sky, and there's nothing like warm sun on your whole bare body to make you feel languorously ready for love. Fleetingly I thought of attacking Arthur beneath the gray-green waters of the lake.

Arthur, however, stayed dressed. He sat under a tree far from the water reading a book. Harley looked terrible in bathing trunks. A thick tube of flesh overlapped the waistband, and his legs were as thin as those of a water bird. He wore a wildly-flowered open shirt his soldier brother had sent him from Hawaii, its pockets weighted with camera gear, and he was everywhere, snapping pictures of this carefree occasion.

Hoffman hadn't emerged from the bath house yet, so Harley focused on me in my new, lemon-yellow suit and promised to give me the picture.

"Wow!" said Venus.

"Wow?" I turned in the direction she was looking and was equally impressed. Hoffman had a taut, nicely-muscled body, and with his curly hair and beard, he looked like a piece of Greek statuary. Why couldn't I just say, "I'll take that one in a larger size."?

He put out his hand to help me up, and we ran into the water. I leaned into a back float as soon as possible to erase the baneful difference in our heights. He stood beside me, hands placed as if he were holding me up, and shivered. The water was cold, but I wasn't shivering.

"See what you do to me?" he said.

I stole a glance at Arthur, who was looking up from his book and gazing into the distance. Not my distance, unfortunately. Hoffman caught my hand, brushing it against his body in what could have been an accidental contact. I chose to interpret it as such.

"My suit will never be the same after today," I said, "it looks like the yolk of an over-cooked hard-boiled egg."

He laughed lightly, but I caught the edge of hurt before the words came, "All right, Semiramis, I won't press."

"Who's Semiramis?" I tried to visualize how it was spelled and arrived at Samearamiss.

"An ancient Assyrian princess said to have founded Babylon—eternal woman."

I moved my arms, interested in their green-opal color just beneath the surface of the water. I could have been a statue hauled up from the depths of Atlantis. "That was a long time ago."

"Not for a geologist. Margaret, will you wear my pin? It can mean whatever you want it to mean."

"I didn't know you had a pin."

"Oh, I picked one up as an undergraduate. Brought it along out here just in case."

"What were you?"

"You're not answering the original question very fast, but I was a Phi Gam. Will that do?"

He *did* say it could mean whatever I wanted it to mean, so why not? "Sure, it will do. Yes."

Hoffman gave me a swift, hard kiss that almost swamped me and started to swim to the raft. I put my feet down on the bottom, a combination of sharp rocks and mossy slime, and watched him. He was so fast, so purposeful, so beautiful in motion.

"Coming?" he yelled.

"No, it's too far for me."

"Then I'll come back to you."

I shook my head, motioning for him to stay, "I'm getting out for awhile."

Venus was sitting next to my towel, guarding the pink yarn.

"Frankly, I don't think anybody will take it," I said.

"Then let's walk in the woods. Put on your shoes."

We left the beach and entered the trees. The light was greenish through the leaves, and I felt cold.

"What are all those umbrella-like plants?" I asked.

"May apples. Look," Venus pushed one of the umbrellas aside to reveal a pure white flower.

I knelt, fascinated by the bloom and its foliage. "I never saw these before."

"They're also called mandrakes."

"Like in the Bible?"

She shrugged, but I sensed that I knew more than I realized I knew. Samearamiss would recognize these flowers.

"I'm taking Hoffman's pin."

"Why?"

"Because it's May."

When everyone got out of the lake, we gathered at picnic tables on the high ground and had supper. Then, as the sun went down, Daddy B started to sing, "Day is Dying in the West," and we all joined in. "Holy, holy, holy, Lord God of Hosts, heaven and earth are full of Thee, heaven and earth are praising Thee, O Lord, most high." The light was the color of spun honey, and then the mauves and purples moved in. No one spoke, and Hoffman pressed something sharp into my palm—the triangle with a star and Greek letters that was the Phi Gamma Delta pin.

"You haven't changed your mind?" he whispered.

"No, but I didn't expect to get it so soon."

He retrieved it from my hand, kissed my palm and fastened the pin to my blouse. Then he was up helping to build a campfire, leaving me to think about it. I decided it felt all right—for now.

"I hope you won't be sorry," Venus said.

The wood was dry and blazed quickly. The gold on the pin glinted in the firelight. Hoffman returned, and we sat back-to-back like bookends in pleasant silent communion as we turned our heads to watch the flames.

Daddy B started to tell stories, "I remember the most difficult wedding I ever performed. This couple arrived with their four-year-old child and a big, black dog.

"I asked which of them had been married before, and the man said, 'Neither.' So I asked if the child were theirs, and they said she was. I commended them on their decision to marry and asked what prompted it."

Someone back in the shadows yelled, "Trouble with the landlady?"

Daddy B chuckled and said, "I'll never know. The bride told me it was none of my blankety-blank business. Then the little girl began to cry loudly, the dog started to growl, and that commotion continued throughout the ceremony. The bridegroom presented me with a Wearever skillet from the line he was selling in payment for my services, and they left. The kid cried and the dog growled all the way to their car, and when they were gone, I realized I had forgotten to say, 'I now pronounce you man and wife.' "

"So are they really married?" Lanie asked.

"I imagine God thinks so, and they don't know any different," Daddy B said, laughing and holding out his coffee cup for Momma B to refill.

He did enjoy life, which was a revelation to me. I thought Baptist preachers were supposed to be miserable in this "vale of tears," hoping to find their pleasures in the next world.

"What are you thinking?" Hoffman asked.

"Gather ye mandrakes while ye may."

The sharp glance he gave me led me to believe that I should look up mandrakes before I started bandying them about.

Summer was almost upon us. The pale chartreuse of spring had deepened, the air was still soft and warm when the sun went down, and the river banks were carpeted with couples. The atmosphere was heavy with sex, and that languor mixed oddly with the pressure of impending final exams.

Hoffman never took me to the river bank. He said, "That's for kids." I didn't mind, because the dutiful good-night kiss I gave Hoffman before I jumped out of his car was enough for me. On one of those heavy, fragrant nights he parked on the street beside the cottage and told me how much he'd miss me when the semester ended. He was going to Wyoming to work on a geological survey and asked how I planned to spend the summer.

I hadn't thought. I only knew I wanted to go home and sleep past those eternal 7:30 classes for at least a month. That wouldn't be possible, though. I'd have to work. Mr. Sommer had a secretary now and wouldn't need me, and I couldn't think of any other job in Harlan.

Hoffman held me a little tighter and a little longer that night, but I was too abstracted to give him my full attention.

Venus had a summer job at the library in Davenport, and she said, "What about the Harlan Library?"

I saw myself padding around in rubber-heeled shoes and hissing, "Shhhh!" like Miss Minnie Brazie and shook my head. "I couldn't. I don't know the dewey decimal system. All I ever did in a library was read and work on my Girl Scout book binding badge."

"Then why don't you go down to U Hall and talk to Mr. Wickson? He has a list of summer jobs in all kinds of places."

I took her advice, though I felt a bit guilty that I hadn't consulted Mom first. I guess I knew that she would veto the idea unless I had a good job to convince her that I should spend the summer away from home.

Loren Wickson was a full-lipped, smiling man whose eyes twinkled behind rimless glasses. He seemed impressed with my credentials and whistled cheerfully as he went through his files looking for something I'd like. He brought several cards back to his desk and pushed one toward me.

"This looks pretty good to me. What do you think?"

"Lake Leisure Resort, Lake LaRue, Wisconsin. Wanted: typist to handle reservation queries." The pay wasn't impressive, but the noon meal and transportation to and from the town would be furnished. Wickson returned to his file and found a brochure on the resort for me to read.

"A gracious vacation inn on beautiful Lake LaRue offering swimming, fishing, golf, tennis and horseback riding. Seven cocktail lounges and a gourmet dining room." The inn looked rustic with a long, screened porch; a flagstone patio with umbrella tables; and a deep, emerald lawn stretching to twin docks where red and white boats were anchored. I put myself into the scene and told Wickson I'd do it if they'd have me. I filled out the application for him to send with a cover letter, and he told me the reply would come to my home address.

I had three finals in one day and then a long lag before the last two. I spent most of my study time in the quiet carels at Shaeffer Hall, though I sometimes went to the zoology library because it was never crowded.

Nita was doing her studying in the cottage with the radio going full blast, and since she hadn't cracked a book all semester, she kept at it all night. Kay tried to stay up with her but kept falling asleep over her books. Rosemary was off somewhere with Charlie, defying the hours rule, but Boots wasn't around to catch her at it. We took the precaution of wadding up blankets to look like a sleeping Rosemary in case Boots should come in.

Reva, Sheila and Sue were staying at their sorority houses, and Dot was dead to the world after a long stretch of drinking at the Airliner.

Venus hung down from her bunk like a two-toed sloth and nudged me. "Are you awake?"

"How could I be anything else?"

"We might as well get up and talk."

We went to our desks and peeled oranges to eat. Venus always had a supply in the bottom of her corrugated paper wardrobe.

"Rosemary isn't coming back next year," Venus said. "She's going to marry Charlie and raise kids."

I said, "I couldn't stand it if I couldn't come back. If I'd never come here, maybe I could just get married and raise kids, but not now."

"I'm not having any kids."

"Never?"

"Never!"

"Because of what you have to do to get them?"

"Partly, but mainly because they might not turn out the way I wanted them to."

"It wouldn't be your fault," I said, thinking of Uncle Stig and how nobody ever blamed Grandma for his wild ways.

"Maybe not, but I want everything in my life to be of quality, and to do that, you have to give up quantity—don't let anything in you can't control. Will you be my roommate next year when we move into Currier?"

I laughed. "Are you sure I'm quality?"

She nodded solemnly, "You're golden—a golden girl."

That's when Boots fell into the cottage, laughing and crying at the same time. Mascara ran down her cheeks, and her lips had been kissed into a pale blur.

"He did it!" She shouted, pulling Venus up from her chair and dancing her around the desks, "He told her! They're getting a divorce!"

Nita and Kay left their bunks to find out what was going on, and Nita said, "Are you sure?"

"Sure, I'm sure!" Boots exulted, "Steve *told* me so."

Nita shook her head. "Most guys will say anything to get in your pants."

Boots drew herself up to her full five feet and sniffed. "Steve is *not* most guys. Now where is everybody? Guess bed check is a little late, but better late than never."

Kay reminded Boots that three had signed out to the sorority houses, Dot and Rosemary were asleep, and she was looking at the rest of us.

"We're happy for you, Boots," I said.

She burst into tears.

"What's wrong?" Venus asked.

"Why in the hell do we all have to be Catholic? She got the white veil, and I get the big sin!"

Venus shook her head. "I guess you'll just have to decide whether he's worth it."

"Damned right, he is!" Boots grinned and marched off to brush her teeth.

I thought about rooming with Venus the next year and decided that I would prefer Elena, but Venus had asked first. I raised one foot high to press the bulge in her mattress and told her I'd do it. The choices I had been making lately weren't the result of wild enthusiasm, but Venus, like Hoffman, was OK. Grandma had told me that you should do either what you wanted with all your heart or the thing that really didn't matter much one way or the other. Only if you felt a strong aversion should you back off altogether. After all, it was choosing something over nothing that made the world go around.

We were just falling asleep when Boots let out a yelp that brought us upright in our bunks.

"Where the hell is Rosemary?"

"Out with Charlie," Kay said.

"I'll have to report this."

"But she's in love—just like you and Steve," I said.

Boots turned out the light and snapped off Nita's radio right in the middle of a Friendly Grainbelt commercial.

Dot left the next day. She found out that she had flunked chemistry and decided to go home immediately.

"I'll never be a doctor now, so I might as well get a job in the Post Office if I can. Have a good life, you guys!"

Nita came up to Dot and kissed her on the mouth. Dot's eyes were bright with tears as she slammed out of the cottage with the small leather case she always called her "doctor bag."

Rosemary, it turned out, was pregnant. The big wedding she and Charlie had planned for June was off in favor of a private ceremony in Iowa City that could be spoken of as "our wedding last spring." She explained, "The folks at home still count on their fingers."

Only four of us would be moving into Currier in the fall, and we might never see the others again. Iowa City was like that. In the cases of Lew and Abdul, this was a plus. Had I met either of them on the campus or in town, I would have blushed and hoped the ground would swallow me, but happily, I hadn't seen them since the traumatic farewells. In a small town where you went to school with people from kindergarten to high school graduation, you had to be more careful about relationships than in this shifting, dazzling academic community.

The saddest farewell of finals week was with Wilson Ling, who was returning to China. He was afraid to go back, but he believed it was his duty.

"I'm sorry I didn't get the sweater finished," I told him.

"No sorry is essential."

"No sorrow is necessary, Wilson, or just plain 'That's OK' will do."

He grasped my hand and pressed it so hard that the glossy wing of black hair fell into his eyes. "Good-bye, good fortune!"

"Please take care of yourself!"

He shrugged. "I follow the Tao."

I sent the last case of dirty laundry home and started to pack. Somehow, I now owned more things than I had brought with me in the fall and had to go to J.C. Penney for some boxes to hold it all. Not wanting to ask Roger for a ride, I planned to take the train to Atlantic, where Uncle Karl would pick me up.

Boots allowed Hoffman to come inside and help me organize my luggage, which he did with great efficiency. I complimented him, and he said, "Anyone who camps out as much as I do *should* know how to organize gear."

He looked at the battered case my grandfather had taken to the Chicago Exposition of 1893 and smiled. "Too bad that thing can't talk."

"Yeah. Mom said my Uncle Stig took it when he ran away to join a carnival. He can tell fortunes by spitting in your palm."

"What's yours?"

I shrugged. "I can't remember—except for the long life-line."

"When am I going to meet your family?"

"No hurry, is there?"

His pupils danced with hurt, and I was sorry I hadn't chosen my words more carefully. Hoffman seldom pushed me, but when he did, I reacted unthinkingly—usually hurtfully.

"I keep forgetting how very young you are, Juno mine!"

"I need to stop at the law school and pick up my check. Is that OK?"

"My time is your time."

When the car was packed, Venus waved good-bye, and Hoffman said, "Are you really going to room with her next year?"

"Yes, why?"

"I don't think she approves of me."

"Maybe she'll find somebody of her own and stop worrying about what I do."

"We'll have to work on that."

Regina regarded me with her usual cold stare and told me my check was in the "out" basket.

"Is the dean in? I'd like to say good-bye."

"He's at a meeting. I'll relay your farewell. You'll be back in the fall?"

"Yes, Will my job still be here?"

She nodded unenthusiastically. "He seems to like you."

"Well, have a good summer."

"Thank you. You do the same."

Gwen was coming back from the lounge as I left, and she hugged me, enveloping me in a cloud of floral scent. "Sure will miss you, Kid! Hurry back!"

As Hoffman drove south on Clinton Street, I leaned out the window to watch the dome of Old Capitol as long as possible. The next time I saw it, I would be a sophomore. This year—so long and so short at the same time—had been enchanted because I was a clean slate receiving each mark with joy and wonder. I would never be that again, I knew, and my eyes grew moist over the loss of a glorious condition so intentionally altered.

Hoffman attended to my baggage while I bought my ticket, and then we had a last meal in the depot cafe where we had eaten so many times before.

"I know you'll come back," he said, "but will you come back to me?"

"Why wouldn't I?"

"If you can't think of reasons, I certainly won't supply you with any! Write to me?"

"Of course, but you'll have to write first and tell me where you are."

The train whistle blew, and I had to leave half my dessert—strawberry and rhubarb pie. The starving Armenians evoked by Mom when I refused to eat as a child rose up to haunt me, and when I told Hoffman, he laughed.

"It *is* funny, isn't it? I always *did* wonder how my eating something could help them."

Hoffman lightly touched his fraternity pin fastened to my blouse. "Don't forget me."

"I won't," I promised, turning to kiss him before we reached the conductor and his little step. I almost wished Hoffman would mount the step to kiss me but dismissed this unworthy thought.

He put a small package into my hand. "Open it on the train."

When I was in my seat, I waved at him from the window and looked away immediately. He wouldn't mind, because I had told him of the Danish superstition about the bad luck of watching people until they were out of sight.

About ten miles west, I opened the package, almost fearful of what I would find. The gray velvet box looked ominous, but when I opened it, I found a green pendant on a gold chain and a note, "Not quite sea-splashed emeralds, but here's a bit of jade to wear around your lovely throat. Love, Hoffman."

What a wonderfully romantic man he was! If there were only more of him. I fastened the chain around my neck and almost immediately fell asleep. Absorbing so much for so long had exhausted me completely. The next thing I knew, the conductor was shaking my arm and calling, "Atlantic! This way, miss."

And there they were: Mom, Grandma, Uncle Karl and Aunt Kam wearing clothes I'd seen before and looking like the family I'd left behind more than nine months ago.

"How tan you are!" Aunt Kam said.

She was the only one who talked. Mom and Grandma just hugged and patted me and looked at me, and Uncle Karl was muttering about "all the junk" I'd brought home.

The drive to Harlan along familiar roads in the mauve twilight was an intense pleasure, and so was coming into the house and smelling the aroma of fresh-baked cinnamon rolls and laundry dried in the sun.

The kitchen faucet dripped with a familiar rhythm, and Pharaoh's daughter still lounged beside the bulrushes on the china plate in the rack above the kitchen couch covered with the scratchy Army blanket.

"So!" Grandma said, "You sailed out."

"Yes, but no farther than I could row back—yet."

"Well," she said, "I never *could* row back, and I lived through it. Do what you must."

"Mama, she's too young to know what she must," Mom said.

"But she has learned much. It shows in her face."

"Does it really?" I jumped up and looked in the flawed mirror above the kitchen sink. Either I couldn't remember how I used to look, or there was no difference.

"Margaret," Mom said, "will you go out and pick the nasturtiums? We have to do that every day, or they'll stop blooming."

That was when I knew I was really home, where something had to be done or else.

When the letter from Lake Leisure Resort arrived, Mom dropped it on the dining room table and gave me a questioning look. I decided to wait until I opened it before I said anything to her about going away for the summer. Possibly they didn't want me.

But they did. Mr. Wickson had recommended me highly, the letter said, and my experience with Dean Ansel Judd of the College of Law was impressive. When could I report for work?

I handed the letter to Mom, and the vertical creases between her eyes deepened as she read it. Grandma watched her in total stillness, her gnarled hands clasped on the table top. The only motion in the room was the dancing glint from Grandma's gold-rimmed glasses set off by the June sun flooding through the windows.

Mom passed the letter to Grandma, who adjusted the thin, gold ear pieces of her glasses before starting to read. Now Mom was still, eyes focused broodingly on some middle distance where I never could join her.

"We've missed you so much and looked forward to the summer," Mom said.

"I'm sorry, but I just couldn't think of a job I could get here. I don't have to take it, you know."

"Almost a shame not to. They really seem to want you. We'll have to figure out how to get you there."

"Karl?" Grandma suggested.

"It's too far. We'll look into the train schedules. But where will you live? They didn't say anything about that."

"I suppose I can rent a room in the town."

"I can't let you go alone."

"Oh Mother, please!" I remembered the times she walked up to the city hall to escort me home from summer band practice, hiding behind trees to keep from "humiliating" me with her concern.

"She'll be all right, Petra," Grandma said, pushing up from the table to peel potatoes and chop green onions for the *frikadeller*.

I hugged them both and rushed to the bedroom to change out of my shorts. I planned to walk uptown and ask Gregory Sommer if I could use the office typewriter to answer the letter.

On my way out the door, I asked, "When shall I tell them I'll be there?"

Mom looked at the big Harlan National Bank calendar on the wall. "Next Monday."

Striding along in my red and white seersucker suit and spectator pumps, I felt all crisp and professional—like the secretaries Merrie and I had imagined we'd be. I hadn't been able to wear the pumps when I went out with Hoffman, and they made me feel like a show horse with ribbons braided into its mane—a high stepper.

I passed the squared bulk of the high school softened by a mantle of green vines and remembered exactly how it smelled inside, a mix of chalk, sweat and hectograph gel. How satisfying it was to be finished with all that.

A strong breeze had blown up, sending the meringue clouds scudding across the sky of blue impossible to achieve in fabric. My friend Wyonne called it "Virgin Mary blue," and it was a shade I never would wear, delicious as it was to view.

The flag at the Post Office snapped in the wind, reminding me that I had missed Decoration Day at home for the first time in my life. No parade, no rifle salute, no once-a-year chance to see inside the big stone mausoleum at the cemetery, no decorating of the family graves—Daddy's, Grandpa's and Uncle Soren's. Until now, Memorial Day probably had been the most dramatic day of all the year. Somebody always fainted during the parade, and each year I tried (and failed) to get up the courage to keep my hands from my ears during the rifle salute.

The buckeye tree at the library had leafed out to create a deep shade. I detoured up the curving walk to contemplate the "Keep Off the Grass" sign and think of all the lucky buckeyes I could have collected had I been willing to disobey it. Now that I was willing, it was the wrong season. Just as I was turning away, a reddish-brown gleam caught my eye, a buckeye from the last crop polished by the winter and nestled in the grass.

I looked around quickly to see if anybody was watching, dashed onto the grass and snatched the buckeye. The heels of my spectators sank into the damp earth and came up muddy, not a particularly auspicious first result of owning a lucky buckeye, but I cleaned them with some leaves from the bushes and went on my way.

Norgaard's Drugstore had a display of suntan lotion and dark glasses; the Frockery's window offered a sundress of deep blue and white stripes and bathing suits of Schiaparelli pink, blue and white laid out in a fan; a hand-lettered sign promising "Lemonaid" was taped to the window of the Hotel Saylor coffee shop. The misspelling bothered me greatly.

A western was playing at the Harlan Theater, Schnepel's Bakery breathed its delicious aroma into the street (I could almost see the stone soldier of the Civil War monument sniff it appreciatively), and the medicinal smell of the yard goods at the Golden Rule wafted from an open door. It was real summer in my hometown, the perfect first weeks of the season, and I was planning to leave it all behind.

Climbing the dark stairs to Gregory Sommer's office, I wondered who sat in my former place at the massive L.C. Smith? No one, it seemed. Or perhaps she had gone on an errand. I could hear Mr. Sommer's voice coming from his inner sanctum and knew by the familiar over-enunciation that he was using the dictaphone. I would not make my presence known until he came to a full stop, knowing how he hated interruption.

The wine-covered law books were just as I'd left them, their dull gold stamping nearly unreadable in the light from the green-shaded lamp on the secretary's desk. Several dictaphone rolls waited on the desk, giving me an uneasy feeling that I should get at them immediately. I pulled the Lake Leisure letter and the paper and envelope for a reply from my purse and waited, listening to Mr. Sommer spell words that any legal secretary should know—like "r-e-p-l-e-v-i-n." When I heard the machine click off, I cleared my throat.

Mr. Sommer came to the door of his office, still abstracted, and I noticed his two-toned brown and white shoes (like mine) before he recognized me and spoke. Sommer's summer shoes. The last time I saw him wearing them, he had terrified me by asking me to recommend my replacement before telling me the reason—I was to receive the Garner scholarship and go to college rather than straight to work.

"Well, hello, Margaret. How was your year?"

I opened my mouth and closed it again before managing a simpleminded "Fine." That wondrous year, that vast catalog of new possibilities could not be described accurately without my sounding uncharacteristically gushy. "I came to ask if I could use your typewriter for a few minutes—if it's all right with your secretary."

"Certainly. Edna comes in at night after she feeds her family and puts the kids to bed. Her husband baby-sits. Of course, we never make the five o'clock mail the day the letters are dictated, and it took me awhile to adjust to that."

"But who answers the phone?"

"The only person you see. Everybody in town thinks I'm too poor to hire a secretary, but actually, I'm busier than ever."

"How is Mary—I mean Mrs. Sommer?" I remembered so well the night he walked me home from the office and told me about the car accident that killed their child and fogged Mary's mind forever. As far as I knew, I was the only person in town he'd told, and I never had spoken of it to anyone. I hoped that my long time away privileged me to ask about her now.

"As ever," he said, tightening his lips and changing the subject. "So you've been working for Ansel Judd. I must have had some influence on you."

"It was an accident, really. We met in a reception line at a freshman tea, and he thought I looked Swedish."

"That explains nothing. What if you did?"

"His wife is from a Swedish family, so he had an impulse to ask if I wanted a job."

"At least you had the sense to be in the right place at the right time."

"And because I knew you, I didn't faint from fright when I found out he was dean of the law school. Thanks."

"You're quite welcome. Judd is a real tartar when he wants to be, but you seem to have survived in his employment."

"Just barely. Regina, the office manager, was convinced I had stolen a Torts test, but one of the other secretaries took it."

"Ah, yes. I know Regina well. The old dragon was there even when *I* was in Law School. If I hadn't bullied you first, could you have handled her?"

I shook my head, smiling. "Probably not. If you'll let me type my letter, I'll do one of those rolls for you."

"Not a fair exchange. Leave it for Edna."

"But I know how you like to make the five o'clock mail. Remember the night of the Carroll game during basketball tournament?"

He nodded, and I knew both of us were seeing a replay of me weeping while I typed, the clock moving inexorably to the bus departure time and then past it. He disappeared into his office for a moment and returned with the fake malachite pen he had used to sign the letters prepared on that awful night.

"I think you should have this as a memento of the dangers you have passed," he said.

"Thank you. That's almost Shakespeare, isn't it?"

"You *have* learned something. I'll leave you to your correspondence."

I typed my reply to Lake Leisure Resort, informing Mr. Arnold Stith that I would be there on Monday. The fat, green pen gave my signature authority. Then I inserted the earplugs and listened to Sommer's recorded voice. I nearly fell off the chair when I realized what I was hearing. Gregory Sommer was going to defend Charles Syrovy, the murderer of Bebe Maxwell.

I pulled the earplugs out and rushed into his office. "Bebe Maxwell lived in the cottage next to mine. How did you ever get the case?"

"Do I hear a note of doubt that I can handle it?"

"No, but you're so far away—I don't see how—"

"I wrote to Mr. Syrovy and told him that the case interested me and that I would represent him without a fee, whereupon he retained me."

"But that isn't your kind of law, is it?"

He gave me a sour smile. "It used to be. What's your opinion of the case?"

"I think he did it, but he didn't mean to."

"Excellent. I share your view. Would you care to give me some help during the trial? I'll need some kind of a secretary while I'm in Iowa City."

"When is the trial?"

"I've succeeded in getting it set right at the beginning of the docket—early September before the students are back intensifying the prejudices of the jury."

"Then I suppose I can. I'll be finished with my job at the lake, and classes won't start for a few weeks."

"One never knows how long a trial will last, but if it's prolonged beyond the beginning of the semester, I can fill in with somebody else." He leaned back in his chair and steepled his hands. "I went to see Syrovy. He's a raving romantic with a Byronic look—destined to suffer largely. What was Bebe like?"

I tried to remember and was shocked to realize how far she had receded in my consciousness in such a short time. I told him that she was pretty, came from a moneyed family and had casual morals as far as any of us knew.

"Whatever happens, our Charles will be just as well off as he would have been had she lived, then?"

"Oh, no! He'll never be able to forget what he did."

"But he was in an impossible situation—in love with a girl who would never belong to him. His condition and aspirations were separated from hers by a bottomless abyss. In death, she'll never belong to anyone else."

I almost rose to the bait, but I recognized Mr. Sommer's old trick just in time. I laughed. "If you want to play Devil's Advocate, you'll have to find somebody else to confuse. I have to get this roll finished and be on my way."

"Leave the roll, Margaret. I'll see you in September. I shall dictate a letter to the Hotel Jefferson reserving you a room immediately."

"Oh, wow! I've never stayed in a hotel before."

He smiled sardonically. "Most world-weary almost-sophomores wouldn't admit it."

"Will you pay me enough that I can afford it?"

"I'll pick up that expense on top of your salary. By the way, you're looking well."

"So are you! Maybe it's because you're suddenly a criminal lawyer. Oh!"

"Oh, what?"

"If you're going to be in Iowa City that long, what about Mrs. Sommer?"

"I've hired a wife sitter. It's considerate of you to think of her, but you really must learn to credit the rest of the human race with a bit of practical intelligence."

I blushed. "Sorry! I can't seem to help playing 'Mommy', and I know lots of people hate it." I glanced at the copy of *Desire Me* on his desk and said good-bye.

Later in the afternoon I went to the swimming pool with Lotus. My yellow suit *did* look like pea soup after its immersion in Lake Mac-Bride, and Lotus was bulgier than ever in her brown one after a year of dormitory starch.

She padded outside the fence to the refreshment shack and bought Coke for us, and while she was gone, Roger walked past and said "Hi," scarcely moving his lips.

"I thought you were going to get out of town this summer," I said.

He shrugged. "Heard you were pinned to a Phi Gam."

"Yeah, but not one of those young jerks who live in the house."

"Watch out for that older stuff."

I nodded solemnly. He ought to know. I wondered if he had fallen back into Florine's clutches.

The hot sun seemed to multiply the beating pulses in my body, and I longed for someone to long for. Too bad it couldn't be Hoffman. At that moment, I knew I'd have to give back his pin, but it would have to wait until I saw him in the fall. One didn't do that sort of thing by mail.

Lotus handed me my Coke and sipped her own reflectively. "Learn anything this year?"

"More than I know, probably. How about you?"

"Nothing spectacular—except that I'm sick of Methodists."

We both lay back on our towels and watched the sun making red and gold patterns on the inside of our eyelids.

"Lotus?" I said, meaning to ask her if she had found someone at Simpson—a male someone—but she was asleep. I supposed it took more energy than Lotus could muster to work through all the half-gods one had to deal with before the gods arrived. Maybe the one intended for me would be waiting for me in Wisconsin.

When Uncle Karl drove me to Manilla to catch my train, the whole family went along. The air was blue from his cigarette smoke because the Jorgen women had a deep-seated dread of drafts from open car windows, even in June. I was feeling carsick in the back seat, as usual.

"I'd feel better about this if I knew where you were going to be," Mom said. "You don't even have an address."

"You can write me at the resort the first time, and since I have to find a place to stay as soon as I get in, you'll know where I am as soon as you get my first letter."

Aunt Kam gave Uncle Karl a slanting look of command which communicated her wish that he'd put out his cigarette. He did. The look continued, and he turned down the volume of the baseball game on the radio.

"One would think they could have arranged that for you, Margaret," she said.

Grandma said, "She'll manage."

I tuned them all out and drifted, wishing I dared to crack the window beside me. I'd shoved a new letter from Hoffman into my purse unopened, but I felt no urgency about reading it. Like the others, it probably would be full of boring details about his geological survey in Utah. He was trying so hard not to press me emotionally that I wished I hadn't asked it of him. I could use a few more "sea-splashed emeralds" around my throat.

The last time we'd ridden this train was when we went to Rochester for my operation—the scarring of my throat that I'd nearly forgotten. Had Hoffman wanted to hide that puckered welt with jewels? Now I was starting to think like Mom with her eternal "reading between the lines."

Aunt Kam was saying, "DuLac isn't very far from Chicago, really. Maybe Marianne can come out some weekend and see how you're getting along."

"She's probably much too busy for that," I said hastily.

"She needn't be. After all, family is family."

Further protest was useless, so I just smiled until Aunt Kam turned and faced the windshield again. The thought of my crabby, perfect cousin picking her way through the umbrella tables at Lake Leisure with an exasperated expression on her face gave me the shivers. I'd never been anywhere with Marianne alone except for the time we were trapped in the creek bed for hours when I was a little kid, and I wasn't eager for her full attention again. She was a tough career woman now and undoubtedly had intensified her youthful fierceness.

I hoped never to spend time with her unless Aunt Kam was around to serve as a buffer. Or Grandma, who knew how to keep Marianne from "ramping and snorting."

The cousin I really wanted to see was Marianne's sister, the glamorous Geraldine, married to Vito Scarpelli when I was in grade school and never seen since—by me. Uncle Karl and Aunt Kam had visited them in California, bringing back tales of unimaginable elegance, but our only connection with the Scarpellis was a yearly Christmas greeting with their name engraved in real gold. We kept them all because they were too beautiful and expensive to throw away.

Gero, as Vito called her, now had a Manx cat, Aunt Kam reported, "just as smart and loving as a dog." I was surprised that Aunt Kam had adopted Vito's name for Geraldine, considering how much she had disapproved of Vito before the marriage. Had all that money won her over? The thought made me pull myself up short—more "reading between the lines," which I was determined not to do.

Jack Russell, the brother of Geraldine and Marianne, was trying to make a go of farming and doing better now than he had in the years when his best crop was babies. Each time Velie went to the hospital to produce a new one, Aunt Kam kept last year's model, and they were adorable babies—sweet enough to dull the edge of Grandma's curse, "May you have a dozen children!"

I hadn't seen my Uncle Stig for years, either. Mom's best pal with the booming laugh and the talent for fortune telling. He had to spit in your palm first, and that cut down on the requests for his services, but if he were beside me now, I'd endure it to know what lay ahead for me.

Mary Lois Engle, who had postponed her first year of college to serve as Worthy Advisor of the Rainbow Girls, had phoned me the day before to ask, "What did you *really* think of the University?"

"I loved it!" I said, adding, "I still do."

"But weren't you completely lost in all those people? I mean, wouldn't you get more attention in a smaller school?"

"I got all the attention I needed."

"But I mean *individual* attention."

"No matter how many people are around you, you can get involved with just so many."

"Well," she said, "I think I'd feel more comfortable if I knew everybody."

"Then you'd better go to a small school, I guess." I let it go at that, surprised at how mellow I felt toward Mary Lois. I could remember the time when she was the worm in my lettuce, the static on my radio, the know-it-all Valedictorian of my class.

"I wonder if I'll feel funny about being older than the other freshmen?" she was saying.

"Who's going to know?"

"Oh, yeah, I guess you're right. I don't need to tell anybody, do I?"

The touch of uncertainty in her voice made me feel downright benevolent. "Look, if there's anything I can help you with, just give me a call."

"OK, Margaret, thanks. Thanks a lot."

Just thinking about the crack in Mary Lois's shell of superiority made me feel better about my own venture into the unknown. For all the assurances I'd given Mom and the rest of the family, I was scared to death, but I knew I was better prepared to face whatever was out there than good, old Mary Lois was.

We made it to the station just as the train came whistling in, and Uncle Karl suppressed a cuss word as he jumped out of the car to get my suitcase from the trunk. "I *told* you we should have started earlier!"

"Now Karl," Aunt Kam said, "there's still plenty of time. The conductor hasn't even put his little step down yet."

All my possessions were in my grandfather's horrible-looking suitcase, which I couldn't wait to shove out of sight. Mom ran into the station to buy my ticket while the rest of us stood on the platform in the tongue-tied emotions of parting. She rushed back, pressed the ticket into my hand and hugged me.

"Be good and be careful," she said.

Uncle Karl laughed. "If she does the first, she won't need to worry about the second."

Aunt Kam's green eyes yellowed with annoyance at the remark, though she pretended not to hear it.

"Don't talk to strangers," Mom warned, and I didn't see how I could avoid it. Everybody would be a stranger to me for awhile.

Grandma patted me with a bony hand, Mom hugged me, and Aunt Kam turned her cheek for me to kiss. Then Uncle Karl vaulted upward with my suitcase and got me settled in the coach car. He started to leave but turned and came back, extending a five-dollar bill folded like a fan. To both of us, this was a lot of money.

He said, "Use it to have some fun."

"Thanks a lot, Uncle Karl."

"Don't mention it."

He looked wistful, as if he could scarcely remember what fun was, and I thought what a hard life he had seeing to the needs of a large tribe of females. He was *the* man of the Jorgen women, and apparently, he believed that Aunt Kam was worth all the aggravation. I supposed it was generous of her to share him, but if I had a husband, I wasn't at all sure that I'd do the same. Still, it was clear that Uncle Karl cherished Aunt Kam by being good to the whole tribe of us. I wouldn't mind a husband who loved me enough to undergo all that. Women alone—women without men—simply got no cherishing.

I waved from the window, noticing how tired Mom looked and how Grandma was shrinking. Grandma had been my height when she was young. We had talked about that when I was shooting up taller than my friends and hating it.

"Walk like a queen and be glad for every inch that God gave you!" she said.

Aunt Kam never was as tall as Grandma or her sisters, and they said that was because she was sick so much as a child. She had the knack of looking right, though. No matter what she wore, it looked stylish—even to the towel she wrapped in a turban after she washed the long hair she wore in a high crown of braids. It pleased her enormously when someone remarked that she looked like Isak Dinesen, the Danish author of *Seven Gothic Tales*. At certain angles, she did, but without the dark and almost frightening aura of the author.

The train started with a lurch and the metallic hiccups of the hitches between the cars. I had to remind myself to look away from the family to avoid bad luck because I had a sudden attack of homesickness and wanted to gaze at them as long as I possibly could. I even imagined jumping off the train and staying behind, letting the historic suitcase travel to DuLac alone. I needed my family and wanted to be with them, and yet I didn't fit back into the place I had vacated. Things had shifted, somehow, until the space was a different size and shape. Eventually, if I stayed away long enough, there would be no space. It seemed that I had to keep moving, because trying to be what I was before was as difficult as smoothing facial tissues back into the box through the oval opening on the top. I settled back in my seat, trying to look both purposeful and mysterious.

No one paid any attention to me. An elderly woman knitted, a salesman of some kind worked on his books, and a young mother rocked her body to lull a drowsy baby to sleep. I looked out the window at fields of young corn, each plant still distinct like green embroidery stitches on a dark brown background. At least this job I was taking would save me from detasseling, the closest thing to going to Hell I could think of with steamy heat and skin-flaying leaf blades.

The ditches were filled with wild roses, saucers of pale pink centered with gold, and hemp still grew where it had been planted during the war when there was a scarcity of rope. The delicate, jagged leaves had a lacy look. I made a wish on several loaded hayracks for a place to live in DuLac and was frustrated by the tight-shut windows of the car that robbed me of the wonderfully sweet scent of fresh-cut hay until it occurred to me to walk onto the platform between my car and the next.

A man was standing there smoking, feet planted wide apart to keep his balance in the lurching motion. I tried to step past and fell against him.

"I'm sorry!"

"I'm not."

Both of us were shouting to be heard above the noise of the train. I expected him to release me immediately, but he held on. His hand was higher than my waist and lower than my shoulder, excusable only on the first bounce. I squirmed until I could reach the bar on the door to the next car and pull myself out of his grasp.

"Let's go into the club car and I'll buy you a drink," he shouted.

"No thanks," I yelled back, "I came out to smell the hay."

He lit another cigarette and looked me over minutely while I scanned the passing fields, irked that I could find no hay. He'd think that I didn't know corn from timothy. But what difference did it make? He was just a stranger I'd bumped into. At last we whizzed past a field of red clover. I caught a few deep inhalations of the summery scent and returned to my seat.

When a white-coated steward came through the car to announce that dinner was being served in the diner, I pulled out the lunch Grandma had packed for me: sandwiches of thin-shaved roast beef and juicy rounds of onion piled thickly between slices of homemade bread, a peach that was pale yellow and rose-tinged and three of the filled cookies I had asked her to make for me when I got home from Iowa City—golden pockets of raisins in a thick, sweet sauce. All of this was carefully wrapped in the printed waxed paper from a loaf of store-bought bread and tied with a piece of string. I found the packet both touching and embarrassing.

"Be sure to eat the peach before you eat the cookies," she had said, "or it will taste sour."

I had discovered that Grandma's practical advice of that sort usually had a deeper application, but she'd never hand it to me on a platter. I had to puzzle it out for myself. Which experiences in life were the peaches, and which were the cookies? I really didn't know.

The train pulled into DuLac while it was still light, and it didn't look like much of a town. Furthermore, the total flatness that surrounded it oppressed me. I needed at least a gentle rise here and there, something to look up to or down from, and the southern Wisconsin fields, spread out like cloth from a bolt, made me feel that I could walk forever and never arrive anywhere.

I lifted my heavy suitcase, and my fingers drowned in the deep, wide grooves my grandfather's fingers had made in the handle—Uncle Stig's, too, probably. The bag hadn't been to many places through the years, but it always had been carried by someone with great expectations.

No one else got off the train, and I was alone on the platform. A few railroad functionaries were taking off mail, and a baker's truck pulled up with rolls for the diner. I looked inside the station, searching for a telephone, but I could see none and there was no one to ask, so I picked up my case and started to walk.

I had to re-cross the track to get into town, and as I was picking my way through the cinders and trying to decide whether to walk the ties or step between them, the heel of my spectator pump got caught in a projection from the nearest rail. I stepped out of the shoe and knelt, trying to see how I could free it without scarring the leather.

The sound of screeching brakes was so close and so startling that I fell over sideways and had just righted myself when a small man with a big cigar jumped out of a big, maroon car with a grill that seemed to be breathing hotly in my face.

"You all right?"

"I'm fine, but my shoe's caught."

"My God, I thought I'd picked you off for sure! Let me see about that shoe." He knelt to inspect the situation, blue smoke from the cigar causing him to squint.

"Can you get it loose without scratching it?"

"With any luck." He worked the shoe back and forth gently, causing the large diamond ring he wore to radiate like a small lighthouse. "There!"

There was only a small dent in the heel, less damage than I would have caused myself, and I thanked him, picking up my case to move on.

"Can I take you somewhere?"

Since I didn't know where, I said, "No thanks."

"Well, then, take my card. If you're ever in Chicago, give me a call."

I held out my hand for it, thinking I'd never be in Chicago. He climbed back into the car, waved and was off. I read "Cadillac" on the maroon trunk and looked down at the card. George Halas. Chicago Bears. The information meant nothing to me, but I put the card into my purse and went on.

About four blocks from the station, I passed a white house with a deep porch that had a "Room for Rent" sign in the window. It looked like a friendly house, the home of someone honest and well-intentioned, so I knocked on the door.

The woman who answered was short and plump with bright, blue eyes and the high, creamy voice that many fat women seem to have. She said "Hello?" with a question mark.

"I'm looking for a room."

She glanced at Grandpa's suitcase, and it seemed to reassure her. She invited me in. I parked the suitcase just inside a living room furnished with a brown plush sofa and two matching chairs protected by crocheted doilies, a floor lamp with three peachy lightbulbs shaped like tulip buds, walls papered with white plumes on a dull green ground and a plaster Sacred Heart so vividly colored that I expected to see it drip on the polished hardwood floor that bordered a gray rug patterned with orange flowers.

The house had the piney scent of cleaning compound, I noticed as I followed the woman to the room she was offering. I didn't know her name, but she didn't know mine, either. She switched on the light from an overhead fixture that looked like a blue glass bowl, and I immediately saw that I couldn't read by it. There was, however, a small lamp that might work sprouting from a three-dimensional, starched doily on the bedside table.

The bed was one of those brown iron things covered by a spread of turquoise chenille, and the mattress dipped in the middle. The Virgin

Mary, eyes rolled heavenward, hung above the headboard, her blue gown quarreling with the bedspread and with the apple-green walls, and just when I was forming a polite refusal of the room, I looked at the wall to the right and changed my mind.

There, against apple-green walls in Wisconsin, were Maxfield and Parrish, the classical ladies of my earliest memory, trailing their fingers along a stone wall and looking at nothing in particular, just as they had done on the Audubon County farm where I was born. I remembered every fold in the draperies that I once had thought were their nightgowns, and their presence here seemed like a sign.

"How much is the rent?" I asked.

The woman hesitated, then said, "I usually ask fourteen a week, but since you're so young and all, maybe I can settle for twelve."

"I'll take it. My name is Margaret Langelund, and I don't know yours."

"Malone. Birdie Malone. I'll just leave you to get settled, then— Honey. Do they call you Maggie or anything?"

"No, just Margaret."

She acted as if she wanted to be friendly but didn't quite know to what degree. I smiled at her and went for the suitcase, nearly spraining my thumbs to release the catches with a noise like a rifle shot. The open case released the smell of home—clothes dried by the sun that shone on Harlan, Iowa; a hint of Mom's Lady Esther powder scent; Grandma's garden smell; the yeasty, human smell of a houseful of women. I breathed deeply, exhaled and blinked away the tears that pooled in my eyes.

When would I learn to stop living in the past or in the future? I deliberately put myself into the moment. This room was mine, the first dwelling place I'd ever secured with my own money, and its imperfections could be loved as a parent loves a defective child. If not, I could alight here briefly and depart as untouched by it all as Maxfield and Parrish up there on the green wall.

Lake Leisure Resort sent a bus to town every morning to pick up employees who lived in DuLac, and the same bus took them home at the end of the working day. I learned about this service when I phoned Mr. Stith, who had hired me, and he told me to be at the drugstore on Chippewa Street at seven-thirty in the morning.

I asked Mrs. Malone where I could buy breakfast, and she said, "Why don't you just have it here tomorrow, Honey? You have so many new things to deal with all at once. Besides, I'd like you to meet Bob."

"Who's Bob, your husband?"

"No, the Mister died twenty years ago. Bob's my boy. He works at the furniture factory. He's a nice-looking fellow, if I do say so myself, so it's not that he can't find himself a gal—guess he's just not ready to settle down."

Living with Mama and working at the furniture factory seemed pretty settled down to me, but I didn't say so. I just accepted her breakfast offer happily and set my Big Ben for six o'clock.

That night I dreamed that Hoffman was sanding a piece of furniture to the rhythm of a poem he was reciting while Harley played "Danny Boy" on the trombone. When I walked into the room, both of them ignored me.

Bob Malone wasn't much taller than I was, but he was, as his mother had promised, a "nice-looking fellow." His features were like those of the men drawn by Charles Dana Gibson in an old book the Farleys had left in our Willow Street house. He acknowledged our introduction politely and addressed himself to the toast, bacon and scrambled eggs. Mrs. Malone kept looking at me, her eyes beseeching me to make more of an impression on him, but it seemed unlikely that I could. Besides, I didn't want to. Even Hedy Lamarr would have trouble being alluring so early in the morning, wouldn't she?

The dark red bus was right on time, and I climbed aboard to take my place among chamber maids, waitresses and grounds workers. The girl I sat beside told me her name was Grace, and she started her day as a waitress at late breakfast in the dining room. She wanted to know what I'd be doing at the resort.

"I'll be working in the office."

"Oh, oh! No tips."

"Do you make a lot that way?"

"Not as much as some. I won't unbutton as far."

The first relief I'd experienced from the flatness of the land was the long, tree-lined lane leading to the resort. The flatness was still there, but it was softened and shaped by the arched branches and the cool, green-black shade. Beyond lay the main lodge, brilliantly white in the sun beyond a circle of white pebbles rimmed by red geraniums.

Arriving guests were unloading their cars at the canopied entrance with the help of bellboys in Kelly-green jackets. I wondered how it would feel to be one of them instead of an unseen cog soon to be fitted into the machine designed to give them a perfect vacation.

A jukebox in the lobby was playing something Hawaiian—a touch that some people associated with leisure, no doubt. Those sliding string sounds had a different effect on me, evoking a touch of decay, something rotten in Denmark. I was similarly affected by the wild, tropical print of the cushions on the rattan lounge furniture and the garish Hawaiian shirt of the desk clerk.

I had a few minutes of freedom before the working day began, and I walked to the windows facing the lake. The brochure came to life— bright umbrellas shading round tables, emerald lawn, long docks and sails white against the water. I didn't have time to explore further, so I sent Hedy out there, watching her thick fall of blue-black hair bounce with the smooth undulation of hips clad in white sharkskin. Then I added the Great Dane she'd been photographed with in a movie magazine I'd cut up to fatten my Hedy scrapbook. I thought I'd given Hedy up, but she was like a teddy bear, resurrected in moments of uncertainty. Now, I made her turn and smile, indicating that this was an all-right place.

I asked the desk clerk where the business office was, and he jerked his thumb at a door behind him, bringing the hand forward again to indicate the swinging gate that would give me access to it. His look was avid but not welcoming. I closed my face to him and passed behind him to the door of the office.

It was a small, crowded room, mostly taken up by the big desk occupied by a large, red-faced man wearing an even more lurid Hawaiian shirt.

"Mr. Stith?"

"Yes?" His tone was short, cross.

"I'm Margaret Langelund."

He had to think about that for a moment, and I decided he must have a lot on his mind to forget someone he'd hired so recently. I had the feeling I ought to salute or something, but I just waited until he figured it out and motioned me to my desk, a small one with a typewriter lurking beneath a cracked, fake leather cover and a wire basket piled high with envelopes.

"Might as well start right in," he said. "Here's the calendar with what's available, and here's the confirmation forms. To names that end in ski, we say yes. To names that end in sky, we say no.

I stared at him, thinking he sounded like something out of "Alice in Wonderland," until he swore and explained.

"No Jews. Get it? If you have any doubts about other names, ask."

A cold ball formed deep in my stomach. I tried to tell myself that I had misheard, but I knew better than that. I sat down and opened the first letter on the pile, relieved to see that it came from someone named Smith.

I typed steadily, working with non-incendiary requests for reservations until I came to one from Daniel Rogalski. "What nationality are the 'ski's?'"

"Polish, probably. They're OK."

"Oh."

Stith looked up impatiently, "Don't tell me they sent me Miss Bleeding Heart of 1948!"

"Does the university know about your policy?"

"It's not something you talk about, understand?"

"Oh yes, I can understand that."

"Well, are you going to do things our way, or aren't you?"

"Of course I am, Mr. Stith." I started to type again, thinking I'd add a note to the "sky" rejections telling them to try again with another spelling if they were really bent on coming to Lake Leisure Resort. Maybe—very probably—they could get by with it. Especially if they looked like Reva Rosendorf. I could do that to assuage my own feelings, but what would it do to theirs? The answer was short and simple—hurt.

I typed on, blaming myself for moral cowardice. When Stith asked if I would do things their way, why hadn't I said, "No!" and walked out? Because Mom had laid down good money for my train ticket, and I needed to make more of it to go to school next year. I hadn't realized what a great luxury moral courage really was.

Employees ate lunch in the least comfortable corner of the dining room with no view of the lake, and they were served leftovers.

Grace brought my plate, a paste of macaroni and unidentified meaty bits, promising that things would be better tomorrow, when today's ham would be reincarnated.

"I brought you iced tea, just guessing," she said, "and I even have a minute to sit down and drink one with you. You're late!"

"They've really got the mail stacked up over there," I said. "Grace, did you know they don't let Jews come here?"

"Come to think of it, I guess I've never seen any."

"You can't always tell by looking, can you?"

"Maybe not, but you sure can by listening. They're noisy."

"Not the ones I know," I said, thinking of the Edelsteins, the only Jewish family in Harlan, and of Reva.

"Get a bunch of 'em together, and they are! Just like a flock of starlings."

I sighed and concentrated on eating my paste. What would happen if I deliberately told some Jewish "guests" their reservation had been confirmed? Surely the resort wouldn't dare to turn them away at the front desk? I wasn't entirely sure, and the thought of such a thing happening made the risk too great.

At the end of the afternoon, I climbed back on the dark red bus and returned to DuLac without ever coming close to the waters of Lake

LaRue. I felt like crying but controlled myself.

With icy resolve, I went looking for a cheap place to eat supper. As long as I had to do something this distasteful to earn money, I meant to keep as much of it as possible. A small diner down the street from the Chippewa Drugstore served a bowl of cream of mushroom soup with crackers for next to nothing. This could be considered a meal that I could eat every night. I tried to convince myself that I was crazy about mushrooms.

Sleepless for hours, I finally dreamed of receiving bushels of letters addressed to Miss Margaret Langelundsky.

Mrs. Malone invited me to breakfast again, saying, "You don't eat enough to keep a canary alive, so you might as well start the day with us. Brightens our morning, doesn't it, Bob?"

Bob grunted and shielded himself with the morning newspaper. He wore a blue work shirt fresh from his mother's ironing board, and the smell of the cloth reminded me of home.

As Birdie brought me a glass of juice, a ray of morning lit the gold wedding band almost buried in flesh that looked like rising bread dough. Her face had the same look, but I performed a mental excavation to her cheek bones and decided that she must have been a pretty girl.

"Think you're going to like your job?" she asked.

What was going on at Lake Leisure Resort really was unspeakable, so I merely said, "I hope so."

I chose Rice Krispies from the half-dozen cereal boxes lined up on the table, delighting in a reprieve from the obligatory oatmeal, and enjoyed the small percussion concert of popping sounds triggered by milk poured from a fat, orange pitcher.

Birdie set a plate of bacon and eggs before her son, whose fork was nearly to his mouth when she touched his shoulder and bowed her head to say, "Bless us, O Lord, and these Thy gifts, which we are about to receive from Thy bounty. Through Christ our Lord. Amen."

They both crossed themselves, and Birdie said, "I guess I forgot to ask what religion you are."

"Protestant," I said, surprised at how private I suddenly considered such information to be.

Birdie sighed but immediately smiled and said, "Oh well, all roads lead to Rome."

I smiled back hypocritically, thinking that I would never even flirt with Catholicism until I was past the age of childbearing. However, there were Catholics and Catholics. Aunt Kam was convinced that Geraldine would become a brood mare when she married Vito Scarpelli, but they never *did* have children.

I made it to the drugstore with a little time to spare and mailed the postcards I had written to Mom and Grandma and to Hoffman. They were pictures of the resort lodge shot from the water, and the umbrella-shaded tables were occupied by beautifully-tanned young people drinking from tall glasses. One of the girls looked like Grace.

When the bus arrived, I mentioned the likeness to Grace, and she said, "Yeah, that's me. Last year Stith made everybody on the dining room crew put on their best stuff and pose. He said the real guests didn't look good enough."

"Well, you do look like somebody in *The Great Gatsby*."

Grace's puzzlement over the reference didn't surprise me. She was going to be a senior at Wisconsin and planned to be a gym teacher.

"Know what was in those glasses?" she asked.

"No, what?"

She laughed. "Water!" Stith was too cheap to fill 'em with anything else. Honestly, Margaret, I don't know how you're going to survive on what he probably pays you without tips."

"By eating less than a canary, I guess. My landlady gives me breakfast—so far—and I have a bowl of soup at night."

Grace clasped my forearm with her strong hand and said, "I'll load your plate at noon."

"Are we ever allowed to swim in the lake?"

"You can do it on your day off—if you can stand to *see* the place when you don't have to. *I* can't, and I'm not crazy about changing in the women's john. Besides, have you seen the lake up close?"

Today, the drive was filled with departing guests. They had peeled noses and a peevish look, as if they hadn't found what they were seeking at Lake Leisure Resort.

I walked through the lobby to the lakeside veranda, trying to ignore the Hawaiian music. The desk clerk, whose name, I had learned, was Howie, was arguing with a man about his bill. Howie wore a different floral shirt today, even wilder than yesterday's selection.

"But you had the suite, Sir."

"That's *your* fault, not mine! You confirmed my reservation for a double room, and if it wasn't available when we got here, that's your problem!"

"You'll have to speak to Mr. Stith, Sir."

I moved out of earshot, weaving through the tables littered with dirty glasses and napkins from the night before to walk out on the dock. My heels brought a hollow resonance from weathered planks better suited to bare feet. My eyes had been focused far out, where the water was blue and a solitary fisherman sat silent and motionless in his small boat. Now I moved closer to the edge and looked down at a fuzzy green mantle undulating obscenely around the pilings. Algae.

The kind of request for reservations I dreaded was halfway down in a pile of mail I opened that morning. Mr. and Mrs. Myron Lansky of Chicago wanted a double with roll-a-ways for two children from August 12 to 19. The letter was impeccably typed beneath the engraved name and address of M.D. Lansky, CPA, and initialled "ds" by some secretary. Lansky's signature was bold and legible.

I went to find the room chart, praying that everything would be booked for those dates, but a second floor corner room was open. Should I confirm and if caught, plead that I had made a mistake because I was so new in the job? It would be so much easier if I could see the Lanskys and decide whether they would (shameful thought) "pass" or determine whether they were tough enough to bear it if they were challenged.

I closed my eyes tightly and prayed, "God, what shall I do?" Hearing no voice from heaven, I grew protective and typed their names on a "regrets" form B. "We regret to inform you that the accommodations you requested are not available on the dates you specified." Form A offered alternate dates, but B was a shutout and in this case, a lie.

Deeply distressed in spirit, I typed a small postscript on the form, "Don't feel bad. The lake is green with algae. M.L."

That helped about as much as handing a candy bar to a Jewish kid on the way to a German shower.

Aside from Gracie, I made few friends among the resort employees, and the working days were so long that few of my waking hours were spent in DuLac. Birdie Malone's hopes of Bob becoming interested in me eventually died, but she'd gotten used to having me at the breakfast table and allowed that arrangement to continue.

When I complained that the town library was reluctant to issue a card to me, she said, "Land's sake, take mine! It just sits here gathering dust because I've got all I can do to get the St. Anthony Messenger read every month before a new one comes."

I thanked her, regarding the loan of a library card as a true token of trust. Why, I wondered, did she have a card if she never used it?

Birdie Malone was fairly intuitive. Her bright gaze picked up questions before they were asked, and now she said, "I'd always hoped that Bob would take to reading, but he don't seem to care for it much."

"Not the stuff *you* dragged home for me," he said, and the sound of his voice was as surprising as the utterance of Balaam's ass. I had forgotten that he might be listening to the talk between Birdie and me. He was just there, like the refrigerator.

"What kind of stuff?" I asked him, but he had disappeared behind the newspaper again, and Birdie answered for him.

"There's nothing wrong with 'The Song of Bernadette' by that fellow—what's his name? Waffle or something like that. Have you read it, Margaret?"

"No, but I've seen it at my aunt's house. She belongs to the Book-of-the-Month Club." I carried my dishes to the sink. "If you'll just leave these until I get home, I'll wash them."

"Land's sake, I couldn't stand to have them sitting there all day! Besides, it gives me something to do."

Grandma said the same thing sometimes, and I couldn't imagine myself choosing dishwashing over daydreaming as "something to do." Was it possible that time—years of it—removed the desire to daydream and replaced it with the urge to do something, anything?

The morning mail was from people with unequivocally Anglo-Saxon names, and most of them could be accommodated. In due course, they, too, would be hearing the jukebox strains of "Sweet Leilani."

The day was muggy with a hazy sunlight. Once in a great while, a half-hearted breeeze would carry the rotten smell of the algae into the lobby, mix it with cigarette smoke and pass it along to the office.

I had an unopened letter from Hoffman in my purse which I meant to read at some quiet moment, but there was no letup until lunch. I crunched across the gravel drive to the dining room, pulling the elasticized neckline of my flowered pique dress down to bare my shoulders. If I had known it would be so hot, I would have worn a strapless bra, but now I had to hide the straps in the puffed sleeves that rode high on my arms.

Howie was the only other occupant of the employees' table, and he whistled at my shoulder arrangement.

"It's hot," I said.

"Sure is!" he leered. "Say, want to catch a movie some night?"

That was the last thing I wanted to do, as I found Howie completely unattractive, but I didn't need him as an enemy. "Some night."

"What about tonight?"

"Sorry, I have other plans." They consisted of hot-footing it to the DuLac Public Library, which had short and capricous hours.

"OK," said Howie, taking a last swipe at his plate and rising, "I'll be in touch."

Being in touch with Howie was a truly revolting prospect, but I managed to smile and wave him off with a casual flutter of the fingers.

Mr. Stith passed the table with a youngish man in white ducks, boat shoes and an open shirt with an ascot tie. I stared because I'd never seen an ascot worn other than on a movie screen. The man smiled at me and followed Stith, who accorded me all the notice due a fly speck.

About an hour after I returned to the office, Stith brought the man back with him, and they sat down to discuss outboard motors. As the visitor started to leave, he paused at my desk and said, "Arnold, you've neglected to introduce your secretary."

Stith scowled and cleared his throat, "Oh. Well, this is Margaret Langelund."

I smiled and waited for the rest of the introduction, but it wasn't forthcoming. Stith had returned to the papers on his desk.

"I'm Gary Johnson, and I liked that dress better the way it was before."

I blushed and put my hand in the big, tanned paw he offered, saying, "Just a bit of temporary air-conditioning."

"Are you from DuLac? I don't believe I've seen you before."

"I'm from Iowa, but I'm living in DuLac—with Mrs. Malone on Beech Street."

He nodded and went out, leaving me to regret the boldness of offering that much information. If Mr. Stith were a friendlier type, I could find out more about Gary Johnson, but things being as they were, I wouldn't ask.

As soon as the bus got back to town that night, I went to the library and miraculously found it open. Not expecting to have such luck often, I searched for a fat book that would last as long as possible and settled on Sigrid Undset's *Kristin Lavransdatter*. I started it over my bowl of mushroom soup, clumsy though it was to handle on the small, teetering table. Before I finished the last cracker, I was deep in the 14th Century. The writing struck some deep chords in me, and I continued to read as I walked to the house on Beech Street. In fact, I was reluctantly closing the book to get ready for bed when I realized that the book mark I was using was the letter from Hoffman, still unopened.

His survey had gone well and would be winding up at the end of the month. On his way East, he planned to stop in DuLac for a short visit—if I didn't mind. Of course, I didn't mind, I told myself, suppressing my shameful enthusiasm for the more than decent dinner I knew he would buy me.

He closed his letter, "A kiss for each almond eyelid and more love than you know."

I conjured up Gary Johnson in the crisp whites that deepened his tan and the pale blue ascot that intensified his eyes, sighed and set my Big Ben to wake me for another day in the 20th Century.

That day was so hot that the landscape undulated before our eyes on the way to work. Gracie kindly offered to make me a sandwich so I could eat my lunch on the dock.

Aside from the ubiquitous Hawaiian music augmented by Howie's tuneless whistling between his teeth, the morning was quiet. The tennis courts were deserted, and the bars were busy earlier than usual. Down at the swimming area, some of the braver guests were wading through the slime to reach cleaner water, but the sailboats were becalmed in the still air.

At noon, I picked up my sandwich in the kitchen and headed for the dock, only to discover that it was too hot for sitting.

"Care to come aboard?"

Gary Johnson stood on the deck of a cabin cruiser, holding out his hand in invitation. I stepped out of my shoes, hiked up a fairly narrow skirt and took a giant step onto the deck of the Cora Jane. Somehow, we collided, and there was egg salad all over his crisp, striped shirt.

I stammered my apologies, but he just grinned and fed the bits of egg to the small fish that swarmed to the pilings when the first fragment dropped.

"Why don't you check out the refrigerator in the galley while I take this baby out to find some breeze?"

"I have to be back in twenty minutes."

He saluted. "Whatever you say, but if that was lunch, you'd better find a replacement."

I nodded, rueful. "It was. And I hate to ask another favor, but will you grab my shoes? They might fall in, and if I show up in the office barefoot, Mr. Stith probably will fire me."

"Then you could come to work for Johnson Marine."

I found a peach and a chunk of cheese in the compact refrigerator and climbed upward to sit in the leather seat opposite his. He handled the wheel with casual assurance, and as the boat turned and headed for open lake, the sun blazed on the wide, gold watchband imbedded in the grain-gold hairs on his arm. What was it about that watch pushed high that was so attractive to me? I could understand it no better than an urge I had to press my thumb into the hollow behind the earlobe of a guy who sat in front of me in the tiered lecture hall of the chemistry building. I didn't want to see his face, especially, but that hollow—rendered familiar by three Biology of Man classes a week—was precious to me.

I took a bite of the peach, and the sweet juice ran down my chin. Gary Johnson would think I was a total disaster anytime I came near food, and I was beginning to believe it. I wiped my chin surreptitiously and took a bite of cheese.

The lake was bigger than I had supposed. When Gary turned the boat again and cut the motor, we were facing the resort, and it looked like the little villages that surround toy trains. It also had regained its postcard enchantment.

"Peaches taste like summer, don't they?" he said.

"Want a bite?" I offered.

He clasped the wrist of the hand that held the peach, and I expected him to bring the fruit to his mouth, but instead, he leaned close and kissed me lightly.

"Double sweet."

I suppressed a sigh, having recognized another half-god. Concentrating on the wrist, I had cherished higher hopes.

"What do you do at the marine place?" I asked.

"Everything. I own it."

"Oh."

"I prefer sailing to motors, however. When I'm out on the water, I don't like noise."

"Is this your boat?"

"Nope. Belongs to the resort. Stith named it for his wife."

Cora Jane Stith. Somehow, I hadn't thought about him *having* a wife. I listened to the waves slapping against the hull and revelled in the cooler air. "This is nice."

"You'll have to come sailing with me on Lake Geneva. Sometimes we stay out all night and come in just in time for breakfast."

Time. I looked at my watch and panicked. In five minutes, I was supposed to be seated at my typewriter repelling Jews.

"I can see that you want to go back."

"Not want—*have* to."

He turned the key and nothing happened, but I wasn't worried. If he owned a marine motor company, he could make the thing work. He tried several times and started to frown. Then he got some tools and started to tinker. I was fifteen minutes late, then half an hour.

"Well," he finally said, "the radio seems to be out too, so we'll have to go for the flags."

I guess I knew that sailors communicated with flags, but I'd never seen it done and thought those bright banners were chiefly for decoration. Gary waved them energetically—a red and white one halved vertically and a blue and red one divided horizontally, then a quartered square of black and yellow on the diagonal and a purple one with a small, white square in the middle.

"What are you saying?" I asked.

"Nothing if nobody happens to be looking. Otherwise, I'm trying to spell 'help.' I've never had to do this before."

No figures were observable on the shore, and no other boats were on the water at this hour. Gary soon grew tired of waving the flags.

"I'll just hoist 'em on a halyard and hope somebody looks this way."

"What if they don't know the code?"

"Then we'll have a long, lazy afternoon out here. Why don't you bring up a couple of beers?"

I fetched the cold, sweating cans, and with my first swallow, I felt the familiar stab of pain in my shoulder. It was as if the whole tribe of Jorgen women were there with us.

Mom: "You should have known you didn't have time. Why did you go?"

Grandma: "Men don't always know as much as we think they do."

Aunt Kam: "Heaven knows what people will think—you two all alone in the middle of a lake all that time!"

Aunt Valborg: "Make hay while the sun shines, Kid!"

Cousin Marianne: "Leave it to you to do something stupid like that!"

"Penny for your thoughts," Gary said, reaching into his pocket for a coin and flipping it into my lap.

I gave it back. "Not for sale." When I didn't want to flirt, I seemed to do it best. I looked away, staring at the expanse of Lake LaRue between us and the toy buildings of the resort. I could never swim that far.

"You're worried about Stith, aren't you?"

"Yes. Even when I do everything right, he seems to be unhappy with me."

"Ever meet his wife?"

"No."

"When you do, you'll understand. Her family owns the place, and after he got a waitress pregnant last summer, the old she-buffalo really came down on him. If he so much as smiled at you, one of her spies would jump out of the woodwork and yell 'Gotcha!'"

I thought that over, finding it incredible that any girl would let Stith get close enough for such an outcome.

"If you'd like to catch some sun, you can find a suit on a hook in the john."

"Thanks, but I think somebody's coming to rescue us." I pointed at the motor boat that was a mere speck in the distance but growing larger as it came toward us.

He smiled crookedly. "Sorry to hear you put it that way."

"Oh—I didn't mean—I mean, I—"

"OK, OK. So you're a nice girl, and you need to know me better. That can be arranged, can't it?"

The alternative was a span of long evenings on the porch with Birdie or reading *Kristin Lavransdatter* until I went blind. His Scandinavian surname was reassuring, and he had a sexy wrist. I smiled and said, "I guess it can."

Mr. Stith had sent the kid with the motor boat after Howie reported that Gary Johnson's boat was "way out, not moving, and flying a bunch of funny flags."

Gary threw up his hands and rolled his eyes.

The kid towed us in, and Gary went back to the office with me to explain.

Before either of us could speak, Stith said, "Where in hell have you been? The phone has been ringing non-stop, and there's a ton of mail that hasn't been touched!"

Gary lounged in the doorway and drawled, "Arnie, I seem to remember a time when you didn't *mind* a little engine trouble on the Cora Jane."

Stith turned redder than his usual shade, bit back whatever he was dying to say and turned his back on both of us.

Gary gave me a jaunty wave and a wink as he left, and I tackled the mail. People whose names ended in "sky" and "berg" seemed fatally attracted to this place, I thought, finding three in the stack of letters. I wrote the same note to each of them: "Better luck elsewhere. This lake is scummy, and the boats don't work. M.L."

I heard nothing from Gary Johnson for more than a week, and during that time, I buried myself deep in 14th-Century Norway during and after the consumption of my evening bowl of cream of mushroom soup. Kristin Lavransdatter took my mind off the bland taste of what I was eating and almost made me forget how dull it looked.

When I got back from the restaurant, Birdie Malone was all excited about the first phone call I'd received at her house.

"It was a man!" she said.

"Any message?"

She shook her head. "I really tried to get him to say who he was, but he wouldn't. I told him you'd be here in about fifteen minutes, and I sure hope he calls back."

"If it's important, I'm sure he will."

Birdie was bursting to review the small events of her day, patting the cushion beside her on the porch swing invitingly. Why couldn't her stupid son talk to her once in awhile?

I was saved by the phone. Gary Johnson said he had "a few people over at the house" and asked if he could pick me up in a few minutes. I was agreeable and went straight to my room to get ready, knowing that the wildly curious Birdie was suffering the delay on the porch swing.

She didn't meet Gary, either. I watched from my window, and as soon as his convertible pulled up, I was out the door and down the steps. He came around the back of the car to put me in, and I waved to Birdie.

"Sorry about the short notice."

"No problem. It was between you and the Middle Ages."

The car was bright yellow and sleek. As we gained speed and the wind took my hair, I felt a twinge of regret about "my darling Arthur" Blair and the convertible that made him believe the war was over. Gary's sexy wrist showed to advantage as he drove with casual authority; right hand on the steering wheel, left on the top of the door.

His house was in a part of town I'd never seen, and it looked very much like its neighbors—new and pastel. The drive was filled with cars, also new and pastel. He rang his own doorbell to demonstrate that it played the opening bars of "Hail, Hail, the Gang's All Here," and a black-haired girl in extremely short shorts and a blouse knotted to bare her midriff came to the door with a glass of something in one hand and a cigarette in the other. She was barefoot.

"Glad you could make it, Gary," she teased, swinging the screen door wide. "Who's your friend?"

"This is Margaret Langelund. Margaret, meet Vivian Carmichael."

I put out my hand and immediately withdrew it, seeing that she had none free. We both laughed, and I decided that I liked her even if she *did* make me feel like a Baptist missionary in my prim skirt and blouse.

Gary's "few people" turned out to be quite a few, and I told him I'd never remember their names. Maybe I could if they'd stay in one place, but they were always shifting—sitting on floor cushions, ambling to the bar and moving around a table loaded with food. They all said "Hi" when we were introduced and went right back to whatever they had been doing.

"Why don't you get yourself a plate of food, and I'll find you a drink," Gary said.

After weeks of gray-beige bowls of mushroom soup, I needed no persuasion. Cherry tomatoes, chips and dip, cheese, and slices of ham and turkey went down singing hymns.

Gary brought me a tall glass of something colorless with a floating lime wedge, saying, "I forgot to ask what you drink. Gin and tonic all right?"

"Great!" I said, never having had one. I made my way to a screened porch and carefully lowered my body into a canvas sling on a metal frame. I managed it without spilling anything, though I doubted I'd be able to get up without help. The chair was shaped like an oriole's nest. The gin and tonic was limeade with a pleasant edge, and I polished it off thirstily. Somebody took my glass and brought me another.

None of the girls wore much, I observed, but what they *did* have on was linen or silk like my cousin Marianne's expensive summer clothes. All of them had bright red toenails. They were deeply tanned, too, but not as dark as the men, who had raccoon masks from wearing sunglasses and talked about C boats and E boats.

When the bodies shifted, I could see a little of the nautical decor of the house: colored glass balls caught in a piece of fishnet, navigating instruments, sailboat pictures. I remembered Grandma saying, "There are land Danes and sea Danes," and I had asked which were we? "Land Danes," she said. From the pleasure I was taking in all this nautical stuff, I figured that I might be the other kind—a sea Dane in the midst of land Danes—a volunteer cornstalk in a bean field.

I'd cleaned my plate, drained my second glass of gin and tonic and was thinking about catapulting myself out of the sling when Gary came out on the porch and apologized for neglecting me.

"That's OK, I'm having a good time." It was true. I had a pleasant buzz in my head and nary a worry. Mr. Stith and his rejection of the world's "berg" and "sky" population seemed like an unpleasant dream.

Gary took my glass and disappeared, and when some squinty-eyed sailor came past and offered me a cigarette, I took it. I hadn't tried one since my early teens, and it made me even more light-headed. The letters in the bottom of the ashtray that read "Geneva Yacht Club" swam in and out of focus.

"You OK?" the sailor asked. His name was Orv—unless that was the brand of his shirt embroidered on the pocket. Where I came from, only filling station employees had names on their pockets. "Need some air?"

"We're *on* the porch," I pointed out, marvelling at his stupidity.

"Look, Honey, why don't you go down and play the one-armed bandit for awhile? Gary keeps the nickels in the fishbowl right beside it, and maybe you'll hit the jackpot. It's cooler down in the basement, and it wouldn't hurt you to move a little bit."

He pulled me out of the sling and propelled me to the downward steps, which I negotiated by clutching the handrail tightly.

The couple that had been playing the slot machine stood aside for me, saying they'd had no luck at all. The girl laughed and said, "Lucky in love, unlucky at gambling!"

"How do you do it?" I asked.

The man took a nickel from the fishbowl and demonstrated. I tried it, and coins cascaded out of the thing.

"Wow!" said the girl, "You really have the touch. Some thrill, huh?"

I shook my head. "Nope, it wasn't my nickel."

"What's the difference?"

With the sensation that I was speaking with exceptional clarity from a bottomless fund of wisdom, I said, "I didn't risk anything."

They laughed uneasily and left me. I started to pick up the scattered coins, got tired of the task and kicked some of them under the rug. Then I saw the couch across the room and zig-zagged over to it. It smelled slightly musty—like the algae on Lake LaRue—but I threw myself down on it and closed my eyes.

Someone was shaking my shoulder gently. I opened my eyes, looking around in confusion.

"Hey, I'd better get you home," Gary said. "Why didn't you tell me you hadn't eaten? I was pouring you doubles."

I sat up and looked at my watch. It was 2:30 a.m. No wonder it was quiet. Everyone else had gone home. "Well," I said ruefully, "I guess we didn't get to know each other any better."

His hand tightened on my shoulder, "It was a temptation, but I'm not that much of a rat. Next time."

Relieved that I would see him again and have a chance to alter the terrible impression I'd made, I swung my feet to the floor and got up so quickly that I felt dizzy. We made our way through the rooms cluttered with dirty glasses, plates of uneaten food and brimming ashtrays.

"Looks like it was some party," I said. "Sorry I missed it," and Gary laughed.

Our next date was for a golf tournament on Sunday. For this occasion I chose a dress that had been Marianne's—lavendar with a plunging neckline—and high-heeled pumps. I hadn't really visualized such an event, but I guess I thought you sat somewhere and watched the golfers go by the way you watched events from the grandstand at the county fairgrounds.

Gary gave me a rather odd look when he picked me up, but it changed to a smile so quickly that I thought perhaps I had imagined it. It had rained the night before, and my heels sank deep into the turf as we followed the favorite. I was no less bored by a perfect drive than by walking to the next hole. Gary was completely absorbed by the play most of the time, and the rest of the time he looked down the neck of my dress. I longed to sit down in some obscure corner where I wouldn't stand out from the spectators in sportswear.

At long last, we went to the clubhouse for a drink. This time, I was wary as well as thirsty. I ordered a Coke and plied Gary with questions about himself. He came from one of the Chicago suburbs, he said, and not until I pressed him to be more specific did he say it was Cicero.

"Why do you act like you're ashamed of it?"

He looked at me in amazement. "You really don't know, do you?"

"I wouldn't ask if I did."

"Because, my sweet innocent, a lot of nasty stuff with guns happened in Cicero. When you say you're from there, people think you're with the Mob."

"Oh." The mention of guns reminded me to ask him, "Were you in the war?"

"Just missed it. I wanted to be a Seabee."

"And where did you go to college?"

"What makes you think I did?"

I shrugged. "I just do. People who haven't are sort of anxious, trying harder to prove something."

He laughed. "Northwestern. Engineering. Say, you're looking mighty pretty today."

"And all wrong. I should have asked."

"Now Margaret," he teased, "you shouldn't be anxious, you being a college girl and all that."

I sighed. "I guess one year isn't enough."

"Maybe not, but when you're as old as I am, you'll realize that first year was the best of them all—the reaching year."

"Reaching for what?"

"Not that kind of reaching. What I'm talking about is sailing on a course with the wind forward of the beam—going like a bat out of hell! That's reaching. If we get the wind, you can see for yourself when I take you sailing."

Later, when I was sitting on Birdie Malone's back steps cleaning the mud off my heels with a stick, she came out to talk.

"I've seen that young fellow around town. Johnson, isn't it?"

"Yes, Gary Johnson. He owns Johnson Marine."

Birdie wiped her plump hands with her apron. "Got money, they say."

"I suppose he does."

"Wouldn't be a bad catch."

"If I felt the right way about him."

"And you don't?"

"Nope, and my Grandma says there's no sense in wasting time with a man who doesn't make your bones burn."

Birdie sighed deeply. "Well, Timothy Malone did that, all right, but he's been gone so long I can scarcely remember it. I thought God gave me the baby to make up for taking Tim so young, but Bobby—well, you know Bobby."

It was true that "Bobby" wouldn't make up for much. A dog or a cat would have been better company.

"Maybe I shouldn't ask, but how did your husband die?"

She smiled sadly. "He was too friendly—too full of the blarney. His pals would never let him leave the saloon on his own two feet, and he shouldn't have tried the night he stepped in front of a car. I called to tell him the pains had started—the only thing in this world that would have brought him. If I could just go back to that day and live it over, knowing what I know now!" Her eyes welled with tears.

I was speechless with pity, thinking of my own grandmother, widowed when she was pregnant with Mom—succeeding generations that never touched.

"Ah well," Birdie said briskly, "it's crazy to keep looking down the road not taken, temptation though it is. I had another beau who was well-fixed, and if I'd married him, I wouldn't be renting rooms today."

"And I wouldn't know you," I reached out and squeezed her plump hand.

"Well, don't be hasty in getting rid of this young man. He may grow on you."

"We'll see."

The sail on Lake Geneva was preceded by a party in the home of Joe and Annette Kirwin, newly-married friends of Gary's who lived in the town. I guess it was a home, though the furniture consisted of a mattress on the floor, some cushions and a card table and chairs. The broad windowsills were the only counter tops in the kitchen, and the loud crash of falling pots and pans was a constant accompaniment to music from the portable record player in the living room.

Joe Kirwin was a daily newspaper reporter, and most of the other guests were connected with the paper in some way—photographers, writers, circulation people. Annette had been a society reporter, but when they married, she had to resign in deference to the paper's anti-nepotism policy.

The main beverage was a huge crock of something called Purple Jesus made from grape juice and grain alcohol, and I told Gary I couldn't possibly drink anything with such a name.

"Are you religious?" he asked, surprised.

"Yes, I guess I am," I said, feeling slightly guilty that it didn't show. It occurred to me that I hadn't tried to evangelize anyone for quite some time.

Gary picked up a fork and struck his glass, quieting the noise in the room, "Now hear this! Anyone crewing for me will save the drinking for later. I want to come off that lake alive!"

Joe laughed. "You may have to sail alone, my friend!"

"Oh, come on, we were counting on you and Annette."

"You can," Annette promised. "I'll watch him!"

I watched everyone, fascinated by fragments of conversation about a business I planned to enter. They sounded as if they hated it, complaining about "lousy editing," "rotten headlines," "crappy assignments," and "starvation wages," but their eyes glowed. They literally vibrated with the proud joy of "being in the know," a privilege withheld from ordinary mortals.

I mentioned this paradox to Annette, and she said, "In this business, bitching about everything is a sign of health."

She gave me more information about the others, reinforcing the brief introductions made when we arrived.

"The little guy with the cigar is Earnest Pease, the religion editor, and that skinny, cadaverous guy in the corner is Chad Miller, the sports editor."

Neither looked right for the job, which led me to believe I was wrong in thinking the plump woman sitting cross-legged on the mattress was the food editor. I was preparing to ask Annette when I felt a sharp pain in my ankle and let out a yelp.

"Charley, I'm cutting you off!" Annette said crossly, bending to grab the mop of curly hair at the level of my distress. Its owner crawled off on hands and knees as she explained, "That's Charley McAffee who writes the editorials. He nibbles ankles when he gets liquored up."

"I'll try to stay out of his way. And that woman over there—" I pointed to the mattress, "food?"

"No, that's Evelyn Gissing, fashion. The last time she bought a new outfit was when Hitler marched into Czechoslovakia."

I looked around for Gary and couldn't find him in any of the rooms. A few minutes later, he came in to announce that the wind was right, and we'd better get on the water.

Annette grabbed a jacket and summoned Joe. I asked her, "Are you just going to leave these maniacs here?"

"Sure, there's nothing they can hurt. We don't *have* anything."

The boat looked sleek but frail. Annette and Joe jumped aboard with casual assurance, but I hung back, measuring the possibilities of its sudden movement when I was in mid-air, until Gary grasped my upper arms and pulled me on.

"Is there anything special I should know?"

"When I yell 'Coming about,' duck."

The sail went up and caught the wind, looking like the giant wing of a pale moth in the shore lights. I was enthralled by our silent speed. I forgot to duck only once, and Gary pulled me down in time.

Eventually, he left the necessary duties to the Kirwins and came to sit beside me. "This is reaching," he said. "How do you like it?"

"I'd like it to go on forever."

He chuckled. "Wouldn't we all? Unfortunately, the wind won't always cooperate."

He laced his fingers through mine, and we leaned back, watching the stars in silence. I was thinking of Birdie's advice; wavering. The wooing of the boat was persuasive.

"Where did you learn to sail?" I asked.

"At summer camp on this lake. I was about ten." He unlaced our fingers and put an arm around me. It felt good in the Mentholatum chill of our fast skim over the water. "That was the summer they sent me home."

"Why?"

"Because I pushed a kid off the dock and stepped on his fingers when he tried to crawl out of the lake. He couldn't swim, and the water was over his head."

Horrified, I said, "Somebody else saved him, I hope."

"Oh, sure. The place was crawling with counselors."

"Did you hate him that much?"

"Didn't hate him at all. Actually, I liked him, and I never *have* been able to figure out why I did that."

I stiffened in his circling arm, and he laughed softly, "Don't worry, you're safe. If you're wondering why I told you that, chalk it up to honesty."

I laughed too, but the sound was forced. Annette and Joe eventually joined us, and hours passed in casual conversation. The wind died as the eastern sky grew pink.

"Nifty maneuvering!" Joe said, "We'll make it to Rattigan's for breakfast."

I drank my first stinger in a knotty pine booth at Rattigan's. It tasted so good and was so warming that I had another, and when the scrambled eggs arrived, I scarcely knew what I was eating. I was still on the lake—reaching—and trying to erase the image of a ten-year-old Gary stepping on a desperate kid's fingers.

Hoffman arrived a day early. Half-dead from lack of sleep, I had nearly finished my lunch in the employee section of the dining room when I looked up and saw him opening a menu at one of the lakeside tables. He smiled and nodded at me, as if it were a pleasant chance meeting, but I had the angry feeling of being spied upon and took my time about going over to his table. I was even pleasant to Howie in my lingering, which shocked him greatly. Usually, I was up and out of there in minutes to spend as much of my short lunch period as possible beside the water.

"Hey, how about that movie?" Howie said.

I glanced over at Hoffman and told Howie I had company from out of town. Hoffman was wonderfully tan, and his beard was luxuriant. Sitting down, he was magnificent. When I could postpone my departure no longer, I paused at his table and said, "I didn't expect you until tomorrow."

"I had to start a day early because of an appointment in Boston, but I couldn't reach you to tell you. The woman who answered the phone said you were out sailing."

"Yes, you couldn't reach me because I was reaching."

Hoffman, being an old salt from the eastern seaboard, laughed. "I kept on trying, and she was a bit peeved when she answered the phone at four o'clock in the morning." He left a significant pause for me to fill which I ignored.

"I have to get back to work."

"What time shall I come for you? We'll have dinner."

"Not here, I hope. I'll get back to town the usual way, and you can pick me up at Mrs. Malone's at six."

"I'll count the minutes."

Grace stopped me near the door and whispered, "You know him?"

"No, Gracie, I just stop and talk to every strange man I see."

"Bite my head off, why don't you?"

"Oh Grace, I'm sorry. I'm so tired I don't know what I'm doing!"

She patted my arm in forgiveness, and I went out into the dizzying heat. This was the afternoon when I confirmed one of the best lakeside rooms for Mr. and Mrs. Hyman Cohen. When Mr. Stith yelled at me, I snapped, "Since when do we turn down the Irish?"

I waited, head bowed, to be fired. It wouldn't be the end of the world, because not that much of the summer was left. He must have had the same thought. Tearing the Cohens' confirmation card in two, he only scowled and said, "Very funny!"

Somehow I made it through the day and back to Birdie's house, but I couldn't take a bath because Bob was wallowing in the tub.

"He has a date!" Birdie said, curling her plump fingers in ecstasy. "Good for him!"

I changed clothes, casting looks of longing at the bed. No time for even a quick nap. I found Hoffman's pin in a tangle of costume jewelry, wondering if he had noticed I wasn't wearing it earlier. Then, in a fit of perversity, I doused myself with Evening in Paris.

The sight of Hoffman's familiar car mellowed me somewhat, reminding me of Iowa City, my paradise lost. The back seat was now full of rocks. Hoffman was dressed in a suit, white shirt and tie, and I was sure that Birdie would be impressed as she watched our departure—if I could manage to jump into the car before he got around the back to stand beside me. At least I let him do the door shutting.

Before he turned the key in the ignition, he turned to me and said, "Hello!" as if we were meeting for the first time in this strange state and kissed the air almost imperceptibly.

We went to the best restaurant in town: white linen and real flowers on the tables and air conditioning like a deep freeze. When I tried to look at a menu the size of a child's blackboard, the words ran together, and I asked him to choose for me.

"Anything will be better than a bowl of mushroom soup," I said, telling him about my nightly economy menu.

"Margaret, that's not even healthy!"

"Do I look unhealthy?"

"I could be arrested for describing the way you look to me."

He ordered wine, which we sipped while he talked about his survey and the exciting mineral deposits he'd found. Exciting to him, maybe. But I grew less critical as the wine warmed me and our seated position put us on the same footing. Footing? More like rumping. I giggled and sang, "I love you for sedimental reasons."

He broke off whatever he was saying with a startled laugh. "I'm boring you stiff!" He reached into an inside pocket of his coat and brought out a small box. "Here. Brought you something."

Please, God, don't make it something I can't resist but can't take!" The box contained a bracelet of linked tortoise shell ovals inlaid with silver boats.

"From the Fiji Islands. I traded a Swiss army knife for it during the war. Never knew what to do with it until now."

"It's beautiful, Hoffman. What kind of boats are they?"

"Outriggers. They have an extra spar for stability."

I inspected the finely-worked silver closely, thinking the extra spar ruined the lines of the boat. Furthermore, this was no craft for reaching. Hoffman reached across the table to fasten the bracelet around my wrist, and I felt imprisoned.

"I shouldn't have it," I said, "your mother or your sister—"

He ignored that because our dinner was being served—mounds of fat, pink shrimp; au gratin potatoes; out-of-season asparagus with a golden sauce; tossed salad that was a veritable garden. He began to eat with obvious pleasure, but after a few bites, I put down my fork.

"What's the matter?" he asked.

"Maybe my stomach has shrunk. Or maybe I'm just tired after spending most of last night on the lake." The room was starting to revolve, and I took a hasty swallow of ice water that stabilized things.

Concerned about me, Hoffman hurried his dinner and signalled for the check. I thought he'd drive straight to Birdie Malone's, but instead, he stopped the car deep in DuLac's only park. He opened the trunk to find a blanket. Parting the trailing branches of a willow tree near the small stream that ran through the park, he made us a bower.

We sat inside, feet straight out in front of us, and leaned back on our hands. The stream made a low, throaty sound; fireflies winked outside the green curtain of branches. I could smell the starch in Hoffman's white shirt and felt sure he was gagging on my Evening in Paris.

"How did you know about this place?" I asked, "I didn't."

"I scouted it this afternoon—right after I saw you at lunch."

Then we were quiet for a long time until he said, "It's not going to work, is it? I met you too soon."

I felt the shape of his pin with my fingers and my other hand came up to work the catch. It was too dark to see, but he seemed to know what I was doing. When I reached for his hand, it was there for me, palm cupped to receive the pin.

"You should have the bracelet, too, and all the other—"

He closed my lips with two fingers. "Please keep them and wear them. I'll enjoy thinking of that."

"Oh, Hoffman!" I sobbed, throwing my arms around his neck and weeping into the base of his throat. His beard grazed my forehead, and I thrust myself against it, wanting the punishment of its wirey texture. A car drove past on the upper road, its headlights penetrating the willow just long enough to light the silver outriggers on my wrist. No stability spar for me.

He took me home, then, or to as much of a home as I possessed in DuLac. Our lips touched lightly in farewell, and Birdie was amazed to see me home so soon. Bob, she reported happily, was still out. Good for him. I fell on the bed in my clothes, too exhausted to wash my face or brush my teeth. In my dreams, I was lost in dark waters, going down with no one to hear my cries.

In the morning, I couldn't get out of bed. My legs were leaden. When all attempts to help myself failed, I called for Birdie in a voice that sounded weak and distant, even to me.

Upon hearing my symptoms, she crossed herself and breathed, "My God, what if you have polio?"

"Do you think you could call a doctor?"

"Look, Honey, why don't we just get you dressed and on the train so you can see your doctor at home?"

"I'm not sure I can make it."

"Sure you can! Bob hasn't left for work yet, and he can drive you to the station. I'll start packing for you right now!"

I turned my face into the pillow so she couldn't see me cry. I could hear the dresser drawers opening, the snap of the catches on my grandfather's suitcase, and Birdie's under-the-breath litany of "Jesus, Joseph and Mary!"

"Bob!" she shrieked, and the sound cut through my skull painfully. I could hear his slow footsteps coming toward my room and pulled the covers over my head.

"What do you want?"

Birdie explained, and he assented with less truculence than usual. His date must have gone well.

Maxfield and Parrish looked down from their perfect environment with disdain as Birdie helped me to a sitting position and thrust the shoes on my feet.

"Lucky that you're all dressed and everything. All you've got to do is run a comb through your hair and put on a dab of lipstick." She picked up my purse and fished for the tube of Revlon. "Got money?"

"Some. Payday is tomorrow."

"I'll go along and buy your ticket. You can send it to me."

"Thank you." I felt grim. Now I knew what biblical lepers went through. What if I *did* have polio? I'd have to spend the rest of my life in an iron lung—if there was anything left of it to spend. I could be cruel and tell Birdie she needn't be in such a hurry because she'd already been exposed, but now *I* was the one in a hurry. I wanted to go home.

Bob whistled "Someone to Watch Over Me" as he drove to the station, and Birdie, despite her anxiety, shot him shining glances. She cradled her arms as if they already held a grandchild.

I remembered that I had left *Kristin Lavransdatter* on the dresser and asked Birdie to take it back to the library for me. I was sorry I hadn't finished it, because it was much too heavy to manage in an iron lung.

Birdie bought my ticket while I waited on the platform, swaying dizzily in the early hours of a day that was hot much too soon. Beads of sweat clung to the down on her upper lip as she handed me the ticket at arm's length. Bob lifted my case onto the train.

"Come on, Ma," he said, "I'll be late for work."

Birdie looked worried about leaving before I was safely out of town, but I summoned all my energy to tell her it was OK and ask if she would call Mr. Stith.

"I'll tell him," she said, blowing a kiss from a distance. I wondered what she'd tell him.

She had explained that I must change trains at Savannah, and I was beyond caring. If I couldn't haul myself off this one, I would just stay on it forever like the Flying Dutchman. They'd come into the car and stare at an old, old lady dressed in the fashion of the late 1940s, wondering how she got there, and I would just stare back, saying nothing.

Just to be on the safe side, however, I caught the sleeve of the conductor and told him about the change I had to make. I asked him to alert me in plenty of time, as I was "feeling a bit peaked." Odd that I would use a term I always avoided—one that I hated to hear on the lips of Mom and Grandma.

I leaned back against the soiled white towel covering the gray-green plush headrest, watching the flat landscape rush past with increasing speed. The car was hot, and I was desperately thirsty, but I couldn't negotiate the bucking connections between the cars to do anything about it.

What if I did have something awful? Something you died from? What if I carried my own death in me at this very moment? I tried to tell myself that everyone carried death from the moment of birth—that it was there, ready to unfold at the right time. Humans were like tulip bulbs, fully equipped for all they were to do and be from the beginning. All they had to do was take root and get on with it.

I tried to steel myself to the bravery with which Bette Davis met blindness in "Dark Victory," but she had a man who loved her to help her bear it. Thinking of that, I felt a rage that rose from my leaden legs to the top of my skull. I would *not* die until my demise devastated a man who was more than a half-god. And I would *not* die until I found a love that was on the side of life. I was sick of "Liebestod" and "Mayerling" and trampled fingers on a dock. I chose life, and having done so, slept until the conductor shook me awake and put me off at Savannah.

How I managed not to lose my grandfather's suitcase is more than I know. The features of my helpers were hazy, but their voices were kind. Other faces and voices attended me when I detrained in Manilla, and Uncle Karl caught me as I fell.

I had an exotic viral pneumonia, the doctor said, brought on by poor nutrition and lack of rest. I was to stay in bed until otherwise advised and take the medicine he prescribed.

As I was recuperating in the bedroom with the black lacquer furniture left by the Farleys, I had a few visitors: Merrilee (I was glad I thought to have Mom put the Evening in Paris bottle on the dresser), Lotus (who brought me chocolate malts) and my old nemesis, Mary Lois Engle (who wanted to know which sorority had the most class).

Reverend Boysen came to call and prayed over me. He said my illness might be God's way of removing me from a sinful environment, and he didn't even know about the Purple Jesus.

I really didn't care who came or went, and Mom was clearly worried. She came in and sat on the cane-seated black rocker, clasping and unclasping her hands as she looked at me. "How did you ever get into such a condition?"

"Oh Mom, I was just trying to save money, and I ended up losing a lot more."

"You've got to learn to look beyond your nose."

I sighed deeply. "I know."

Grandma came in, wiping her hands on her apron. She smoothed the bedcovers and stood there clutching the footboard. The black wood had such a high gloss that both sides of her ancient fingers were on view.

"I had a thing like this once," she said, "just before I married your grandfather. They thought I'd die. Sometimes we learn so much so fast that there must be a settling—a quiet time to let it sink in. If your mind won't say yes to it, your body must."

I laughed weakly. "So it wasn't the mushroom soup?"

"Not altogether," Grandma said.

I nodded. "It was the reaching."

Mom asked, "Reaching for what?", but Grandma seemed to understand.

I gained strength slowly. Mom got *Kristin Lavransdatter* from the library for me, and I picked up where I had left off, propping the heavy volume against a bread board supported by my knees. As I read, I sipped from the cup of elderberry tea Grandma kept filled for me.

The day I nearly choked on one of the big pills the doctor prescribed, I finally washed it down with nearly a quart of that tea. I felt the pill go down, and yet I had the sensation that it was still there. For days, I swallowed compulsively, trying to get rid of that lump-in-the-throat feeling. When the doctor came for what he said would be his last house call, he peered down my throat, aided by a small flashlight and wooden tongue depressor, and pronounced the passage clear.

"Then why do I feel there's something there?"

He shrugged. "It's an idiopathic condition."

"What does that mean?"

"Something with an obscure or unknown cause."

After he left, Grandma came and sat on the edge of the bed. She stroked my throat, and her touch was surprisingly soft, considering that her hand seemed to be all bones.

"Something's bothering you, Margarethe."

"It certainly is!" I said crossly, "This dumb throat!"

"Did something happen up there in Wisconsin that's sticking in your craw?"

I thought hard. Not the break with Hoffman, which had been inevitable. Not my horror at discovering a hidden streak of murder in Gary Johnson, because I had no plans for letting him into my life. Not Birdie Malone's eagerness to get rid of a renter with a possibly dire disease, because I wasn't as useful to her plans (thank God!) as she had hoped I might be. What, then?

"Something at your job, maybe?" Grandma suggested.

That was it! I told her about Mr. Stith's refusal to accommodate Jews and how guilty I felt that I hadn't had the courage to quit as soon as I found out about it.

"Margarethe, I think you dealt with it in the Danish way. Denmark is a tiny, little country, you know, and we have learned to survive by smiling as we twist the knife. Our victims are never absolutely sure that we did it—or meant it—and they are too confused to do anything at all to us."

"But *I* didn't do anything at all!"

She laughed. "I can just see your face when he told you what was going on! If the man wasn't made of stone, he was ashamed, and every time you typed one of those lying refusals, he felt it in the air. Don't tell me he didn't! Oh yes, Margarethe, you *did* something!"

"That's a cowardly way to fight!"

"It's a way to bend and not break—and to stay alive for the next battle. The Danes didn't get all those Jews to safety in Sweden by acting tough with the Germans!"

Mr. Sommer came to our house one evening to talk over my early return to Iowa City to help him with the Syrovy trial. He wanted to assure Mom and Grandma that it would be perfectly proper.

"You'll be driving?" Mom asked.

I cringed, aghast that she hadn't remembered he never *did* drive— not since the awful accident that killed the child and damaged his wife forever.

He shot me a quick glance that had a puzzling flavor of approval and said, "No, we'll take the train from Atlantic. I can use the time to go over some papers."

"Then she'll have to come back here for her school things, I suppose," Mom said. "The dormitory won't be open that early."

"I'm sure that storage arrangements can be made, but I thought Margaret would like to spend a little time at home before the semester starts—if the trial winds up in time, and I'll do my best to see that it does." He turned to me. "You're sure you're well enough?"

"Oh, yes!" My idiopathic throat was still carrying on, but that was my secret. I was beginning to wonder if I had inherited Aunt Kam's fits of choking anytime something disturbed her. If so, it probably served me right for all the scorn I'd secretly heaped on her for that idiosyncrasy.

We all had coffee with Mom's elegant lemon meringue pie, and when Mr. Sommer left, I walked out on the porch with him to say good-night.

"I'm sorry that she asked you about driving," I said.

"I'm not. It shows that you understand confidentiality. As for my feelings, I've forced myself to think about all that so deeply and persistently that it can't hurt me anymore. I've hired a driver to take us to Atlantic, and you can take as many or as few of your belongings as you wish."

"What if I can't find a place to put them until school starts?"

He gestured impatiently. "That's unlikely. We'll deal with it immediately—so we can concentrate exclusively on the defense of Mr. Syrovy."

How grand it was to have a man take charge and vanquish one's vague worries about practicalities in unknowable circumstances. Our household of women moved into each tomorrow with slight apprehension, unlike Aunt Kam, who knew Uncle Karl stood between her and any possible difficulty.

I wore my seersucker suit and spectator pumps for the journey and slipped a stenographer's notebook into my purse in case Mr. Sommer wanted to dictate anything on the train. I had gained some weight during my convalescence, which kept me from looking like the secretary I had envisioned when Merrilee and I spun our futures from magazine ad images, but Aunt Kam said not to worry. She said I looked "lush."

Sommer had retired his two-toned shoes early, returning to the English leather pair that looked better with his dark suit. He presented such a distinguished appearance that I was proud to be seen with him.

The hired driver was Alfie Swensen, a lineman for the Farmer's Mutual phone company who happened to have that day off, and after he loaded my things, he stood there on the curb, looking hard at Mom. She'd said "hello" to him, of course, but then she ignored him. Alfie was the one who had rushed her home from work in his truck the day I fell out of the maple tree and split my head open. He took me to the doctor's office, too, and didn't seem to mind the blood I got on the truck seat. When Mom thanked him, he said he'd do anything for her—anytime. Why had it taken me so long to see the reason?

As we drove south, Alfie joked, "You look a lot better now than you did the last time I gave you a ride!"

"When was that?" Mr. Sommer asked.

It took until we got to the County Home, which most people called the "Poor Farm," to explain it, and then I fell silent. I wanted to think about how I'd feel if Mom ever got interested in a man. Was it possible that she might? She was so old—well over forty—but you wouldn't know it from the way Alfie looked at her. Unlike Mrs. Hess, Lotus's mother, she still had a waistline, and she had less trouble keeping her stomach flat than I did.

I could see why she wasn't interested in Alfie. A toothpick protruded from a corner of his mouth, he had a farmer tan from his outdoor job, and he smelled sickeningly of Old Spice. Every time we passed a farmer working in the field, he honked and waved his pointer in what we laughingly called the Shelby County salute. He was, pure and simple, a hick.

I giggled at the thought, remembering Venus's haughty pronouncement, *"I'm* no hick, I'm from Davenport!" Place wasn't the big thing in the making of a hick, I was convinced, but Venus was right—she wasn't one. I thought about rooming with her at Currier Hall and supposed she wasn't my worst bet among the inhabitants of Cottage 15. Actually, I would have preferred Elena, but it was loo late to have regrets about that.

When we got to the Atlantic railroad station, I jumped out and ran around to the trunk to get my own bags, but Mr. Sommer signalled ever so slightly, and an older man in a billed cap pulled them out and put them on a wheeled cart. All I needed to do was step onto the train unencumbered.

After we were settled in the coach, Sommer pulled a legal pad from his briefcase and started to look at his notes. I carefully avoided looking at the page. Whatever it was my business to know, he would tell me.

Finally, I could stand it no longer. I said, "I know I shouldn't ask this, but is he guilty?"

"Yes," he said, looking at me unblinkingly.

"Then how can you—" I broke off, "I'm sorry, I *really* shouldn't ask that, because I know the answer. Everyone is entitled to a defense, right?"

"Right. But there's a difference here. Syrovy killed your friend Bebe."

"Oh, I didn't really know her that well."

"Be that as it may, he did kill her, but he is not guilty as charged, and I will prove it. I killed my daughter, but I was not charged as guilty. Which is worse?"

I shook my head.

"No matter what happens in this trial, Syrvoy will pay and pay and pay—just as I have. Justice will be done."

I swallowed hard and to no avail. As Grandma put it, something was sticking in my craw—something I could do nothing about.

We had lunch in the dining car, a new experience for me. While acting as if I were quite accustomed to such niceties, I admired the real carnations, the white linen cloth and the cunning, silver coffee pot. I paid close attention to the way he wrote our orders so I'd know how to do it should the occasion ever arise.

As I was cutting up the tenderloin he'd ordered for me, he asked, "Are you tough enough for murder, Margaret?"

"If you mean committing it, no. Otherwise, I'd better be—if I want to be a reporter."

"That's what you've decided?"

"I think so—although the ones I met this summer were crazy as they come. Most of them."

He smiled. "The Fourth Estate gets almost as little respect as the Law. Good luck!"

"And this isn't the first time I've bumped into murder. Remember Fern?"

"The woman who ran the dress shop."

"I saw them in all the blood, and my friend's mother said I was cold because I didn't scream and cry." The scene came back to me, complete with the dog, Licorice, whimpering over his dead owner, and I pushed my plate away. I swallowed painfully, again and again.

The waiter brought ice cream, which slid over and around the idiopathic lump, and then we were coming into Iowa City. The sight of the station cafe reminded me of Hoffman, and I felt more elegaic than pained.

Sommer found a cab to take us to the Hotel Jefferson, and as I ascended in the elevator with a bellboy, I savored being a non-student in Iowa City. The room was small but glamorous because it was my first, and I'd seen enough movies to tip the bellhop. From my west window, I could see the golden dome of Old Capitol. Almost a year ago, it had beckoned me to learning, and it still did, but in the meantime, I had a job to do.

The phone rang, startling me, until I realized it could only be Mr. Sommer.

"If you'll meet me in the lobby, we'll visit our client."

Our client! "I'll be right down."

The Johnson County jail was forbidding, but I supposed all jails were. It occurred to me that I'd never really looked at the jail in Harlan. It had been there since the last century, but I had no reason to walk that street or care about its inhabitants.

Mr. Sommer signed for us, and we were let into the cell of Charles Syrovy and locked up with him. I backed into a corner to get out of the way, but Sommer insisted that I take the only chair while he sat on the hard bunk beside Syrovy.

"This is Miss Langelund, my secretary," he said. "Margaret, Charles Syrovy."

Syrovy acknowledged the introductions with a quick dip of his head. His eyes were red-rimmed like a rabbit's, and his face had a puffy, pasty look. I had thought him handsome in the newspaper photographs at the time of the murder, (I must remind myself to stop calling it that, even privately) but the only surviving feature of his good looks was his luxuriant hair, still combed in a deep wave.

"Charles," Sommer said, "you did love Bebe, did you not?"

Syrovy nodded miserably.

"And you still love her memory?"

"Yes," he spoke for the first time in a voice that seemed cracked from disuse, "I think of her all the time—every minute, especially at night."

"Take that down, will you, Margaret?"

I recorded his words in shorthand and waited, pencil poised, for more.

Sommer said, "We will win this case by telling the truth, Charles, do you understand?"

I didn't understand, since Mr. Sommer had told me Syrovy did it, and the client looked at him dully. He said, "I tried to grab the cop's gun and go with her, but he—" Tears welled in his eyes and spilled to his cheeks. He twisted his body and buried his face in the limp pillow on the cot.

"Charles," Sommer shook his shoulder gently, "your defense will involve a great deal of expert testimony. Are you ready to cooperate with doctors, psychiatrists or any other professionals who can help?"

"Whatever you want. I don't care."

"But you have a mother, a family—people who care about you. What about them?"

"Nobody mattered but Bebe."

I wrote that down.

After we were let out by a guard with a key, Sommer asked, "Do you feel sorry for him?"

"Yes, of course."

"Good!"

We took a cab to the rooming house where Bebe met her untimely end, a shabby, three-storey building on Dubuque Street jokingly called the Empty Arms. No one lived in the fatal room, and the landlady let us in with a skeleton key. The air was stale, and the light was sickly through greenish translucent window shades pulled to the sill. The dirty, olive-green walls added to the undersea atmosphere. A bed from which the imprint of Bebe's body had been smoothed; a dresser that once held Syrovy's belongings; a table cleared of the exotic meal copied from the book, *Desire Me;* and two chairs from which Bebe and Charles meant to regard each other with love as they dined were the only furnishings.

"Do you feel violence in this room, Margaret?"

I stood still between the bed and the table, trying to decide. What I *did* feel was a worsening of my idiopathic lump, which was unsurprising, considering how Bebe died. Finally, I said, "What I feel, I think, is a grief beyond words."

"Excellent! That's what you *should* feel here. There's an ambiance like the Gettysburg battlefield or the site of the Battle of the Little Big Horn. Tragedy and loss that weren't really necessary."

Now I felt it even stronger, swallowing and swallowing with an increasing sense of panic. Why was Mr. Sommer asking *me* about such things? I'd never been anywhere or done anything—except come to the university and spend part of a summer in Wisconsin. I asked if he wanted me to take notes of any kind, and he shook his head.

"Just wanted to verify my feelings about all this. Let's go back to the hotel, and you can put on some walking shoes. I want you to run over to Psychiatric Hospital with a note for someone."

I reddened, thinking we could have walked to the Empty Arms if I hadn't been wearing such high heels. It was kind of Mr. Sommer to indulge me. I also planned to change into something cooler. The day had turned hot.

The cab that brought us was waiting at the curb, and that in itself was a thrill for someone who'd scarcely ever ridden in one. As we passed a book store, Sommer asked the driver to stop. He jumped out and went up to the window, which was crowded with multiple copies of *Desire Me* and a hand-lettered sign, "The book that doomed Bebe!"

When he came back, I asked, "Will that help or hurt?"

He laughed. "It should help the poet, at least. If that book hadn't been found in Syrovy's room, it probably would have sold a dozen copies. Have you read it?"

"No."

"Well, don't bother. It's pretty bad. While you're gone, I'll make some arrangements for getting your stuff to the dorm."

It sounded simple the way he put it, but if I had tried to buck the rules and regulations, I couldn't have managed it. I thanked him, hoping that gratitude would substitute for assertiveness now and then—at least until I developed more of the latter.

Psychiatric Hospital with its quaint, vine-covered architecture looked like the setting for a British mystery. The light inside had a greenish glow, probably because of the vines. When I asked for the doctor Mr. Sommer had specified, the receptionist said she'd give him whatever I had for him.

"I'm sorry, but I've been instructed to deliver it to him personally."

She gave me a cross look and went down the hall to push the buzzer at the door of a locked ward. When she was let in, I could hear a loud babbling that sounded like the biblical speaking in tongues. However, when I looked through the glass panel, the people sitting on sofas appeared to be quiet and sane.

I was curious about the message I carried. Would Sommer try to prove that Charles Syrovy was insane? I'd never personally encountered anyone who was—unless it was Jess, the hired man of my early childhood whom I could scarcely remember. Mom said he used to pick me up, high chair and all, and whisper things to me that I seemed to love hearing. I couldn't remember what they were. Jess had been taken to the insane asylum at Clarinda, where he died.

Eventually, the doctor returned with the receptionist. He had an absent-minded look, as if he were still thinking of the patient he'd just left. He tore open the envelope I handed to him, read the contents and said, "Tell Mr. Sommer the appointment is confirmed."

Having completed my task, I wanted to stroll back to the hotel, soaking up the ambiance of Iowa City on the way, but I supposed I shouldn't. There never seemed to be time to contemplate the pool below the Law Commons with its rugged rock wall, to cut through the art building and smell the paint, to mosey across the acres of formally-patterned carpet in the Union ballroom.

I did have time to notice the girls who were back early for sorority Rush Week. Hot as it was, they wore sweaters so new that they still showed fold marks from the store. The pleats of their long, swinging skirts were knife-sharp, even in the back. I might feel like a hick in my summer dress, but I certainly was more comfortable than they were.

I thought of Florine Hammond, who had tried to persuade me to pledge her sorority. Once she had come back to Iowa City early for Rush, wearing new clothes too warm for the season and mercifully unaware of her future. How many of these lovely, shining girls would turn out like Florine—wanting admiration so much that they would risk comtempt to get it?

Mr. Sommer used me chiefly as a courier, though I did take notes before the trial and was asked to record the actual courtroom action in shorthand. I couldn't see why that was necessary, there being an official court reporter who was much faster than I was.

At first, I was afraid that I would be so busy with the mechanics that I'd miss the sounds, the sights and the feelings that hung so thickly in the chamber. However, these things reached me and were stored until I could replay them from memory later.

When the black-robed judge entered the courtroom, the bailiff loudly intoned, "All rise!" The first time it happened, I was so startled that I dropped my pad and pen with an embarrassing clatter. After that, it became as commonplace as rising for a hymn in church, but I did wonder how it would feel to inspire such a gesture of respect. Did Judge Bonner feel he deserved it, or did he think, "You folks wouldn't do that if you really knew me."? He had small tufts of hair growing out of his ears that gave him a troll-like appearance, and he spoke in a slow, measured manner in a reedy voice.

The prosecutor, Daniel McGuire, had a square jaw and oiled his hair heavily, trying to control a stubborn cowlick. The knot of his tie was always slightly off-center, and his suit needed pressing.

In contrast, Gregory Sommer was impeccably groomed, dressed in a gray pin-striped suit or a navy one with white shirts and assorted maroon ties. He never pulled at his collar as McGuire did, and when he sat at the defense table listening to testimony, his hands were still—unless he was taking notes. I was proud to be associated with him.

Mr. Sommer had sent me out to buy Charles Syrovy some shirts and ties, and the defendant looked as good as a person in his situation could hope to look. I had asked if we should do something about his red eyes, and Sommer said, "Absolutely not. They're an asset."

All in all, Syrovy was marked by his grief, but anyone could see that he had been a handsome young man, a guy Bebe Maxwell could have loved.

His parents were in the courtroom daily, driving back and forth from Cedar Rapids for the sessions. Marta Syrovy was thin and dark. She wore a tailored suit and an Eleanor Roosevelt hat, holding her head at such an angle that the reflection from her glasses hid her eyes. Benesh Syrovy was bald, but one could envision a wave of hair like Charles's on his head. His suit jacket did not conform to his body, probably because it was seldom worn. His eyes were a faded blue, and they looked tired. Daily, the Syrovys greeted their son with an intense look across the room, and when court recessed, they came to him for a kiss and a few words. His eyes were redder after his parents took their dignified departure.

Each day, the walk leading to the courthouse was lined with spectators, and after some were turned away because the courtroom wouldn't hold them all, they began to come earlier and earlier.

For the most part, they were sympathetic. When McGuire told the jury that he would prove "premeditated murder motivated by sexual interest far beyond the ordinary," there was a low murmur that seemed to be in Charles's favor.

A police officer testified as to how Bebe was found. "She was layin' on the bed on her back."

McGuire asked, "And what was she wearing?"

"A long, white dress and gloves that came up over her elbows."

"And when you booked Mr. Syrovy, how was he dressed?"

"Objection!" Sommer said.

"Overruled."

McGuire smiled, repeating, "How was Mr. Syrovy dressed?"

"He had on a tux and a topcoat but no shirt or undershirt."

"Did this lead you to conclude that he had been engaging in—"

Sommer interrupted, "Objection!"

"Sustained."

McGuire pulled at his collar and shot Sommer a look of disgust. "I have no more questions."

Sommer decided to cross-examine, asking, "Officer, was Miss Maxwell's gown disarranged in any way?"

"No, Sir. It was all pulled down nice and smooth—like she was laid out for burial."

Syrovy groaned.

Sommer continued, "Is it not possible that Mr. Syrovy tore off his shirt to be unhampered in his efforts to resuscitate the victim?"

"Objection!" McGuire shouted.

"Sustained."

At first it puzzled me that Sommer was so untroubled by sustained objections. Then he explained that it didn't matter. The seed had been planted in the minds of the jurors.

McGuire continued with his roster of witnesses, bringing out the details of the tragic night in such detail that Syrovy winced and hid his face in his hands. The lobster, the burgundy, the single flower on the table, the drape of Bebe's white gown bought especially for his fraternity's spring formal, the radio that went on playing in the room when Bebe was beyond hearing any of the sounds of this world.

The State's key witness was Dr. Norbert Shafer of the psychology department, who testified, "regretfully," he said, that, "Charles Syrovy came to me weeks before the murder to tell me of an impulse to commit a murderous assault upon a girl he was seeing."

McGuire said, "And you had reason to believe that the girl was Bebe Maxwell?"

"Objection!" Sommer said.

"Sustained."

Then Sommer began to call witnesses. The first was the cook at the Amvets bar where Syrovy worked, and he said, "I just couldn't believe that he would kill anybody. He was always friendly and considerate."

Sommer called the manager of the Amvets bar and began to question him about the connection between Syrovy and Bebe. "Would you say that they were attached to each other?"

The man nodded. "A guy and a girl don't sit together three or four hours at a time three or four times a week without being attached. They were attached, all right."

Another police officer was called, and I was to wonder how in the world Sommer had found out what this man knew. So was McGuire, no doubt.

Sommer asked the officer, "Will you please tell us what the coroner said and did after you informed Mr. Syrovy that Miss Maxwell was dead?"

"Yes, sir. The coroner wadded up her dress and her underwear and shoved them in the guy's face, and he yelled, 'Come clean! We know you did it!'"

"And it was after this that Mr. Syrovy fled the police station and ran to St. Mary's church?"

"No, sir. The coroner did that after he was locked up."

"When did you first see Mr. Syrovy the evening of April 20, officer?"

"It wasn't April 20 anymore—it was after midnight. He came running into the station hollering, 'Send for a pulmotor, a doctor, a fireman—somebody!'"

"Then you drove him to the rooming house?"

"Yes, sir."

Sommer stepped back, deferring to McGuire. "Your witness."

McGuire moved very close to the witness. "Didn't you think it strange that Mr. Syrovy would take the time to come to the police station personally rather than call?"

"No, sir. Most of the students don't have phones."

"While you were trying to revive Miss Maxwell, what was the defendant doing—if you recall?"

"He grabbed the wine bottle and threw it out the window. He was crying, and I could scarcely make out what he was saying, but it sounded like 'That damned stuff!'"

After two and a half weeks, I had almost lost track of the way the trial was going. Whoever testified last seemed the most believable.

Sommer put the psychiatrist who had tested Syrovy on the stand to establish Charles's normality. I was mentally referring to him as Charles now, indicating where my sympathies stood, and the spectators seemed to be of the same mind. Every morning when the guards brought him in, there were soft greetings of "Hi, Charlie!" or "Hang in there, Chuck!"

McGuire tried to rock the psychiatrist by questioning him about psychology majors (Syrovy was one), wanting him to admit that they went through periods of imbalance as part of their learning experience, but the doctor scorned such a theory.

Then Sommer put Charles on the stand before a packed courtroom. He was wearing one of the ties I had chosen for him, patterned with the heads of knights in armor. He'd need all the armor he could get.

Encouraged by Sommer, Charles told of his boyhood days in a modest house on a shady street in Cedar Rapids—growing up with five brothers and sisters and going to Mass every Sunday. He spoke of a high school teacher who encouraged him to go on to the university, which he had done until his studies were interrupted by the war. He had seen Merchant Marine service in the South Pacific and had been so touched by the psychic wounds of soldiers affected by violence and death that he had returned to the university to change his major to psychology.

I watched the jurors as he spoke in a low voice, seldom raising his eyes from his clasped hands. Seven were men—farmers, small businessmen and a banker. Five were women—three housewives, a teacher and a secretary. The teacher was beautiful, but the other women were not. Sommer had told me he had hoped to get rid of the beauty, who might identify with Bebe and blame Charles for her death, but it hadn't happened that way. The other women might think Bebe got no worse than she deserved and forgive Charles for the unfortunate accident that took Bebe's life. What about the men? He hoped they would think Charles had been punished enough already and root for him to escape the bonds forged by having to do with women in any way. At any rate, all of them were listening to Charles attentively.

The attention sharpened when Sommer led Charles into his meeting with Bebe.

"It was at a fraternity party after the Purdue game." He dabbed his eyes with a handkerchief. "She had on a blue sweater and—and a—I can't, Mr. Sommer! I just can't stand to talk about her!" He put his hands to his face and sobbed.

Sommer turned slowly and dramatically, his eyes searching the rear of the courtroom.

"Is Dr. Peale in the courtroom?"

A white-coated man stood, and I recognized the doctor I had delivered Sommer's message to at Psychiatric Hospital. He came forward.

"If it please the Court, this is Dr. Randolph Peale of the University of Iowa College of Medicine. He will administer sodium pentathol, better known as truth serum, to the defendant before we continue with the testimony."

Judge Bonner's eyebrows rose, and he said, "Mr. Syrovy, do you accept this procedure willingly?"

"I do, Your Honor."

"Very well, doctor, you may proceed."

Dr. Peale helped Charles out of his jacket and assisted him in rolling up a shirt sleeve before he unsheathed the hypodermic and punched it into the bend of the left elbow. The silence in the courtroom was heavy as everyone watched for the effect.

After several minutes had ticked away, Sommer spoke softly to the jury, "Charles Syrovy will now recall details that have been blotted out by shock."

He came close to the witness chair and said, "Now, Mr. Syrovy, we are in your room at the Empty Arms. It is the night of April 20. Tell us what is happening."

Charles spoke tonelessly, as if in a trance. "We're standing in the middle of the room, kissing. We've been dancing to the radio. Now Bebe puts her hands on my throat, pretending to choke me. I tell her that isn't the right way to do it, and I show her. She asks me if that's the way to play blackout, so we do that for a little while.

"I'm really out, and as I'm coming back, I see that she has a strange, surprised look on her face. She throws up her arms to break my hold on her throat. I take my hands away, and we start to dance again."

"How long did you dance?" Sommer asked.

"I don't know—it might have been a few seconds or a few minutes. I notice a sort of gasping or moaning sound, and she's sort of twisting in my arms. She staggers and falls—hits the chair. The next thing I know, she's lying on the floor, and I'm sitting next to her, too weak to get up. There's a whistling in her throat, and I'm scared—there's a drop of blood at her nose and froth coming from her mouth—my God, I have to get help!"

"So you picked her up and put her on the bed?"

"I think so. Couldn't leave her on the floor."

"Thank you, Mr. Syrovy. Would the Prosecution care to cross-examine?"

McGuire stood, hands in his pockets, lips pursed. "Mr. Syrovy, if you wanted to save the girl's life, why didn't you find a phone and get help quicker? It's a long way to the police station from the Empty Arms."

"Not far when you drive. We had Bebe's car."

"Is it not true that Bebe Maxwell's family disapproved of your relationship and she was trying to end it?"

"They didn't like me, but she loved me. She was willing to go against them."

"No more questions," said McGuire.

Medical testimony was offered by a doctor called by Sommer who said, "The victim did not die of strangulation; rather from a sharp blow on the neck as she fell away from the defendant and struck a chair."

That's what did it, coming right after the truth serum testimony, and the jury wasn't out long. When they announced their "not guilty" verdict, Syrovy cried, his parents cried, and perfect strangers cried and cheered. I just sat there thinking about love and death and watching McGuire push his way through the crowd to Mr. Sommer to shake hands.

"Hey, Greg, you give grandstanding lessons?"

"The one today was tuition-free."

"Oh, what the hell! Congratulations! I wasn't crazy about putting the poor bastard away for life anyhow."

"He'll take care of that himself," Mr. Sommer said. "I'd like you to meet my secretary, Margaret Langelund."

McGuire acknowledged the introduction with a short nod. "I'd better go talk to the Maxwells. You know something? You country boys are dangerous!"

Sommer grinned. "Thanks."

Then Charles Syrovy fell on him, sobbing and thumping his back. "I'm so goddamned grateful!"

Sommer smiled grimly, shook hands with the parents, and started out of the courtroom. I followed him as closely as I could, blinking in the explosion of flashbulbs.

We had a good dinner to celebrate—at the Lark in Tiffin. Mr. Sommer ordered wine and limited me to one glass. I didn't mind, because it tasted sour to me.

"Probably too dry for you."

"Wine sounds better than it tastes. Sort of like Evening in Paris."

"You may develop a taste for dry wine, but I doubt that Evening in Paris will grow on you."

I was amazed that he knew about Evening in Paris, but I shouldn't have been. Gregory Sommer knew everything. I raised my glass and said, "To Charles Syrovy. May he live happily ever after!"

"He won't. Margaret, you're a born romantic, I guess."

"Is that bad?"

He shrugged. "Maybe I'm just jealous because I can't seem to live in a world of my own making. Reality always intrudes."

I thought of Mom and Grandma and Aunt Kam. They were realists, weren't they? Of course they did have their occasional flights of fancy, but Danes were like that—spinning fairytales while eating bacon and eggs.

After dinner, Sommer went to call a cab, and when we pulled up to Currier Hall, I was embarrassed. Early as it was, enough girls had arrived to create the May fly effect of kissing couples around the entrances.

"Young love," he said sardonically. "Have you been having any symptoms of it?"

"No, I'm waiting for the gods to arrive." I could see that he knew what I was talking about.

Venus was settled into our third-floor dorm room with a view of Currier's flat, gravelled rooftop at a lower level. My stuff completely obscured the blue bedspread, but hers was neatly put away with nothing but a heart-shaped pincushion and a bottle of Yardley's lavendar hand lotion on her half of the dresser top.

When I came in, she was doing exercises to firm her "bust," and they made her joints crack.

"Did you have a good summer?" she asked.

"I don't know how good it was, but it was an experience! How about you?"

"Oh, the usual. Typed all day at Alcoa and read at night. I did go to the Col one night."

"What's the 'Col?'"

"The Coliseum Ballroom. I went with a couple of girls from work to hear Vaughan Monroe."

"How did he look?"

"Old."

I shook my head. The owner of that sonorous baritone would be young enough for racing with the moon forever. "When did you get in?"

"Just after lunch. After I unpacked, I went down to the Union to see Rosalie."

"Who's she?"

Venus laughed. *"She* is a painting—by Miro. It's called something like 'Rosalie, Asleep Under a Rose Bush, is Awakened by a Drop of Dew Falling From the Wing of a Bird.' It cost a chunk, and a lot of people are mad about it."

"Why?"

"Because it's abstract, and they say a kindergarten kid could have done it."

"What did you think of it?"

"I liked it."

"Venus, have you ever thought of majoring in art?"

She sighed. "Yes, but I couldn't make a living."

Venus was living out that old Danish proverb, "Don't sail out farther than you can row back," and it saddened me. She ought to have someone like Grandma to tell her, "Never mind the rowing back, sail!" I told her that.

"You're still going to do journalism?" she said.

I thought of the crazy bunch in Lake Geneva, wavered a bit and then took the reckless plunge. "Yes."

"I guess I'll just go along with you."

"Anybody else from Cottage 15 here yet?"

"Elena is on Currier South. Dot isn't coming back, I guess. She said if she couldn't be a doctor, to heck with it, and she's getting some kind of Civil Service job."

"What about Nita?"

"Oh, she's here, all right! I walked past her sorority house during a serenade, and she was all done up in her sweater and pearls making obscene gestures at the guys behind the backs of the other girls."

"You haven't talked to her, then?"

Venus shuddered massively. "No! But she also came through the Union ballroom while I was looking at 'Rosalie,' and I heard her telling someone what she was going to do to the pledges—make them crawl from the top floor of the house to the basement with their mouths full of water to put out a fire in the furnace."

I needed a straight pin to hang up a skirt and took one from Venus's pincushion. She came over immediately and respaced the heart design to eliminate the gap.

I wrote a letter home before I went to bed, telling Mom and Grandma that Mr. Sommer had defended Charles Syrovy successfully and that I was settled in Currier Hall. Venus was fine, but if she was as fussy about other things as she was about the placement of pins in her pincushion, it would be a long semester.

After breakfast, we headed for the Fieldhouse to register, and Venus asked me if I could pick out the freshmen.

"I guess so," I said. "They have a bewildered look, and everything they're wearing is brand-new."

A runner came toward us as we were crossing the bridge. He was thin and blond with a spiky crewcut, and he wore steel-rimmed glasses that looked like Army issue. The high reach and thrust of his legs was beautiful to see, reminding me of drawings of Mercury, messenger of the gods.

As he passed, our eyes met for an instant, and I felt that I knew him. I asked Venus if she did, and she shook her head.

It wasn't until I was signing up for a course in semantics that it came to me. He was the basketball usher who called in the big football muscle when the loud-mouthed fan refused to get rid of his cigarette.

He simply couldn't interest me, I thought. I was looking for a Latin lover type after growing up with a town full of towheads. Still, I found myself settling a winged helmet on that spiky crewcut and affixing wings to those mercurial heels. *We'll see*, I told myself.

When I'd signed up for seventeen hours, I met Venus at the appointed spot, the west door of the Quadrangle, and we started back to Currier.

She took me through the Union to look at "Rosalie," and I was bemused. The painting was smaller than I expected it to be, and the eye that was its focal point caught me and held me.

"What do you think of it?" Venus asked.

"I doubt that thinking has much to do with it. I feel something, though. As long as I live, I'll always see that eye."

Venus clapped softly. "Lester Longman would be proud of you. He must have taught you something in that survey."

We chugged up the hill from the union, feeling the pull on our leg muscles, and Venus said, "How can you tell the difference between an SUI coed and one from Iowa State College?"

"I give up. How?"

"The one from SUI has fatter calves. They don't have hills like this on the Moo U campus."

We met four girls in sweaters, pearls and long, swingy skirts coming down the walk in an unbreachable phalanx. I started to step aside, but Venus grabbed my arm.

"Let *them* get off the walk. They're freshmen."

They parted like the Red Sea and flowed around us, giggling and talking in high, nervous voices. Venus and I, infinitely older and wiser, exchanged a significant look.

"Don't you feel sorry for them?" she said.

"No, because they're reaching."

"Reaching for what?"

"Not that kind of reaching. I mean, they've caught the wind just forward of the beam, and they're sailing fast. They've never sailed this fast before, and they never will again. It's scary, but it's wonderful."

"I didn't realize you knew about stuff like that."

"I didn't until this summer."

The winds would always shift, but I hoped I'd be able to tack my way to wherever I wanted to go. I'd need the help of a lot of sailing teachers. And I knew one thing for certain. I'd never row back. In spite of what they said about hanging onto that option, no Jorgen woman ever did.

-The End-